Mated to my Bully

Jade Rivers

Contents

Chapter 1 11
    TYLER 12
    RAIN 14
Chapter 2 15
    TYLER 15
Chapter 3 18
    RAIN 18
    TYLER 21
    RAIN 22
Chapter 4 23
    Tyler 23
Chapter 5 25
    TYLER 25
    RAIN 28
Chapter 6 29
    TYLER 29
    RAIN 31
Chapter 7 34
    TYLER 34
Chapter 8 38
    RAIN 38
    TYLER 39
Chapter 9 43
    RAIN 43
    TYLER 45
Chapter 10 47
    RAIN 47
    TYLER 48
    RAIN 49
    TYLER 51
Chapter 11 53

- RAIN 53
- TYLER 56

Chapter 12 58
- RAIN 58
- TYLER 59
- RAIN 61

Chapter 13 63
- TYLER 63
- TYLER 66

Chapter 14 68
- RAIN 68
- TYLER 69
- RAIN 70

Chapter 15 72
- TYLER 72
- RAIN 73

Chapter 16 74
- TYLER 74
- RAIN 76
- TYLER 77

Chapter 17 79
- RAIN 79

Chapter 18 81
- TYLER 81
- RAIN 82

Chapter 19 84
- TYLER 84

Chapter 20 88
- RAIN 88
- TYLER 90

Chapter 21 92
- RAIN 92
- TYLER 94

Chapter 22	96
RAIN	96
Chapter 23	98
TYLER	98
RAIN	99
Chapter 24	102
TYLER	102
Chapter 25	105
RAIN	105
Chapter 26	109
RAIN	109
Chapter 27	113
TYLER	113
Chapter 28	116
RAIN	116
Chapter 29	119
TYLER	119
Chapter 30	122
RAIN	122
Chapter 31	125
TYLER	125
Chapter 32	128
RAIN	128
Chapter 33	130
TYLER	130
RAIN	131
Chapter 34	133
TYLER	133
Chapter 35	135
BECCA	135
Chapter 36	138
JORDAN	138
BECCA	139

Chapter 37	141
TYLER	141
Chapter 38	144
RAIN	144
JORDAN	145
Chapter 39	148
RAIN	148
BECCA	149
JORDAN	150
TYLER	151
Chapter 40	153
BECCA	153
JORDAN	156
Chapter 41	158
RAIN	158
TYLER	159
Chapter 42	162
RAIN	162
Chapter 43	166
BECCA	166
JORDAN	167
BECCA	169
Chapter 44	173
JORDAN	173
Chapter 45	176
JORDAN	176
Chapter 46	179
BECCA	179
JORDAN	180
Chapter 47	182
BECCA	182
Chapter 48	184
JORDAN	184

- Chapter 49 186
  - BECCA 186
  - JORDAN 191
- Chapter 50 193
  - RAIN 193
  - TYLER 194
  - RAIN 195
- Chapter 51 198
  - BECCA 198
  - TYLER 200
- Chapter 52 202
  - MATHIS 202
  - RAIN 203
- Chapter 53 206
  - JORDAN 206
- Chapter 54 209
  - BECCA 209
- Chapter 55 211
  - MATHIS 211
  - HEATHER 212
  - RAIN 213
- Chapter 56 215
  - JORDAN 215
  - MATHIS 216
- Chapter 57 218
  - TYLER 218
  - RAIN 219
- Chapter 58 222
  - HEATHER 222
- Chapter 59 225
  - JORDAN 225
  - BECCA 226
  - JORDAN 230

- Chapter 60 232
  - MATHIS 232
  - HEATHER 234
  - MATHIS 235
- Chapter 61 238
  - HEATHER 238
  - MATHIS 240
- Chapter 62 243
  - HEATHER 243
  - MATHIS 246
- Chapter 63 248
  - HEATHER 248
  - MATHIS 250
- Chapter 64 252
  - MATHIS 252
- Chapter 65 255
  - RAIN 255

Copyright © 2022 Jade Rivers

All right reserved. This copy is intended for the original purchaser of this book only. No part of this book may be reproduced, scanned or distributed in any printed or electronic for without prior written consent from the author.

This book is a work of fiction. The names characters, places and locations are either the product of the author's imagination or used fictitiously, any resemblances to actual persons, living or dead, business establishments, events, or locales is entirely coincidental.

This book contains descriptions of BDSM, spanking and dubious consent. This book describes sexual situations. If any of the forementioned topics offend you, please do not read. This book is fiction and not be used as a guide. The author will not be held responsible for any harm, injury or death resulted from use of the information contained within.

Note from the author:

This is the first book in the Mated to my Bully series. This book was originally published under the same name as an Amazon Vella Series. It is an ongoing series.

Thank you!

Mated to my Bully

Tyler

It had to be her. Of all people. The misfit, the weird one, the unpopular one. The runt of the litter in a pack where it was survival of the fittest. Why did I spend all those years making fun of her and pulling stupid pranks? Now she won't even talk to me. How do I convince her to give me a second chance when I never gave her a first one?

Rain

It's as if destiny wanted to help Tyler play one last cruel prank on me. This has to be a joke. The only thing getting me through the last weeks of school is the thought of getting the hell out of Praxley. I can't be mated to the future Alpha. Well, Tyler is definitely in for some surprises, I'm not exactly what I seem.

Chapter 1

TYLER

"Here comes the losers of the pack," Max says. Before I even look, I already know who he's talking about. Rain and Becca, the most unpopular shifters in our school, walking down the hallway towards us. Rain is the smallest member of our pack and Becca isn't much bigger. They are much weaker than an average shifter and being such get picked on by the other teenage members of the pack. If my dad was here, he would give me some lame lecture on how it would be our responsibility to protect the smallest member of our community. But at Praxley High School it's always been survival of the fittest.

"Hey losers can you hear us? I'll be alpha of our pack soon. Show some respect," I say joining in with the other jocks. As the next in line for pack alpha, I am at the top of the social pyramid. Rain looks over at me with a look somewhere between disappointment and something else, maybe resignation. She passes me too quickly to tell, scurrying off to her next class. It gave me the weirdest pang in my chest.

On top of being the runt of the litter, Rain goes out of her way not to fit in. She dyes her naturally brown hair all sorts of bright colors. The latest is purple highlights. She wears dark clothes. Today she was wearing a black mini skirt with a loose dark red shirt that hung off one shoulder with fishnet stockings and combat boots. Becca is her only friend, although she at least attempts to be a part of the pack. I have never seen Rain at any of the pack meetings or get togethers. Not that she's overly welcomed. Her and her family live in some creepy gothic style house surrounded by woods with no close neighbors. I think she has older brothers, but her family only do the bare minimum to be members of the Praxley Pack, so I don't really know her home life.

"That is one uptight bitch," Max says.

"I wonder if the carpet matches the drapes," Kevin says, another member of the football team.

"I wouldn't risk it to find out, she probably has fangs down there," I say.

"She would be kind of cute if she dressed like a normal person," Max says.

"She's a weak shifter," I say.

"So, I like when my female is submissive," Max says.

"What female?" I tease. Being on the football team makes us high school royalty, and any of us could get any girl we chose.

"Hey Tyler," Heather says walking down the hallway. Heather is one of those girls the entire football team has been with at some point. However, she has been an on again off again girlfriend of mine for the past six months. She's captain of the cheerleader squad. It is so cliché that it hurts, but she would be my perfect match, on paper at least. She comes up to me putting her manicured fingers on my chest.

"Are you going to take me out this weekend?" She asks bating her eye lashes.

"There's a big party at the pack grounds this Friday night," I say. Heather has been hanging off of me because she knows I turn eighteen the following weekend, and she's convinced she'll be the next Luna of our pack, as my mate. Wolf shifter males can start sensing their fated mate once they turn eighteen. Luna is a coveted position that comes with respect and authority that Heather craves. I can't imagine what that would mean for our pack. I mean she's an alright lay, but I can't imagine actually spending my life with her.

"Yes, I should go to that, practice my hosting skills. I will be throwing several parties when I'm Luna," she says before giving me a kiss and walking off to class.

"Can you imagine Heather being your fated mate. Jesus, she's hot, but she is psycho," Max says.

"I fucking hope not," I mumble, making my way to class.

RAIN

"Those guys are such assholes," Becca says. I know she's actually bothered by what they say. I couldn't care less but Becca wants to be a part of the popular crowd, so I feel bad when they tease her. The popular kids have been picking on me since elementary school. Praxley is a small town made up exclusively of wolf shifters. We all grew up together, so I have had the misfortune of knowing Tyler and his jackals pretty much all of my life.

"Don't let it get to you. We're almost done high school and then we'll never have to see those assholes again," I say.

I plan on doing some traveling when I graduate, maybe a backpack across Europe. Somewhere not highly populated with shifters. My father hasn't agreed to it yet, but my mom is fully supportive of my ambitions to wander. Although my mom is a romantic at heart and wants me to find my true mate and have several babies too.

I just can't see myself living in a small town for the rest of my life. I want to go to art school and be around people who can appreciate what I create. Instead of these closed-minded assholes that'll only ever see me as too weak and too small.

Chapter 2

TYLER

 It's finally Friday, and everybody's counting down the days left of school. I'll kind of miss high school. Although I know I'll still see everybody, it'll just be different. I walk up to my locker and Heather's waiting for me. I need to get rid of her. There's no way this woman's my mate, and her personality's getting old. Still, she's part of the popular circle, and it would not benefit me to piss her off. Plus, she is an easy lay.

 Male shifters claim their fated mates by biting their necks. When a male shifter is in the presence of his fated mate, his canines will elongate, and he'll produce a hormone that he imbeds into his mate's neck, so she carries his scent. Whenever Heather has sex with me, she isn't subtle about offering up her neck for me to claim. But I feel nothing with Heather. We haven't even slept together in a while. She doesn't really like me; she just likes the idea of being the next Luna.

 "Hey losers do everybody a favor and just leave already," she says when Rain and Becca walk by. Rain just smiles with a laugh and keeps walking, which just pisses Heather off more.

 "She thinks she's better than us even though she's a social pariah, someone should really take her down a notch. You know what'd be funny? If you guys pretended to be interested in those social outcasts and get them to show up at the party tonight. We could pull a Carrie, but instead of blood, throw a bucket of warm beer on them when they show up," Heather says. The exact reason she should't be Luna.

"That's not funny," I say.

"You just don't think you could get her to come. Come on, it will be funny. You guys have been pulling pranks on those two losers for years," Heather cackles. It's true, we have done all sorts of wicked shit to them. Filling their lockers with jello, stealing their clothes when they were showering in the locker rooms. Once we found Rain's cell phone number and wrote it in the bathroom of a bunch of gas stations saying it was the line for an escort.

"Fine. I'll see if I can get them to come. But we're not throwing anything at them," I say.

"I'll try to get Becca to come you try to get Rain," Max says.

After school I see Rain alone sitting next to a tree reading a book. Against probably my better judgment, I approach her.

"Hey Rain. Did you hear about the party tonight?"

"No," she says without even looking up at me.

"Well, there's going to be one. I was thinking I've never seen you at one, maybe you would like to come with me," I say. She starts laughing.

"No, I would not like that," she says. For some reason I thought she would swoon over me if I gave her a little attention. Most girls fall over themselves just to talk to me.

"Come on. I always thought you were kind of cute. We can just hangout. It'll be fun," I say. She finally puts down her book to look at me. She has intense deep blue eyes with long natural lashes.

"Tyler, you and your team of assholes have pulled pranks on me since elementary school. I know this is another one of your cruel jokes. Don't worry the second I graduate from this awful high school I plan to move as far away from this pack territory as I physically can, and would you like to know why?"

"Why?" I ask.

"Because you'll be the next leader, and you're not an alpha I would ever want to follow," she says gathering up her stuff and storming off. That hurt more than I thought it would.

Chapter 3
RAIN

I'm still upset with Tyler when I walk up to our Victorian styled home after school. The people who have seen my house think it's creepy, but it has always been home to me. Opening the front door, I see my brother Rex in the living room watching TV.

"You okay?" he asks.

"Yeah, I'm just ready to be done school."

"Do you need me to kill someone?" Rex asks without even a hint of humor which actually lightens my mood.

"No reason to get homicidal. Thank you for the offer and if I ever need someone to be killed, you're the first person I'll call, but I'm fine. I'm just going to go read until dinner," I say

"Okay nerd," Rex replies.

"God not you too," I say under my breath.

"So, there is someone I need to kill," and although the thought of Tyler going up against my brother makes me a little giddy, I know that would be an overreaction, because Tyler would not stand a chance.

"No seriously, there's no one bothering me," I say escaping to my room for a few hours before my mom calls me down to dinner. My father and brother are already sitting at the table. They're both intimidating men and I'd be nervous around them if they weren't my family.

"How was school my darling," My mom asks. I take after my mother in stature, but I inherited most of my attitude from my father.

"I'm ready to be done," I say.

"Have you thought more about your plans for after school?" My father asks.

"I still want to take a few weeks traveling," I say stabbing my food with my fork.

"No," my father says.

"Why not, Mathis and Tanner travel all the time," I say. My two oldest brothers both travel for work.

"Yeah, and they're strong enough that I don't worry about their safety," my dad says cutting into his steak.

"I can just go to places that are mostly human," I say. Shrugging. My dad glares at me with his almost black eyes.

"You think you are stronger than a human male?" he asks arching an eyebrow.

"Human females travel all the time, and I'm definitely stronger than them," I say.

"I think it's romantic. Maybe she's being called to her mate," my mom says.

"Your mate will eventually be drawn to you no matter where you are. Look Rain, you have been blessed to take after your mother in size and disposition. One day you'll be mated to a fearsome male of our kind and if he allows it, you can travel all you want with him by your side," my dad says. I don't even bother trying to explain to him how insane what he just said is.

"You can take art classes at Praxley College," Rex says.

"I'm so over shifters though," I groan.

"Yeah, but Praxley is a safe place to be," my dad says.

"It'll all work out, whatever the fates have planned for you will unfold in time regardless of our actions," my mom says making my dad smile at her indulgently.

After dinner I plan on spending the rest of my Friday night in my room reading, one of my favorite pastimes. At around 11pm I hear pounding at my window. I open it to see a drenched Becca crying.

"Becca what happened? Are you okay?" I help her into my room.

"It was all a mean joke," she says. Shit. I didn't even think about Becca falling for their dumb prank. A deep sense of guilt washes over me. It hadn't even occurred to me that they'd ask her too.

"What happened?" I say gently.

"You know I've had a crush on Max forever? He came up to me after school today, and said he always had a crush on me, and that with school ending he wanted to get to know me before he missed his chance. He invited me to a party down on pack grounds." She says sniffling.

"What did they do?" I ask.

"I found him, and he was talking to me like we were friends, asking questions about me, flirting even. Then all of a sudden, Heather and Kelly come up behind me with a cooler filled of beer and dump it over my head. They started laughing at me for being so stupid," she says sniffling.

"I'm so sorry Becca," I say giving her a sticky hug.

"Would you like to take a shower? I'll give you some pajamas to wear, and we can talk about the slow death we would wish on each of the popular kids."

"Yes, thank you Rain. I should have realized it was a prank. I am so stupid."

"Wanting to have friends isn't stupid. It'll be fine. There's only a couple more weeks of school. We can come up with a plan to avoid them."

TYLER

"Can you believe how stupid that Becca girl was? The look on her face was priceless. Like anybody would ever be interested in her. I just wish Rain came too. Oh well," Heather says. I keep replaying Rain's words in my head. How I was supposed to be a leader, and here I was pulling mean pranks on someone I should be protecting. I guess all my father's lectures were finally taking hold.

"Tyler, why do you look so upset?" Heather asks.

"No reason," I say taking a drink of my beer.

"Well, I think I could cheer you up, how about we sneak off and find a dark corner and I will make you feel better," Heather says seductively.

"I don't feel like it tonight, plus I didn't bring any condoms," I say. I didn't have hooking up on my mind. The closer I get to eighteen the less interested I am becoming in Heather.

"That's okay. We don't need to use a condom," Heather says.

"Absolutely not," I scowl.

"I'm on the pill," she says.

"No, you're not. Why would you lie about that?"

"Well, we're going to be fated mates, we should start trying to have a child. It'll be expected of us," Heather says. This girl must be out of her mind.

"I think I'm done for tonight. I'm going home."

"Oh, good I will come with you."

"Not tonight, Heather," I say leaving.

RAIN

Becca stays with me over the weekend. She decided not to tell anybody from either of our families about what happened. Rex could sense something was up but knew better than to push her for details. She ended up ditching school Monday and Tuesday but decides to go back the rest of the week. I told her to arrive early and leave early and she would avoid those assholes that pranked her. She got through the rest of the week unscathed.

"Are you okay?" I ask Friday after school.

"Yeah, you were right, I was able to avoid them, and it wasn't that big of a deal," she says.

"Good," I say lightly squeezing her arm.

"The crappy part is for a few hours I felt so good about myself," Becca says.

"Soon our crappy high school experience will be over, and we'll never have to see any of these people again."

"But we will. They'll still be part of our pack and we'll still be at the bottom of the social pyramid."

"Maybe you can come and travel with me," I say.

"I never really considered it before, but I think you're right. I'm tired of trying to fit in with people who will never accept me."

Chapter 4
Tyler

Turning eighteen is a big deal in the shifter community. It means I'm an adult member of our society, but it also means I'll be able to scent out my mate. Since I come from a long line of alphas, it also means that I'll be able to use an alpha command. I'll be able to compel people to do things with my voice.

The celebration for turning eighteen is kind of like New Year's Eve, where everybody stays up until midnight the night before the actual birthday. Most of my class is at my house to celebrate, especially the girls. My parents went all out and decorated the entire backyard for this party.

"Mate?" Heather looks at me expectantly when the clock strikes midnight. Her smile drops when she sees the face I make. Her scent is repulsive to me.

"No," I say.

"What? What do you mean? Maybe you just can't tell yet. We have to be mates."

"No definitely not mates," I say shaking my head.

"You're joking right, very funny. Such a funny alpha," Heather says, clearly losing it.

"I'm sorry Heather, you're not my mate," I say.

"You'll pay for this asshole," she says storming off crying. All the high school girls around me swarm in.

"Am I your mate?" Kelly asks.

"No." I take a deep breath. "I'm sorry none of you are," all the girls look disappointed. I don't like the idea of being tied down, but I'm kind of disappointed too. It's weird, exactly at midnight I got this new sensation, an impulse, that says find your mate and claim her. My wolf is unsettled that she's not around us. I don't feel like celebrating anymore, but I can't exactly leave my own party.

"You fucking dodged a bullet with Heather," Max says.

"Yeah, so did our pack," I say.

"Who do you think your mate will be? Every female in our age range was here tonight," Max says.

"I don't know, but my wolf is going to go insane if she takes too long to find. I already have this overwhelming impulse to find and claim her. I can't fucking imagine what it'll feel like if I don't find her," I say. It's close to 2am before people start to leave.

"I'm pretty tired, I think I am going to head to bed, thank you for the party" I say to my parents.

"Happy birthday son. Don't worry, you will find her, I guarantee it," my dad says.

Chapter 5
TYLER

I spent the rest of the weekend in an anxious daze. I ignored all fifty of Heather's texts. Of course, I knew I couldn't avoid her forever, but I did manage not to talk to her until the end of the school day on Monday when she corners me at my locker.

"Hey, I'm sorry I ran off on you Saturday, I think we both said some things we didn't mean. But I'm ready to accept you as my mate," Heather says.

"Heather I'm very sorry, but you're not my mate," I say. Once the words leave my mouth, I get hit by the force of a mack truck.

"Hey, where are you going," Heather calls after me, but I can't even hear her. I have to find the source of the scent. It's exactly how everybody describes it, my fated mate is here somewhere. I turn the corner at the end of the hallway, and there's Rain in front of her open locker.

"Fuck," I say. Of all the fucking people. It had to be her. She just ignores me, continuing on putting her books away. I approach her, and her scent is addictive. I have to stop myself from touching her.

"Rain," I say her name like a prayer.

"Tyler," she says dryly, but just hearing her say my name does very unexpected things to me.

"It's you," I say.

"You got to be fucking kidding me Tyler. Is this some kind of sick joke?" Heather asks, coming up behind me but I tune her out.

"It's no joke, Rain's my mate," I say. Rain turns to look at me with her dark blue eyes, and my heart stops.

"If you are serious the joke is on you, because I don't want shit to do with you," she says slamming her locker, trying to walk around me. I grab her arm, and she must feel the connection because she just closes her eyes for a second, like she's trying to reign in her temper.

"That's really unfortunate for you Tyler. I rather die alone, than be mated to you," she says before pulling her arm out of my hold.

"Rain wait," I say with an unintentional alpha command.

"Don't you fucking dare alpha command me," she says, pushing through the command.

"Rain, you have to at least give me a chance," I beg. She turns back to me.

"No Tyler, you were the one who never gave me a chance," she says before turning to exit toward the parking lot.

"Tyler, are you serious? You picked Rain over me?" Heather says.

"You know how this works Heather, I didn't pick anybody, fate decided that Rain is my mate," I say. No point in denying it, everybody will find out soon enough. I feel compelled to follow her. It only takes me a minute to catch up with her, a block away from school. I follow at a distance until she turns into the long driveway that I know leads to her creepy house.

I walk closer to the house. It's large and dark, two stories high. I sneak around the back not really knowing what I'm looking for. I know I'm being irrational, but my wolf is on fire. He doesn't understand why our mate doesn't like us. He wants me to claim her and force her submission. I'm surprised to find what looks like what could be her room on the first floor. I try to open the window, but it's locked. Her room is covered in colorful art. I was expecting something darker from her.

I decide I have to try and talk to her one more time, so I go around front and knock on the door. Rain answers. It makes my chest hurt when seeing me immediately makes her frown.

"Rain I'm sorry, but you're my mate now, you can't just ignore me," I plead.

"Yes, I can," she says, trying to shut the door but I prop it open with my foot. She takes a glimpse back into the house then comes outside.

"You're going to get yourself killed coming here," she says.

"I will eventually go insane if I don't claim you, you know this," I say.

"Well, you don't have much going on upstairs, so it won't me much of a loss."

"I'm serious."

"So am I. You will go crazy. I will be fine. So how I see it, this is your self-made problem not mine."

"You can't ignore me forever," I say.

"I guess we'll see." I can't suppress the growl that comes out of my throat. I step closer, and Rain backs up against the closed front door. I reach and gently wrap my large hand around her slim neck. She is so tiny with such delicate features, with her stunning eyes.

"Please don't hurt me," she says, and it physically hurts me that she is afraid of me. I pull my hand away.

"I would never hurt you," I say.

RAIN

He sounds so sincere that I almost believe him.

"You can't expect me to just forget everything you've done to me. Please leave," I say. He lets out a frustrated breath. Being here alone with him, I am acutely aware of the size difference. Tyler is an over six feet tall mountain of muscle. On top of that, he can alpha command me if he wants. Not that he would need to, he could physically overpower me with ease. Shifters are stronger than human, but I am so much weaker than an average shifter. Mostly because I am not just a shifter. Tyler is an alpha shifter male in his prime. He's the top of the food chain, and I am the bottom.

With his long wavy hair, and dark brown eyes, he's very attractive. That's not the problem. The problem is he's an asshole. Being close to me I can feel his pheromones at work too. But we're just too different. This could never work.

"I at least want your phone number," he says. I let out a sarcastic laugh.

"Right because it worked out for me so well the last time you got a hold of my cell phone number. You realize I had to change numbers after that prank," I say.

"I'm sorry. I will never do anything like that to you again," he says.

"Oh, I know you won't because I will not give you the opportunity to," I say.

"Give me your phone," he says with an alpha command. I try to fight it, but he's too strong. I reluctantly hand over my cell phone. He texts himself then hands it back.

"I will go, but this is not over," he says before turning and leaving. He's going to put up more of a fight than I was expecting.

Chapter 6
TYLER

I walk back to school to get my car. I'm tempted to shift and run back to let off some energy, but I decide to wait until later tonight. I want to talk to my parents first, then I want to go on a very long run. When I get home, I find both my parents in the kitchen, making dinner together. I just watch them together. I never really appreciated the relationship they have. My parents were fated mates that met during high school too. You can tell by how they interact how much they love each other.

"Darling what's the matter?" my mom asks when she sees me.

"I found my mate today," I say taking a seat at the kitchen table.

"How exciting, who is she?" My mom asks.

"Rain," I say. I can tell my mom is a little surprised but still happy.

"She really is a very beautiful girl, why didn't you bring her over?" my mom asks.

"Yeah, son you two should be inseparable," my dad says.

"She wants nothing to do with me," I admit. My mom sits next to me grabbing my hand.

"How could she not want anything to do with you? You're very handsome and will be the next alpha," my mom says.

"I spent the last 13 or so years bullying her," I say. It sounds so horrible, and I know I really fucked this up.

"Tyler, I thought I taught you better than that. The entire reason we have a pack is for protection. It's your duty as one of the strongest members to protect all the people that are weaker than you. People shouldn't want to follow you because you bully them, they should want to follow you because you inspire them," my dad says, and I know he's right. This is the same lecture he has been giving me for years, but now it really hits home.

"What do I do?" I ask my mom.

"Give her time, prove to her you're worthy of being her mate," my mom says.

"I have to go for a run, my wolf is going insane," I say.

"Eat some dinner first, it's already ready," she gets up and brings me a plate. After I quickly inhale my food, I go outback strip off my clothes and shift into my wolf form. My wolf is huge, the size of a small horse with shaggy gray hair. I take off running with no particular direction in mind, or so I thought. It doesn't take me long before I find myself in Rain's backyard, looking into her window.

With my shifter eyesight, I can see into her bedroom clearly without being so close that she can see me. She's getting ready for bed. Her back is to me as she takes off her top. I never really noticed how curvy she is. She takes off her top but puts on her pajama shirt before turning around. Then she pulls down her pants, and I see her lacy black underwear. She takes them off and I get a glimpse of her ample bottom. She slides on her pajama shorts with nothing underneath and crawls into bed. I will be masturbating to that image later. I can't believe I ignored her obvious beauty for so long. Not only did I ignore her beauty, I terrorized her. I watch her sleep for a few hours, before running back home.

RAIN

I dread having to interact with Tyler again. I turned my cell phone off as soon as Tyler left yesterday. After getting dressed and eating a quick breakfast, I head out to walk to school.

"Good morning, Rain," Tyler says as soon as I open the door, his car parked in front of my house. Shit. I don't even get the walk to school to mentally prepare for this interaction.

"Tyler," I say. I briefly consider going back inside and locking the door, but I don't want to hide from this asshole. I didn't do anything wrong; he should be the one hiding from me.

"I don't appreciate you ignoring my texts," Tyler says.

"That's really unfortunate for you," I say with a fake grin.

"Let me drive you to school," Tyler says.

"I'm not getting inside your car," I say walking past him.

"Alright I'll walk you to school then," he says, matching my pace.

"I'm not really in a position to stop you. You'll just alpha command me to do whatever you want," I say petulantly.

"Rain, I'll do whatever I have to do to claim you," I stop to turn and look at him.

"Claiming happens during sex Tyler, and I'll never let you have sex with me. So what? Are you going to force me to have sex with you?"

"I didn't mean it like that Rain. Please just give me a chance. Let me take you out on a date." I turn to continue the walk to school.

"Although I appreciate the offer, I'm actually busy whatever night you wanted to take me out," I say. When we get to school everyone turns and looks at us. I can hear everybody whisper; some people are even pointing. I meet Becca in front of her locker. Our lockers are right next to each other.

"Good morning," she says to me, eyeing Tyler curiously.

"We are safely at school, you may leave my side now," I say to Tyler. His group of Jackals are down the hall just staring at him.

"I want to make sure you get to your first class," he says.

"Do you really think I am going to get attacked on the way to first period? Before yesterday, you were the only person I worried about harming me," I say. The look of regret on his face almost gets to me. Almost.

"Fine. Have a good day in your classes," he says before walking off. Although he stays close enough where he can still see me while pretending to be nonchalant about it.

"What was that about?" Becca asks.

"Tyler's my mate," I say.

"Are you serious? Are you sure it's not another cruel joke?"

"Unfortunately, no. I could tell when he grabbed my arm yesterday. I felt the connection," I say.

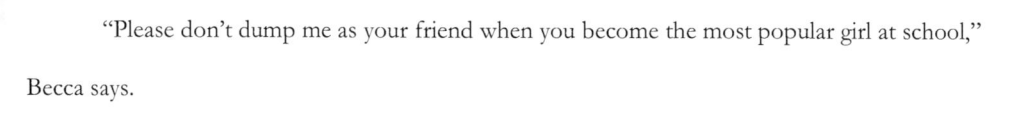

"Please don't dump me as your friend when you become the most popular girl at school," Becca says.

"Becca I would never do that. I doubt I'll be winning any popularity contest anytime soon and even if I did, I'm not the type of person to ditch my only friend," I say.

"Of course, I know you wouldn't. I just am still vulnerable from that last prank," Becca says.

"Besides, you know I can only take so much of shifters," I barely whisper knowing Becca will be able to hear me.

"I would have sworn Tyler was full blooded shifter," Becca says.

"Come on let's get this school day over with," changing the topic. This is not a conversation we should be having in public.

Chapter 7
TYLER

"What the hell was that about? Why were you walking with that freak?" Max asks. It takes every ounce of self-control not to kill Max for talking poorly about my mate.

"Rain is my mate and your future Luna," I say. Max starts to laugh but stops when he sees how serious I am.

"Seriously?" Kevin asks.

"Yes. So spread the word. Rain is the new queen of Praxley High," I say.

"Fuck man, all those stupid pranks we pulled," Max says.

"Yeah. I highly recommend making amends with every single female you have wronged before you guys turn eighteen. She wants nothing to do with me and I did this all to myself," I admit.

I leave class early to walk Rain to each of her classes. I am spending every minute I can with her. At least Becca doesn't seem to hate me as much. At lunch time, Rain heads her way outside instead of to the cafeteria.

"Where are you going?" I ask.

"To go eat lunch," she says without stopping.

"Why don't you come and eat inside with me?"

"No," she says without even looking at me. I know where she usually sits, I go to the lunchroom to grab lunch and tell the guys I am eating outside. Kevin and Max follow me out, which means Kelly also comes following Kevin out. I head to the tree where Rain and Becca sit.

"Absolutely not. Tyler I'd maybe put up with you lurking around, but that asshole Max has to leave," Rain says. Fuck, I should have realized she would be upset about what they did to Becca.

"I'm sorry," Max says to Rain.

"I'm not the one you should be apologizing to," Rain says.

"Becca, I'm sorry. It was a stupid prank that wasn't even funny. It wasn't even my idea," Max says.

"It doesn't matter if it was your idea or not, what you did was cruel to someone who has only ever been kind to you. It would be poetic justice for Becca to be your mate Max so you would have to prove yourself to her. How would you feel about that? As far as I am concerned you are not even good enough to be her friend," Rain says.

"I'd be thrilled if Becca was my mate, like you said she's one of the kindest people I know," Max says. I can see why the fates chose this woman to be the next Luna. Rain whispers something to Becca. I can't hear but I'm pretty sure she is telling her she would get rid of us if Becca wants. I need to make sure I get in good with her friend. I need all the help I can get.

"Fine, you may join us, no more pranks though," Rain says.

"Thank you," I say.

"Why do you guys always eat lunch outside?" Max asks.

"Well, it used to be a peaceful place to have lunch," Rain says glaring at me.

"You don't have any meat for lunch," I say when I notice Rain only has fruits and vegetables packed set out in front of her.

"I'm a vegetarian," Rain says.

"What? You're a wolf, you have to eat meat," my wolf is on edge, and I get an overwhelming urge to feed my mate. "Here have some of my lunch I brought ham sandwiches," I say frantically. Shifters are meant to eat meat.

"Tyler, I haven't eaten meat in years. It's fine," Rain says.

"No that's not fine. You're going to need to eat meat so our babies can grow strong."

"Tyler that was such an insane thing to say that I don't really know how to respond," Rain says, and I let out a low growl.

RAIN

I can't explain to him in front of all these people that I have about a drop of shifter blood running through me and as such don't eat meat. He'll eventually find out about my bloodline and will probably learn some shocking facts about his own heritage, but not right now. I want to change the subject, so he'll drop it, but I've never talked to any of Tyler's friends before. The upcoming graduation seems like a safe enough topic, and we make light small talk all the while Tyler watches every single thing I eat. It's unnerving.

Just like my morning classes, Tyler escorts me from classroom to classroom. The entire school must know by now. Everybody is treating me like their best friend, and it's kind of annoying. By the end of the day, I am exhausted, and sneak out of school early to run to the comfort of my home. The entire walk there, I keep looking behind me expecting Tyler to pop out from nowhere, but I make it to the front door unbothered.

TYLER

I trail Rain home from a distance, to make sure she gets there safely. I'm still on edge thinking about the possibility my mate is malnourished. The image of force feeding her meat while she is bond to a chair comes unprompted to my mind. I file that thought for later though. After leaving Rain, my parents find me pacing back and forth in our kitchen, barely suppressing a growl.

"How are you holding up?" My mom asks with concern in her eyes. I know how unhinged I must seem right now. I stop pacing, loudly sigh, then take a seat at the kitchen table before answering.

"We had lunch together," I say.

"That's a start," my dad says. I run my hands through my hair.

"Yeah, I guess" I say.

"You're upset," my mom states.

"I only have so much time until school is out. I need to convince Rain that I'm worthy of her, but it's hard since I can't get her alone," I say. My parents look at each other, first with a smirk that turns a little heated.

"What?" I ask, but I don't really want to know.

"Oh nothing, just thinking about all the alone time we spent together as a newly mated couple," my dad says.

"You know I think I'll call Rain's mom, I think it's time I formally introduce myself to her," my mom says.

Chapter 8
RAIN

"Who are the extra place settings for mom?" I ask even though I already know the answer.

"Rain I'm so excited to meet your mate's family officially," my mom says right before the doorbell rings and my mom excitedly runs to answer it.

"Alpha and Luna Grant welcome to our home, my name is Miza" my mom says to Tyler's parents "and Tyler we're so happy to have you here tonight," my mom says always the peace maker. I'm not even sure how she knows about us being mated, I certainly didn't tell her.

"Please call us Jeff and Amanda," Tyler's dad says. My dad approaches with a scowl on his face. He isn't thrilled with my future mate.

"Tyler," he grunts and narrows his eyes.

"My husband Trace is very excited about having you tonight as well," my mom says. I can feel the energy radiating off of him and Rex, but I wonder if Tyler's able to perceive it.

"Thank you," Tyler says, oblivious to the threat my family poses to him, or just ignoring it.

"There's a lot we need to discuss," my dad says.

"Trace that can wait until after we get to know each other a little," my mom says.

"No Miza," my dad barks to my mom.

"Well, we can at least sit around the table first, please follow me to the dining room and take a seat" my mom says leading the way.

"I assume you want to discuss our children being mated," Jeff starts, once we are all seated.

TYLER

I've never interacted with Rain's family before, so I never noticed that they're a little off. I can't sense Trace's wolf, but he has mine on high alert. My wolf perceives him as a lethal threat.

"What do you know about chimeras?" Trace asks. My dad inhales deeply through his nose.

"No, how's that possible? I thought chimeras were all extinct," my dad says.

"Not extinct, just hidden and Tyler must have chimera somewhere in his ancestry or he wouldn't be the mate of a half-blooded chimera," Trace says glancing over at Rain.

"What's a chimera?" I ask. I feel like I'm missing something important here.

"A chimera is another species. We can manipulate energy. A male chimera is much stronger and more dominant than a male wolf shifter. It's the reason your wolf is so afraid right now, it recognizes me as a more dangerous predator," Trace says.

"So, wait. Rain you are a chimera, not a wolf shifter?" I ask confused.

"I'm a fourth shifter, a fourth fae and half pixie. Rain is the perfect combination of each," Miza says.

"Thanks mom," Rain says. It's interesting how different her parents are. Her mom is a petite, delicate almost angelic looking woman contrasting against her dad the huge evil predator. He sneers at me like he can read my thoughts.

"I can read some of them," he says, arching a brow at me, pulling his wife's hand to his mouth for a tender kiss.

"What the fuck?" I mumble.

"Tyler watch your mouth," my dad says.

"Sorry, what does this all mean," I mutter, still processing everything I just learned.

"Well for starter, once you two mate, Tyler any dormant chimera blood you have is going to make itself known," Trace says, Rex chuckles.

"God that's all he needs," Rain says rubbing her forehead.

"How so?" I ask.

"It's going to depend on how much chimera blood you have. If it's a lot, it's possible you will grow in size and become similar to a full-blooded chimera and will be able to manipulate energy like we can. If you only have a little, it's still going to be like you shot yourself up with a mixture of steroids and testosterone. All your dominant, aggressive impulses are going to be amplified. Either way, it's a lot of masculine power that you will all of the sudden have," Trace says.

"Yeah, it's hard enough growing up with it. I can't imagine having to learn how to control that much power as an adult," Rex says.

"We could just not mate," Rain offers. Trace sighs.

"Not claiming his mate will activate any latent chimera genes just like mating you will. Only he'll be insane," Trace says.

"Tyler's the next alpha of our pack," Amanda says.

"He'll most likely have obligations to the chimera community too. It's also possible you're going to have some chimera males challenge you to be Rain's mate. You two need to mate sooner rather than later because right now a chimera male would kill you without even trying Tyler," Trace says then turns to his daughter.

"Rain I'm not thrilled about you mating with a wolf shifter, but the fates put you two together for a reason, and I don't want to risk your future happiness," Trace says.

"I hate him. I'd rather die alone than be his mate," Rain says.

"Rain no," Miza says with a pained expression.

"Jeff, I think the two of them need to be put in seclusion together," Trace says.

"Dad no," Rain says.

"I agree," my dad says.

Rain being upset rattles my wolf. When she becomes so upset that she gets up and runs to her room, I am compelled to follow even though I'm the last person she is going to want to see. I leave our fathers to further discuss our seclusion, so that's what my dad was hinting at earlier.

"Leave me alone," she says through unshed tears sitting on her bed.

"Stop," I command, "this is certainly not what I expected, but we're mates now and we're going to be together," I say, grabbing her shoulders.

"And what I want doesn't matter? I don't even like you, but everybody wants me to make a lifetime commitment to you," Rain says standing up to me.

"Of course what you want matters. Nothing matters more to me than making you happy. But I'm not going to leave you be. You heard your dad, I might turn into some rabid, insane chimera if we don't mate. I'm going to be making a lifetime commitment to you too. I promise I'll do everything within my power to make you love me," I stare down at her beautiful eyes, and I don't think I just act. I crush her with my lips, dominating her with my mouth. I must catch Rain off guard because she doesn't try to push me off her. I grab her ass with my hands and lift her up to place her back on the bed and start to crawl over her. Her mind might hate me, but her body recognizes me as its mate.

"Wait Tyler stop. I don't want this." I lower my forehead to hers and just enjoy the moment with my mate in my arms.

"I want to prove to you that I can be worthy of being your mate. I want to be in seclusion with you where we can just get to know each other," I say as she looks up into my eyes.

"I don't think it's a good idea," Rain says curling her hand into my shirt.

"We don't really have much of a choice," I say before giving her one more kiss on the cheek and getting up.

"I know," she sighs.

Chapter 9
RAIN

It took them less than twelve hours to find a cabin in the woods outside of town and have it prepared for our seclusion. Despite my best efforts, I find myself trapped in Tyler's car, heading out to said cabin. Of course, since this is a shifter town and Tyler is the next alpha, we both got excused from school for the rest of the year.

"Are you nervous?" Tyler asks.

"That's not really the word I'd use to describe how I'm feeling," I say looking out the window.

"Why'd you dye your hair back to dark brown," Tyler asks, making me laugh.

"I didn't dye my hair," I say he glances over at me, and I shake my head turning my hair to rainbow colors then back to brown.

"What the fuck?" Tyler exclaims.

"I guess there's no point in hiding anything I can do from you anymore."

"That's fucking awesome, why would you hide that?" Tyler asks.

"The same reason shifters hide from humans. It's safer. My father and brothers are fierce warriors but none of my talents can protect me."

"I'll always protect you," Tyler growls with a ferocity that I think even startles him and I don't know how to respond, so I just nod and look back out the window.

"I think this is it," Tyler says pulling up to a quaint little cabin. He doesn't let me get my own bag from the trunk, insisting on carrying all the luggage. When he opens the front door it's much more modern than I was expecting. The front door opens into an open living room and kitchen and when I walk further in, I see the king-sized bed.

"Why is there a bed in the living room?" I ask. Tyler looks sheepish.

"Tyler why is there a bed out in the living room?" I ask again, a little more urgently.

"We're meant to spend this time together, and we can't do that if you just hide away from me in separate rooms. There are no bedrooms and the only privacy you'll get from me is using the bathroom," Tyler says.

TYLER

Rain gives me a look that would scare lesser men. But I'm an alpha, and after her dad explained to me about chimeras, I must admit I feel the urge to be dominant growing the more I spend with Rain. I just need to claim her before I do something to make her hate me.

"Phone," I say holding out my hand.

"What?" Rain looks at me puzzled.

"Give me your phone," I say with a gentle alpha command. I've been practicing scaling back my alpha commands. She hands it to me, and I put our phones and the keys to the car in a combination safe against the wall. I want to make sure she has no way to escape me. Seclusion is pretty common among shifters, and this cabin has been used in the past for that exact purpose.

"Are you hungry?" I ask, the primitive part of my brain is obsessed with making sure my mate is taken care of. Rain follows me to the kitchen.

"The pantry and fridge are supposed to be stocked and they'll be delivering food weekly," I say.

"Jesus how long do they expect us to stay here?" Rain asks.

"You're not leaving until we're mated," I say staring directly into Rain's eyes.

"No pressure though, right?" Rain says sarcastically "Tyler there are barely any fruits or vegetables here," Rain says looking through the fridge.

"You need to eat meat," I say.

"I'm more pixie and chimera than I am shifter. I don't have the nutritional needs that you do," she says grabbing an apple.

"Okay, my wolf can accept that reasoning. I'll make sure the next delivery has more," I pull out the ingredients to make a sandwich and we both sit at the kitchen table eating our lunch.

"I'm sorry I never took the time to appreciate how amazing you are," I say.

"You're kind of all over the place Tyler. Maybe you're already going insane," she says.

"We better have sex now then," I say with a playful smirk, although my wolf really likes that idea.

"I'll take my chances," she says taking another bite of her apple.

"What was it like growing up with your father. He seems intense and can he read your thoughts?"

"Yes, he and my brothers can read people's thoughts, but growing up with him I learned to block it. He's intense but he's fair, and my mother definitely calms him down."

"Yeah, I thought they seemed like an odd pair," I admit, finishing off my sandwich.

"Chimera males are known to be dominant and aggressive while pixies are known to be docile and submissive. My dad protects and cherishes my mom. He might have last say in any disagreements but he'd also move mountains just to please her," something about that description resonates and I forget why I ever wanted a physically strong partner.

"I want to protect and cherish you," I say. She flashes me an actual smile and it feels like my heart is going to beat out of my chest. Rain finishes off her apple and my eyes are drawn to her luscious lips, and I am reminded of our kiss last night.

"So, what do we do now?" she asks.

Chapter 10

RAIN

"Well, you're part forest pixie, right?" he asks.

"And we happen to be in a forest," he continues, pointing to our view through the living room window. "Wait that wasn't insensitive to say right? I have to admit I feel very inadequate knowing so little about you and what you are, would you like to go for a walk?" Tyler asks, reaching out a hand that I hesitantly take. He leads me outside to a mostly overgrown trail.

"So, what does being a pixie mean?" he asks.

"Now Tyler, I'm not just going to tell you all my secrets. Remember, you are still the enemy," I say but with humor in my tone. I'm nervous that he's growing on me so quickly.

"Why don't we start with the basics then? We can work our way up to all your secrets," he says with a smirk, he pushes a low branch out of our way.

"Being a pixie, I can have a calming effect on the people around me. Like I said, pixies are usually benevolent. Any attitude I have definitely came from my father's side."

TYLER

"So, tell me more about your chimera side," I say. I have this deep need to know everything about Rain, so far she has been a tough nut to crack, but I feel like I'm finally making progress.

"You already know chimera males can manipulate energy. They can suck the life source out of somebody and absorb their energy or they can pull energy from one source and use it as a weapon," She explains.

"So, you could attack me?" important information to know.

"No. Chimera females can also manipulate energy but in a different capacity. I can use energy to heal somebody or to calm somebody, but I can't manifest it into a weapon like a male chimera can. The males can read minds and teleport too. I can't do either, but I can change my hair and eye color." The trail dead ends into a small clear pond, with an old wooden picnic table and bench.

"So, tell me more about you Tyler, is there anything more to you than muscles and nice hair?"

"You like my hair?" I ask with a grin, to which Rain just sighs, but I see her small smile. I'm definitely making progress. "What would you like to know?"

"Well, you are future alpha, right? How do you feel about it? Is it something you look forward to?"

"To be honest, I haven't taken it too seriously up until recently."

"Yeah, I can tell," Rain says with no emotion.

"It just always seemed like it was so far in the future, that it almost didn't seem real. Things just became so much more serious once I turned eighteen…….. I don't even know your birthday. When do you turn eighteen?"

"A month before you did."

"I just assumed you were younger because you're so small," Rain swats at my arm.

"Hey, I'm the perfect size, thank you very much." I let my gaze drift down her body.

"I'd have to agree." She might be petite, but she definitely has a grown-up body.

"Stop looking at me like that," she says.

"Like what? Like a wolf who wants to eat you?" I sense the faint scent of arousal, but Rain looks slightly uncomfortable, so I back off.

"We should go swimming," I say pointing to the pond in front of us. Rain looks at me for a second until she processes what I said.

"Oh uh, yeah maybe. We should go back to the cabin, it's starting to get dark out," she says.

RAIN

Tyler stares at me like I'm crazy.

"I'm the fiercest predator in these woods," Tyler says.

"Yeah, that's what I'm afraid of," I say standing up, heading back in the direction of the cabin. I hear Tyler walking behind me. The silence between us feels heavy. He sighs.

"Rain," I keep walking until he grabs my arm and turns me to face him.

"I've made a lot of stupid mistakes with you that I'll regret for the rest of our lives. But I'm going to prove to you that I'm sorry and that I'll never hurt you again. I know you're not ready to forgive me yet, and I'm not asking that of you. I just wanted you to know," he says, taking my hand to hold again.

He's right, I'm not ready to forgive him, but my stupid pixie nature makes it hard to hold a grudge. When we get back to the cabin, I sit down on the couch.

"I'll get us some food to eat and then we can watch a movie," Tyler says, walking over to the kitchen. Out of sheer pettiness, uncharacteristic of myself, I pick the sappiest romcom I can find. A move that backfires when we have to awkwardly sit through a sex scene together. Tyler just smirks. I expected him to pull a cheesy move and try to put his arm around me, but he didn't. I've been painfully aware of the half inch of space between us. It seems intentional. Whatever games we are playing, Tyler seems to be winning. Worse is that he knows he's winning, and a tiny dangerous voice in my head wonders if that would be so bad.

"You ready for bed?" Tyler asks and I know it's time to have the conversation I've been putting off all day.

"There's no way I'm sharing a bed with you," I say, getting up and turning off the tv.

"Yes, you are," Tyler says.

"We can split up the bedding and I can take the couch," I say. I can tell Tyler is trying to reign in his temper. He takes a couple of deep breaths before coming over to where I stand, right in front of me, putting his hand on the back of my neck to halt my retreat.

"Rain. I won't insist on fucking you tonight, but this is nonnegotiable, you are sleeping with me every single night for the rest of your life," he says and that reality hits me in the gut. He must feel my panic because his eyes soften.

TYLER

The fear in her eyes has my wolf on high alert and I have to comfort her.

"Don't worry I'll take it slow with you for your first-time, when we get there," I say.

"My first time?" Rain asks.

"Your first-time having sex," I say.

"My first-time having sex with you. I'm not a virgin," I'm consumed by a flash wave of blinding irrational rage.

"What? Who the fuck did you sleep with?" I growl.

"Who have you slept with?" Rain challenges back.

"That's different, those women before you meant nothing," I hiss, my feral side taking over.

"Seeing how none of the men I've slept with before you were my mate, I'd have to argue that they were meaningless too," Rain says.

"You never dated in school."

"I may make a shitty shifter, but I'm a highly coveted to the male chimera population," Rain explains.

"Wait? You had sex with a chimera male?" I say trying to put together the pieces in my rage addled mind. For some reason that bothers me even more.

"I welcome you to try and mate with any of the single shifter females from our grade. Maybe Heather? I bet she's still a virgin," she says glaring at me. I have to get out of here, I know I'd never hurt Rain, but my wolf is beyond control right now.

"Where are you going?" Rain asks but I leave without responding stripping when I get outside and shifting into my wolf self. I take off in no particular direction, running through the forest until my muscles are tired. It takes a couple hours of sprinting, but I'm finally worn out enough to sleep. I head back to the cabin and Rain is sound asleep in bed. I pull on a pair of boxers and join her. She unconsciously snuggles into my side and that did more to calm me down than the last few hours of grueling running did. I give her forehead a quick kiss before falling asleep with Rain in my arms, where she belongs.

Chapter 11
RAIN

I wake up with my face against a firm chest. I look up and Tyler's sleeping. I cringe before gently trying to release myself from his grip, to which he just squeezes me tighter.

"Where do you think you're going Little One," He asks, his voice laced with sleep.

"Where did you go last night?" I counter, trying not to sound jealous. I know he wasn't meeting up with any girls or anything, still it hurt more than I thought it could how we left things.

"I went for a run, why did you miss me?" he asks with a playful grin.

"No, just wondering where you could've possibly gone in the middle of nowhere," I say trying to sound uninterested.

"My wolf needed to run," he says looking down at me with a questioning look.

"I've never seen your wolf," he says.

"Yeah," I say, not really liking where this is going.

"I'd like to see your wolf," he says.

"You just want to see me naked," I say.

"Yeah, well that too," he says, pushing his erection against my leg.

"I need to pee," I say, needing an escape from this situation.

"No, you don't," Tyler says, not loosening his grip "why don't you want me seeing your wolf?" he asks.

"You want to chance me having an accident?" I ask.

"Fine but keep the bathroom door open," he says.

"No, pervert," I say, but he gives me a stern look and I don't want to be in this bed anymore having this conversation. I run to the bathroom and keep the door open an inch then turn the water on. I don't want to look at myself in the mirror, so I just stand in the bathroom for a minute, when I turn around Tyler's standing at the door with an eyebrow arched. I've never seen him without a shirt on and I'm embarrassed by how much I like the sight. He sniffs the air, and I might just die of embarrassment.

"Do you like what you see Rain? I smell how aroused you are," he says stepping closer to me.

"No, I don't" I say, blushing. Tyler towers over me placing his hand around my neck, forcing my chin up so I'm staring up at him.

"Never lie to me," he growls. I nod my agreement but should've realized that wouldn't be enough.

"No, I want to hear you say that you will not lie to me," Tyler says.

"I will try not to lie to you," Tyler just sighs before turning me around and bending me over the bathroom counter. He peels down my pajama shorts. I try to swat at him, but he just grabs my hands and holds them at the small of my back with one of his hands.

"I love that you don't wear underwear to bed. Soon I'll insist on you sleeping naked though," he whispers into the shell of my ear. He slowly traces one finger from his free hand through my slit then holds the hand in front of my face.

"If you don't enjoy seeing me without a shirt on then who are you wet for?"

"Nobody," I say.

"Wrong answer," Tyler says before he lands a firm swat on my butt cheek. I squeal more from being surprised than from being in pain.

"You just agreed not to lie, so let's try this again, who are you wet for?"

"You, okay. Your looks are not the problem, the fact that you're an asshole is," I say.

"No name calling or cursing," he says before smacking my ass three more times.

"Do you understand?" he asks.

"Yes," I say.

"Good," he says before raining down five more swats. I'm dancing up on my toes by the time he's done. It takes me a second to process that he stopped spanking me and was rubbing my backside instead. He massaged my pink flesh and with each swipe he comes closer and closer to my center, until finally his fingertips lightly kiss my wet folds. The shock has me bucking my hips, but Tyler uses the hand holding my hands at the small of my back to keep my pelvis in place.

"Such a pretty pink pussy you have, does it need my attention?" I groan in response, not able to bring myself to admitting I want him to touch me. He wraps his arm around me and focuses in on my clitoris, making lazy circles, not quite giving me what I need.

"You must want me to stop then," he says then slows down.

"Please," I say desperately.

"Please what Rain?" I see his reflection staring at me in the mirror in front of me.

"Please touch me," I pant. His grin is wicked but with a soft chuckle he returns his hand to where I need it, this time with more pressure.

TYLER

"No pretty girl, you need to be more specific if you want me to do something," I say, slowing down my movements even further.

"Please, Tyler, make me come," she says.

"All you had to do was ask," I whisper in her ear. I pick up my speed again, she widens her stance to give me better access between her thighs. I kiss her long slender neck, the exact spot where I will eventually claim her.

"Tyler," Rain says alarmed, as though reading my thoughts.

"Soon, Rain you belong to me," I ignore the urge to claim her by focusing on her pleasure. I need to taste her though. She lets out a gasp of disappointment when I remove my hand. I grab her hips to turn her then lift her on to the bathroom counter, dropping to my knees in front of her spread legs.

"You are so fucking gorgeous," I mumble, nuzzling her silky thigh.

"Please Tyler," she pants. I make eye contact with her before lowering my mouth to her warm center. We both moan. Rain closes her eyes, close to coming undone, but I want her complete attention on me. I want her to know who owns her body and her pleasure.

"Look at me," I growl. Her pupils are so dilated I can barely see any blue at all. I insert a single finger in her tight channel, and she immediately clamps down on me, calling out her release. I let her ride out her climax, continuing to gently lick her folds until she becomes too sensitive and pushes me away. I stand up to claim her mouth so she can taste her own arousal. She slowly slides down from the counter, gracefully lowering to her knees in front of me.

"You don't have to, it's not why I did it. I just wanted to give you pleasure," I say even though I am painfully hard.

"I wouldn't offer if I wasn't sure about it," she says. That's all I need to hear. I help her lower my boxers, as my erection springs free. Rain's eyes grow wide.

"I kind of figured you'd be huge," I chuckle before grabbing her hair to gently guide her to my cock. Her hair is still dark brown, but I don't have the presence of mind to dwell on it now. Her small mouth closes in on my length. It's so much better than prior experiences, it's not even comparable. It's a struggle not to immediately come in her mouth. I grit my teeth and she doubles down on her efforts, taking me as deep down her throat as she can manage. With my free hand I push down her pajama tank top so I can see her full breast and her hard pink nipples.

"You feel amazing," I say, and she rewards me with a hum of approval. I'm careful not to pull her hair, but I still hold her firm. I want this moment to last longer, but I was already so turned on before she started.

"I'm going to come," I warn. The image of pulling out and finishing on her tits pushes me over the top. She didn't pull away, so I come down her throat, and after she licks me clean. We both lock eyes in silence. I know she feels the intensity between us, but she isn't ready to accept it fully yet, so when she turns away, I let her have her reprieve. She pulls back on her pajamas.

"I should go get dressed for the day," she says before scurrying out of the bathroom.

Chapter 12
RAIN

I kick myself mentally for running away like a coward, but I needed a moment to process what just happened and how I felt about it. I also needed both of us to have clothes on to have that conversation. I quickly dress, and escape to the kitchen to make some breakfast, not that it's much of an escape since there are no walls inside this cabin. I heard the shower running, so I wasn't surprised when Tyler exits the bathroom in just a towel. But thankfully, he quickly grabbed some clothes and went back to the bathroom to change. The lack of privacy in the cabin slightly grating on my nerves.

"You made me bacon?" Tyler says grinning when he joins me at the kitchen table.

"Yeah, kind of peace offering of sorts," I say eating the fruit salad I made.

"Oh, I thought the blowjob was the peace offering," he smirks and despite myself, I laugh too.

"I enjoyed what we did, and I don't regret doing it, I just don't want to give you mixed signals about where we stand in our relationship," I say.

"Rain, I promise I'll never do anything you aren't ready to do, if you had told me to stop, I would have," Tyler says with a level of sincerity that I haven't seen before.

"I know Tyler, it's just that I don't want you to think that I'm ready for you to claim me. I might be okay with………exploring, but I don't want to make a commitment that I'm not ready to make," I say.

"And I won't make you before you're ready," Tyler says.

"Sure, you say that now, but just wait until your chimera genes kick in." The last thing I need is a supercharged bully. I know he's trying but I can't just forget all the stupid pranks and all the mean names I endured because of him.

"I'll just have to earn your trust before that happens," Tyler says, and for both of our sakes, I hope he does. I'm not sure even the mating bond could save us if he were to claim me against my will.

TYLER

My primitive brain is telling me it's a good sign she made food for me, but the logical side of my brain knows I have a long way to go and a short time to get there.

"So, tell me more about chimeras. Your dad said something about me having obligations to the chimera community, what does that mean? Where even is a chimera community?" I ask.

"Most chimeras live among humans and shifters, they teleport to what is considered the chimera community, I'm not really sure where it is, female chimeras can't teleport and I don't really know what role you'll fill," Rain says.

"If the chimera gene is so dominant, why are none of my ancestors chimeras?"

"Oh, you absolutely do have an ancestor that was a chimera, the gene was passed down from your maternal side, so it wasn't as obvious and was diluted throughout the years and eventually completely suppressed."

"Why are you able to do what you can then?" I feel like I'm in biology class.

"Since my dad is full blooded chimera and my mom is only a fourth shifter, it overrode the shifter gene," Rain says.

"So, if we had a son, he'd most likely be a chimera but if we were to have a daughter, she'd most likely be a shifter," I say.

"That's a huge if. I don't even know if I want kids," she says.

"I never really thought about them before. God, I didn't even think about it, we need protection before we mate," seclusion happened so fast, I didn't really have time to prepare.

"It's okay, I'm on the birth control shot," she says.

"Crisis averted then," I say willing myself not to think about why she needed to be on the shot. "So, what would you like to do today, I'm game for anything but I'd really like to run with you as wolves. Wait, can you even shift into a wolf? Is that why I've never seen you in wolf form?" Rain seems like a puzzle I don't quite have all the pieces to.

"No, I can shift. Yeah, I think I'd like that. Now that you've seen me naked, it doesn't seem like that big of a deal anymore," Rain says. I put our dishes in the sink, then grab Rain's hand to walk outside together. I strip first, but despite what she just said, she still looks hesitant to get undressed. I turn around to give her a little bit of privacy, until I hear the sound of her undressing. When I turn back around, standing in front of me is a completely white wolf with violet-colored eyes. Her coat looks iridescent. It's not like anything I have ever seen.

"I see why you've never come on runs with us, I'd definitely know there was something different about you," her head tilts to the side. Anxious to run with my mate, I let the change overcome me until I am on all fours. I nudge her gently with my nose then start to run. Rain is small but very fast. She has no trouble keeping up with me, even though my wolf is massive compared to hers.

RAIN

My wolf has never been so happy, she's all in already. She doesn't understand what our hold up is and why Tyler hasn't claimed her yet. We run for almost an hour, until we find a clearing in the woods, and it's obvious that Tyler's wolf wants to stop and play. It starts out as playful rolling around, until I can feel Tyler's natural inclination for dominance taking over as he easily pins me to the ground.

I don't even think, I just shift. It's kind of terrifying being pinned by a giant wolf, but I know he won't hurt me. Tyler licks my face then shifts too.

"I didn't think about the fact you'd be naked on top of me if we both shifted," I cringe, trying not to think about how it feels to have his penis against my bare thigh.

"Why'd you shift?" Tyler asks.

"Can you get off of me before we talk." He hesitates for a second before rolling off me, so we can sit side by side.

"Happy? Can we talk now? I felt your panic, what happened?" He asks.

"The position we were in, it was just a little too close to being mounted and claimed. It's your natural instinct in wolf form," I say. Being claimed in wolf form is just as binding as in human form. Tyler gently grabs my chin to force me to look at him.

"I meant what I said, I won't claim you until you are ready, and I'd never do it in wolf form. I want you to be completely aware of what's happening. In fact, I'm going make you beg for it," he says holding me with his intense gaze. "Were you really afraid of my natural instinct to claim you or were you afraid of your natural instinct to be claimed?"

"Both," I whisper, more to myself than to him.

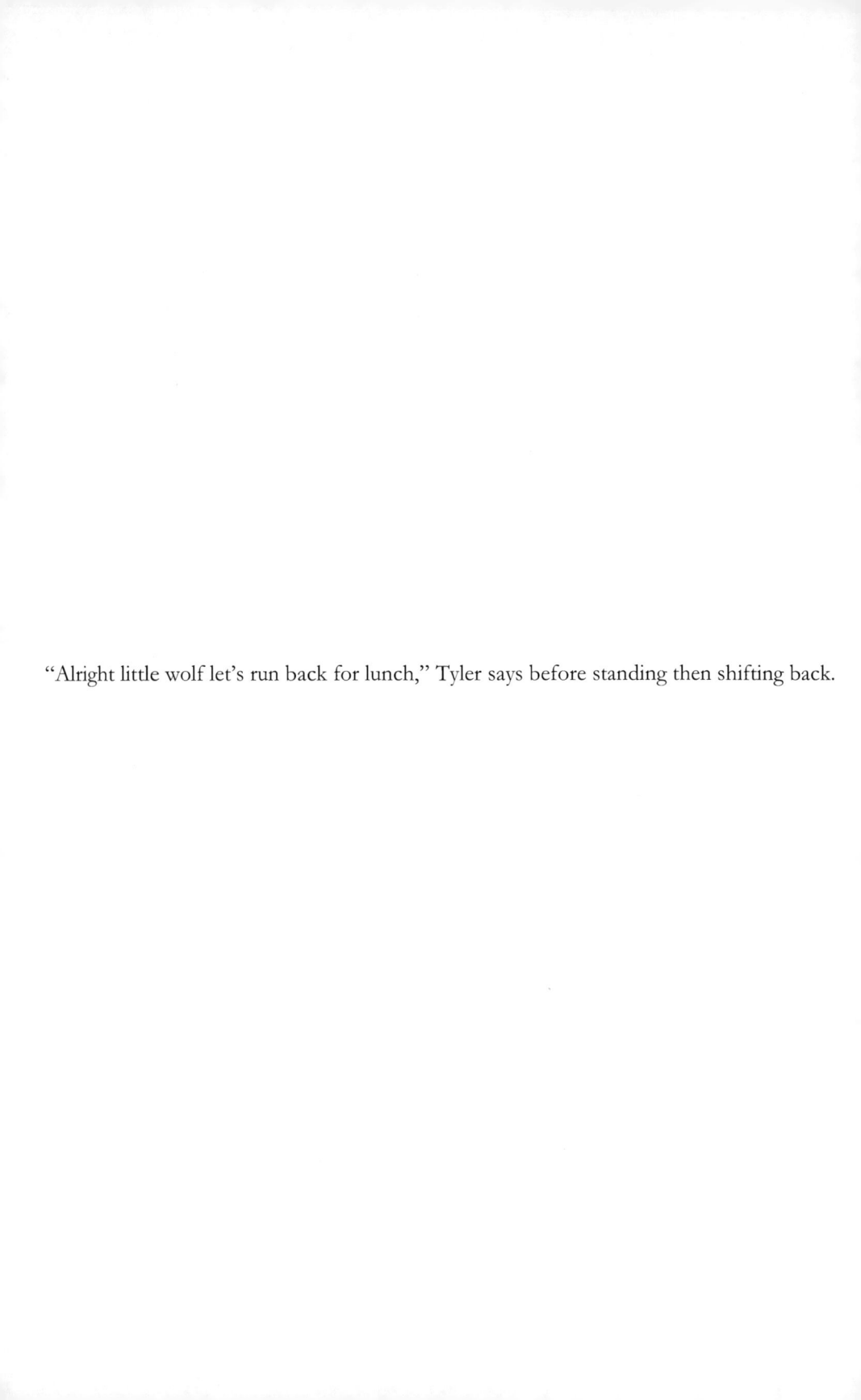

"Alright little wolf let's run back for lunch," Tyler says before standing then shifting back.

Chapter 13
TYLER

The past few days have felt like a standstill. We kind of formed a comfortable routine but Rain has been distant and not receptive to anymore….exploring. It feels like she wants to get close to me but is fighting herself. Sitting and watching her in the living room I can practically see her thoughts broadcasted across her delicate features. I just don't know how to get her out of her own head. I startle when someone knocks on the door.

"Weird we shouldn't be getting another food delivery already," I say standing up to answer the door. Something has my hackles raised, and I see why when I open the door and two huge figures are standing there. I've never actually talked to them, but I do recognize the two as Rain's brothers. The spitting image of their father, they have the same build and dark hair, only they have their mother's light eyes.

"Mathis? Tanner?" Rain says, jumping from her seat to run to the front door. "What are you guys doing here?"

"We had to make sure our little sister was okay," Mathis says pushing past me to enter the cabin, with Tanner right behind him. Rain looks so tiny standing by her brothers.

"Why wouldn't I be okay?" Rain asks. She had been overly polite the last couple of days, so it's nice to see some of her spunk back.

"Just making sure your mate is treating you the way he should be," Mathis says.

"And we never formally introduced ourselves to your……..mate," Tanner says, eying me suspiciously.

"He seems kind of whimpy, are you sure he's your mate?" Mathis asks.

"Yeah, Sis no one would judge you if you weren't interested in being claimed by him. Say the word and I'll get rid of him for you."

"Well thank you. Like always I appreciate your offer to kill for me but like always, it isn't needed." Rain turns towards me, "Tyler, meet my brothers, Mathis and Tanner, I'd make up some excuse for them but they're going to be your family now so might as well get used to them," Rain says. There's something I find weirdly arousing about Rain standing up to two guys that are three times her size.

"In all serious Rain, are you okay? Your hair isn't colorful like it usually is," Mathis says.

"It's not a freaking mood ring," Rain says.

RAIN

I try not to get frustrated with my brothers. They've always been overprotective; it's ingrained deep in their DNA. They mean well.

"I appreciate you two checking in on me, I really do. We're just getting to know each other. I promise you that I'm fine, and I trust Tyler," I say. My brothers stare at me a minute before they seem satisfied that I'm telling the truth.

"Okay, Rain if you need anything at all just let us know," Mathis says to me before turning to Tyler "Tyler if you so much as harm a piece of hair on her head I'll disembowel you and I'm not exaggerating." Mathis and Tanner turn to walk towards the door "Oh and Rain, Jordan wanted us to tell you he said Hi," Mathis says right before leaving. I inwardly cringe.

"Who's Jordan?" Tyler asks.

"No one," I say. He looks like he wants to push the issue, but thankfully he seems to let it go.

"Well, you didn't ask your brothers to kill me, so I'm going to take that as a good sign," Tyler says.

"Their bark is worse than their bite," I say, which isn't really true. I take a seat in the living room, Tyler sitting beside me.

"Oh, so they were kidding about disemboweling me?" Tyler asks.

"No, they were being very literal with that threat. I'm pretty sure they wouldn't hurt you without my approval though," I say.

"Pretty sure?" It's funny seeing the fearsome Tyler looking concerned.

"They're adult chimera males, it's hard to know what they'll do," I say.

"Great. Was there any truth about them asking about your hair color? Does it indicate your mood?"

"No," I sigh. "A little. It's reflecting the indecision I feel," I admit.

"Indecision? About us? What's there to decide?"

"I just…….can't.." I don't know how to articulate my turmoil. I don't know how to explain that I'm afraid of how close I am to giving myself to him completely and then living with the permanent consequences of that decision.

"It's just a part of you wants to stay mad at me. A part of you doesn't trust me yet. It's okay. I understand," he says. "Come on, I'll make us dinner, and then we can watch a movie. I'll even sit through another awkward sex scene for you," Tyler pats my leg before getting up to the kitchen. Great, all I need is awkward sex.

TYLER

After dinner, I picked the movie. I chose a neutral old comedy, one that I had seen before, so I knew it was safe. Although maybe I should've picked something a little spicy for some inspiration. Rain didn't try to resist me when I put my arm around her shoulders and pulled her close to me. She has already changed into her pajama shorts, which means she probably doesn't have underwear on.

I torture myself with that thought. The thought of her being bare underneath the thin layer of fabric. I snake my free hand underneath the blanket we are sharing, I just need a little bit of contact with her skin, resting my hand on her soft stomach. I mindlessly draw small, lazy circles on her belly. My hand travels down to the edge of her pajama shorts on its own accord.

The hitch in her breathing and the slight scent of her arousal is the only encouragement I need. She slowly opens her thighs, giving me easy access to my end goal. With my left arm still wrapped around her shoulders, I pinch her hardened nipple with my left hand, while kissing her neck. She gasps when I make contact with her wet center with my right hand.

"I can make you feel good if you just let me," I whisper into her ear before lightly biting it. I focus all my attention to her clit adding a little bit more pressure and speed when she starts moving her hips. A voice in the back of my head says I should bring her to brink of release and pull back. I should stop and force her to beg me to continue. But when she starts to pant heavily, I can't bring myself to stop. I need to see her come just as much as she needs to come.

I could push this. I could make her submit to me and she'd let me claim her when she's mindless like she is now. But no, I told her I was going to make her beg before claiming her, and I meant that. I dip one finger in her channel, while still massaging her clit in tight fast circles with my thumb. A few pumps and she comes undone on my hand. When she recovers, she tentatively places her hand on my abdomen, but I stop her.

"You don't…want…" she looks at me with uncertainty.

"I want you to give yourself to me completely," I say holding her gaze.

"I…"

"I know Rain, you're not ready," I say.

"That's not fair Tyler," she says.

"You're pretty upset for someone I just made orgasm," I say. She loudly sighs, and I pull her back into my arms how I had her before. "Besides, I never agreed to playing fair," I say before kissing her forehead. She falls asleep before the end of the movie, so I pick her up and gently place her on the bed. I'm hard past the point of pain, but hopefully I made the right call, and my sacrifice will pay off.

Chapter 14

RAIN

Tyler approaches me holding a long deep blue dress while I'm sitting in front of the window, a forgotten book open in my lap. I had been thinking about what happened last night. Still processing how I felt about it.

"It's beautiful but I don't think it'll fit you Tyler," I tease. The dress must have come in the delivery earlier today.

"It's for you."

"I don't know if you noticed, but that dress is a little too formal for hanging out around the cabin."

"Although I love the idea of you dressing up for me, this is for the graduation party tonight," Tyler says.

"Fuck no," no way.

"Rain, like it or not you are still the future Luna of our pack. You're going to have to make appearances to events that you don't want to."

"Does this mean seclusion is over?"

"Nice try. No, we'll be returning back to our little love cabin after the graduation party. Like I said when we arrived, the only way out of this cabin permanently is by you being claimed."

"I thought we were excused from school," I sound whiny even to myself.

"We were, this isn't school this is a party," he leans in towards me putting his hands on the chair behind me caging me in "I don't have a problem forcing you to do this," he says dead serious.

"Fine, but I'm not wearing heels," I say. He stands back up.

"Wouldn't dream of it," he chuckles.

"And the bathroom is mine to get ready," I say.

"Any other demands Princess?"

"I'll let you know if I think of any others," I say sarcastically.

"Great, we leave at 6pm," he says before bending down and kissing my nose.

TYLER

At 5 minutes until six I'm about to start pounding on the bathroom door. It took me all of ten minutes to get ready, in my slacks and dress shirt. Just as I stand up to walk to the bathroom door, Rain comes out with her makeup done perfectly wearing the blue dress that fits her like a glove. She even has matching blue highlights in her hair with soft curls framing her face.

"You look beautiful," I say.

"You're not so bad yourself," she says.

"Shall we," I say offering my arm, which she accepts. The graduation party is at school which is around a twenty-minute drive from the cabin.

"You are good at doing makeup," I say.

"Thanks. I don't find it much different than my art," she says, looking out the car window.

"Right. So, what's your dream job?"

"It fluctuates. Sometimes I want to be a famous painter, sometimes I want to be a famous writer. I have a lot of creative energy that I need an outlet for," she says.

"Yeah, I can see that," I say.

"How about you? Is pack alpha the dream job?"

"I think it might be. I don't know. I guess we'll find out soon enough. I'll be expected to attend council meetings pretty soon now that we are done high school," I say.

We drive the rest of the way in silence.

"Behave tonight, Rain. If you try to escape, I will find you and take my displeasure out on your ass, so you understand?"

"Yes, Tyler. I'll be on my best behavior," she rolls her eyes. The brat.

RAIN

Tyler immediately gets pulled away to talk to his buddies. The graduation party is in the overcrowded hall at our school, and I quickly lose Tyler to the crowd. For a second, I consider making a run for it, but I didn't act fast enough. Kelly and Heather find me by myself, and they're the absolute last people I want to talk to. I wish Becca was here. If I knew about the graduation party, I would've made sure she came.

"So are you enjoying Tyler's large penis," Heather asks with a sneer. I expected as much from her. "Oh, but I don't see a claiming bite," she says pretending to examine my neck. "I guess he couldn't get it up for you. Funny, he never had that problem with me. How does it feel to be practically the only female here who hasn't slept with Tyler?"

"Heather what are you trying to accomplish here? Do you have so little going on in your life that you have to put other people down to make yourself feel better? No, I don't have Tyler's bite, but he's still my mate, not yours," I say before walking away. I try not to think about what she says, but it is disheartening being in a room full of women who have slept with my mate when I haven't yet. I walk towards the entrance when I see Becca coming in.

"Becca. I'm so happy to see you," I run up giving my closest friend a hug. I didn't realize how much I missed her.

"I wasn't expecting you here Becca. How've you been?" I ask.

"Wonderful," she says grinning. "Thanks to your mate, I'm now one of the most popular girls in our pack. Tyler was the one who made sure I came tonight. He wanted me to be here for you for emotional support," she says giggling.

"Seriously?" I ask.

"We all know how taxing being nice in social settings is for you," she says.

"Here you are, I was worried you were trying to escape," Tyler says coming up behind me wrapping his arms around my waist. I turn as Heather approaches the three of us.

"Hey Tyler, if you need another release just call me," she says with a wink.

Chapter 15
TYLER

I am so over this bitch.

"See that's why you're not my fucking mate Heather. You're petty and vindictive. It's why I didn't want to sleep with you even when we were dating," I turn towards Rain.

"I haven't slept with Heather for months," I say. I'm not going to let Heather ruin everything I have built with Rain.

"Heather, you try to start shit with us again I'll banish you from the pack," I say.

"You can't do that," she huffs.

"Yes, I can. You don't think conspiring against the future Alpha and Luna is grounds to be banished? Apologize now and tell the truth," I said. She grumbles but turns towards Rain.

"I'm sorry for trying to start drama. We haven't slept together in months. Even when we were dating," she says cringing.

"I forgive you," Rain says with almost no emotion. She knows she won this fight and is being the bigger person now.

RAIN

Tyler is unusually quiet on the drive back to the cabin. Aside from our little run in with Heather, our night was pretty uneventful. It really wasn't as terrible as I was expecting it to be.

"Thank you for making sure Becca was okay and having her come tonight," I say.

"I know how much she means to you," he says.

"Are you okay?" I ask.

"I just see how quickly you forgave Heather, and it makes me wonder why you can't forgive me," he confesses.

"I do forgive you…..somewhat," I say.

"Then why are you still fighting our mating?" he asks exasperated.

"I'm nervous about how powerful you're going to become. You're already so much stronger than me but once we pair, that power imbalance is going to become much worse. I want to trust you, I really do, but you hurt me for years. That doesn't just go away and it's hard for me to willingly give you that power over me," I try to explain.

"I understand. You're right. I don't deserve your trust yet," he says pulling into the driveway of the cabin. His beautiful face contorts like he's trying to put together the last couple pieces of a puzzle.

"Wait…. Is Becca a chimera?" Tyler asks.

"Well, she definitely isn't just a shifter," I say getting out of the car.

Chapter 16
TYLER

It takes all my self-control to stay out of the bathroom when I hear Rain taking her shower. All I can think about is the water cascading down her petite body. I hear the water cut off and wait for her to come and join me in bed. Rain emerges wearing nothing but a towel, her dark hair still damp framing her beautiful face. I lift up the blanket so she can join me in bed, and she covers herself with the blanket before removing her towel.

"You're playing with fire Little One," I warn, but I don't let her second guess her decision, capturing her lips for a gentle kiss. I pull down the blanket, exposing her dark pink nipples. She moves to cover her perfect breast, but I stop her by grabbing her wrists.

"No, let me see you. You're so fucking beautiful," I lower my head to take a nipple into my mouth while lightly pinching her other one. I kiss a trail down her flat stomach, pulling down the blanket to completely uncover her. She parts her legs for me, and I take my place between them, kissing the tops of her thighs, leaving a glistening trail. When my mouth reaches her slit, I open her up with my fingers. We groan in unison when my tongue finds her needy center. She runs her hands through my hair, and I devour her, grinding against the bed while she grinds against my face. She writhes beneath me, and I add a finger to her entrance while I suck on her clitoris, plucking her nipple with my free hand. Her coming undone is the most erotic sight I've ever seen. I feel her channel spasm around my fingers. I'm half feral by the time she has ridden out her orgasm.

I crawl over her with my much larger body, lining up my hard cock to her drenched entrance. I stare down at her, taking a moment to make sure this is still what she wants. It might physically kill me, but I'd try and pull away if she wasn't ready for sex. She gives a slight nod, and that's all the permission I need, I slowly but steadily sink into her warm cunt. She winces when I'm about halfway in, so I stop to play with her clitoris until she's squirming beneath me, then continue until I'm fully seated. I give her a minute to adjust to my girth but start to pull out when she starts wiggling her hips. I hold her steady with my hands and plunge into her, building up momentum.

"You're better than I imagined, your pussy was made for me," I whisper against her ear, giving her kisses up and down her neck before latching onto one of her taut nipples. She arches her back up into me. She grinds her clit against my pubic bone, and I feel her channel start to squeeze around me. It feels too good, and I can't hold off anymore, once she calls out her release, I plow into her chasing my own.

"Ask me to claim you Rain," I demand.

"Please, Tyler. I want you. Claim me," she says.

I kiss back up her neck to where I'll mark her with my claiming bite, and I clamp down the same time I come deep inside of her. It's the most intense sexual experience of my life. It takes me a minute to catch my breath. Once I do, I release her neck and lick the wound clean that's already starting to heal.

The second I claimed Rain, it was like a switch flipped and my universe exploded. I can feel all the latent chimera genes activate. I can feel my muscles start to stretch and I've never felt so virile and powerful before. They weren't joking, it was like getting a hit of testosterone directly in my veins. At the same time, I feel the calming presence of the mating bond tethering me to my Rain.

RAIN

"God you are huge now," I say. It looks like Tyler grew about fifty pounds of muscle overnight and is a few inches taller. I still haven't processed the complete magnitude of the decisions

I made last night. I try to drag myself out of bed to start the day, but Tyler pulls me back into his chest. His arm is like an iron bar.

"Where do you think you're going?" he asks, his voice laced with sleep.

"I was going to get up and get dressed," I say.

"You're not allowed to leave the bed unless I give you permission," he growls, sounding much more awake.

"Tyler this is your chimera side rearing its head. You're going to need to learn to control it," I can see the thought process playout across his face and see the moment when his chimera baser instincts win the argument.

"No. I can't protect you if I don't know where you are, and I don't ever want to wake up to an empty bed not knowing if you are safe or not. You're to ask permission before leaving the bed and I'm to know where you are at all times," he says. I know right now I'm not going to win this argument, so I decide to table it.

"May I get out of bed?" I ask with fake sincerity.

"Yes, you may," he says. I quickly scurry to the bathroom to take a shower. When I finish with the shower, I step out and startle when Tyler is standing there, leaning against the counter watching me.

"I have to go into town for a little while, future alpha business" Tyler says.

"Shouldn't we pack our stuff up then. We're mated now, seclusion should be over."

"No," Tyler barks.

"Tyler we can't stay out here forever." Tyler steps in front of me holding my chin up to look at him.

"If I want to keep you all locked up for my own personal use there isn't a damn thing anybody could do to stop me. We'll move back into town in a house together when I say we're ready to," Tyler says. I shouldn't find possessive Tyler as attractive as I do. That's probably my pixie side reacting to his dominance. It's scary because deep down I have this growing desire to please him.

"I'll be back as soon as I can, no leaving the cabin. Do you understand?" he asks.

"Yes, Tyler," I say.

"Good," he kisses me so hard I think it might lead to a quickie before he has to go, but he pulls away before leaving.

TYLER

I hate leaving her, even just for a short while. I stop myself from tying her to the bed. She seems to like my more dominant self, but there are still some limits I don't want to push. I drive to the clubhouse where most shifter council meetings are held. I'm required to attend now that I'm finished with high school and will be expected to be more involved.

I see my father waiting for me out front when I pull into the parking lot.

"Jesus Christ Tyler, you're huge. Shit this is going to be hard to explain," my dad says.

"Do I need to hide that I'm a chimera now?" I hadn't really thought of it.

"That's maybe something you should discuss with your mate and your new in-laws, they would probably have more insight than I do," my dad says.

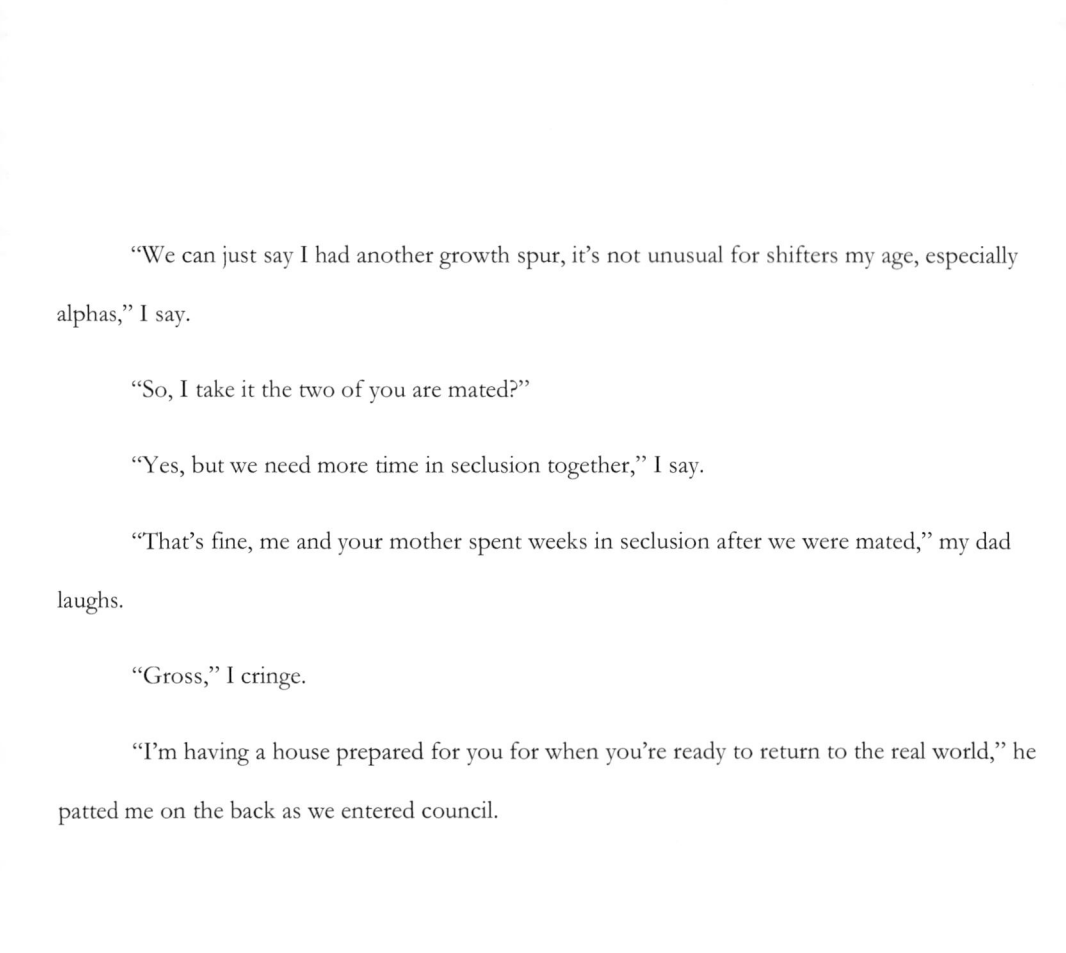

"We can just say I had another growth spur, it's not unusual for shifters my age, especially alphas," I say.

"So, I take it the two of you are mated?"

"Yes, but we need more time in seclusion together," I say.

"That's fine, me and your mother spent weeks in seclusion after we were mated," my dad laughs.

"Gross," I cringe.

"I'm having a house prepared for you for when you're ready to return to the real world," he patted me on the back as we entered council.

Chapter 17
RAIN

I stayed inside for all of fifteen minutes before I got antsy and decided to go for a walk outside. A small part of me knows it's an act of rebellion, trying to prove to myself I'm not going to do everything Tyler tells me to.

"Well, hello beautiful," I hear a familiar voice.

"Jordan?" I ask before seeing his large frame appear from thin air right in front of me. Of course, he doesn't have a shirt on, just a pair of jeans, I'm sure to show off his chiseled abs and chest. His blond hair is longer than last time I saw him.

"Rain. I heard from your brothers that you've taken a mate," he says scrunching his face, "A wolf shifter," he spits out like a curse word.

"Well, he's more chimera than shifter now. What are you doing here?" I ask.

"I wanted my chance to claim you for myself," he says.

"You're a little too late, I'm already claimed, and the bond is formed," I say.

"I'm not concerned, that's undoable," he says.

"No Jordan, I have more mate than I know what to do with already," I say. I turn to walk back to the cabin; Jordan grabs my arm to stop my retreat though.

"Rain, you're one of the women with the highest percentage of chimera blood who's mating age, you deserve someone equal to your own pedigree," he says. I stop myself from laughing. Jordan was never one short on confidence.

"And you think you qualify as higher pedigree?" I know I shouldn't be baiting a chimera male like this but I'm not able to stop myself. "There's a reason I never went on a second date with you Jordan," I say.

"Yeah, because I was busy with work. Now I'm ready to take a mate so here I am," he says. That would be how he remembered it. I still remember how terrible that date was. An entire night of Jordan talking nonstop about himself, then he was rude to the waiter and asked if I wanted to go home with him. I feigned a stomachache and bolted then dodged his texts for weeks. Of course, he had to be friends with my brothers, which meant awkwardly warding off his advances every time I saw him.

"Well, I'm sorry you came all this way, but I'm truly not interested.," I say trying to dislodge my arm from his grip, but I already knew there was no point.

"Again, I'm not concerned. You not being interested isn't going to stop me either," he says. I knew exactly what he was about to do, but there was no way I could stop him. Even with me struggling against him, he quickly was able to grab my other arm and the next second I felt the pull of the teleport portal. He was taking me to his home in the chimera community.

Chapter 18
TYLER

Council wasn't really what I was expecting. I'm not really sure what I was expecting, but a line of pack members with mundane problems wasn't it. The five council members sit in a row behind a long rectangular table in front of a row of seats. Pack members address the council one at a time. Some people then sit and watch the rest of the meeting, some quietly exit.

"What can we do for you Mrs. Thomas?" my dad asks warmly to the frail old lady. She had to be close to ninety by now. I remember her from when I was a kid, she used to teach the young shifters about our heritage. She was the last in line for today's meeting.

"I'm sure it's pretty obvious, I'm not getting any younger. As you know, I've taught several generations the history of our pack," she says.

"Yes, we're aware. The impact you've had on our pack is immeasurable and you are owed a great debt of gratitude," my dad says.

"Thank you, although I'm not here for flattery. I came to council with a problem. When I die, countless stories of who we are will die as well. I need a way to preserve our history. Yes, all the shifters have listened to my stories, but I want a more permanent record for when I'm gone," she says.

"If I may, I would like to help Mrs. Thomas on this project," I say. It sounds like something Rain would be perfect for.

"Sure. Mrs. Thomas, Tyler will be at your disposal," my father says, then turns to me "just let me know if you need any help from the rest of council," my dad says before addressing the crowd to wrap up the meeting.

My skin is already crawling to see Rain again and it's only been an hour. I exit as politely as I can, the other council members all have mates and take pity on me knowing what it's like being newly mated.

When I get back to the cabin, I sense something is off before I pinpoint what it is. Subconsciously I know Rain is gone, but the logical part of my brain doesn't want to consider what that means. I almost broke the front door of the cabin, only to confirm what I already knew. I can see the bathroom door is open, the only place someone can hide, and Rain isn't there.

Outside I catch her scent on the wind. I follow her trail until I smell something else. A week ago, I wouldn't have picked up on the second scent, but now I do. It's subtle but definitely chimera.

RAIN

God even his house is pretentious. There's just always been something vaguely off putting about Jordan. He teleported us to his gaudy living room, with an overwhelming décor of gold, red and black. It's typical for a male Chimera to be full of themselves, but Jordan is a little next level. The furniture looks new, but the oversized sofa I'm sitting on is stiff and uncomfortable. I have a bad feeling about the living room being closed in the way that it is too, with only one door to exit.

"So, what's your game plan here Jordan?" I ask while Jordan paces in front of his extravagant fireplace. He still doesn't have a shirt on, and I can see how tense the muscles in his back are.

"Well as you probably know, I'm in the running to be a ranking officer of Imperia," Jordan says.

"What's a ranking officer and what's Imperia?" I ask. He stops to glare at me.

"Rain If you're going to be my mate, you're going to need to brush up on your Chimera heritage. Imperia is the city we are currently in. A ranking officer is a political position. I told you all about this on our first date," he says.

"Right, of course," as though I remember a single thing he said. "Why exactly do you need me?" I ask. He stands right in front of me, and I feel awkward sitting.

"It's easier to get elected as a mated male. Unmated Chimera are viewed as too unstable to make it to the higher ranks," he explains.

"I'm not going to let you claim me and I'll never be your mate Jordan," I say. He slowly lowers his face until we are eye to eye, caging me in with his arms holding the back of the sofa.

"You have very little time until I officially claim you. There are still things I need to do first, but you need to quickly get used to the idea of being my mate. I want to be very clear with you Rain, that I expect you to do whatever I tell you to do. I don't have a problem forcing you, but I promise, you won't like the consequences of disobeying me," he says with a level of dominance I had never seen from Jordan before. It's too easy to forget how dangerous he can be.

"Now I want you to be good and sit here quietly while I go do some work," he says walking to the only door "Rain, don't try to escape, there's no way for you to get out," he says before shutting and locking the door.

Chapter 19
TYLER

The drive over happens in a blur, before I can process what's happening, I'm standing in front of Rain's house aggressively knocking on their front door.

"Tyler, is there a reason you are pounding down my front door?" Rain's dad Trace answers "I see your latent chimera genes have activated, where's Rain?" he asks, looking around.

"That's why I'm here, she's missing." I say trying to control my panic. Her dad narrows his eyes at me before opening the door wider so I can come inside, closing the door behind me.

"What do you mean my daughter's missing?" he asks, eerily calm.

"I had to go to a council meeting. When I came back, Rain was gone. I followed her scent outside and picked up the scent of a Chimera," I explain. He sighs and turns to walk into the living room with me on his heels. All three of Rain's brothers were sitting around watching tv.

"What did you idiots do?" Trace asks.

"What?" Rex asks not taking his attention off the TV.

"Rain is missing," Trace says, and that gets their attention.

"I knew he wasn't a good mate," Mathis says.

"Yeah, how did you lose her already? Or maybe she just left you," Tanner says.

"I smelled a chimera out in the woods. Someone took her," I say.

"You two know anything about that?" Trace asks. Mathis and Tanner eye each other.

"I might have mentioned to Jordan that Rain was mated," Mathis says.

"And I might have mentioned to Jordan the location of the cabin they were staying in," Tanner says.

"Seriously? You thought Jordan was a better candidate?" Trace asks.

"What's wrong with inspiring a little healthy competition?" Mathis asks.

"Rain hates Jordan you idiot. The three of you are going to help Tyler bring her back," Trace says.

"I wasn't involved," Rex says.

"Now," Trace shouts.

"Fine, we'll help him. Tyler, I'm assuming you haven't learnt how to teleport yet right?" Mathis asks.

"No, I haven't," I say.

"Do you feel the power source inside of you that turned on when your genes activated?" Mathis asks.

"Yes," I say.

"Okay, close your eyes and focus," I do as he directs.

"Can you feel our power source?" Tanner asks.

"No," I say.

"You're too agitated, you need to calm down," Rex says. I take a couple of deep breaths and try to concentrate. It takes a couple of minutes, but I start to feel what started as a glimmer of energy from each of Rain's brothers.

"Okay, I feel it, what do I do now," I ask.

"Hold on tight," Mathis says with a chuckle and before I can ask it feels like I'm being pulled at warp speed. It's like being on an impossibly fast rollercoaster going through a tunnel of lights. Just when I feel like I'm going to puke, the world stops spinning, and we're standing in front of a house in someone's yard. I wobble but brace my hands on my knees before I fall over.

"What the hell was that? Where are we?" I ask looking around.

"We just teleported. This is Imperia, and we are in front of Jordan's house," Tanner explains.

"Who is Jordan anyways? Is he an ex?" I ask.

"They dated briefly," Mathis says.

"They went on one date and Rain hates him," Rex says.

"So, what are we doing? How are we going to get her back?" I ask.

"We're going to knock on the door and if he doesn't answer we're going to teleport in and grab her," Mathis says, walking past me to the front door and knocks. After a couple of seconds, a man I presume is Jordan answers.

"What do you want?" he asks, looking down his nose at me.

"Where is she?" I ask, barely containing my rage. I was already on edge before I realized Rain was missing, just from being away from her. With each second that passes it becomes exponentially worse.

"My new mate is none of your concern," he says, trying to shut the door, but I push it open before he can.

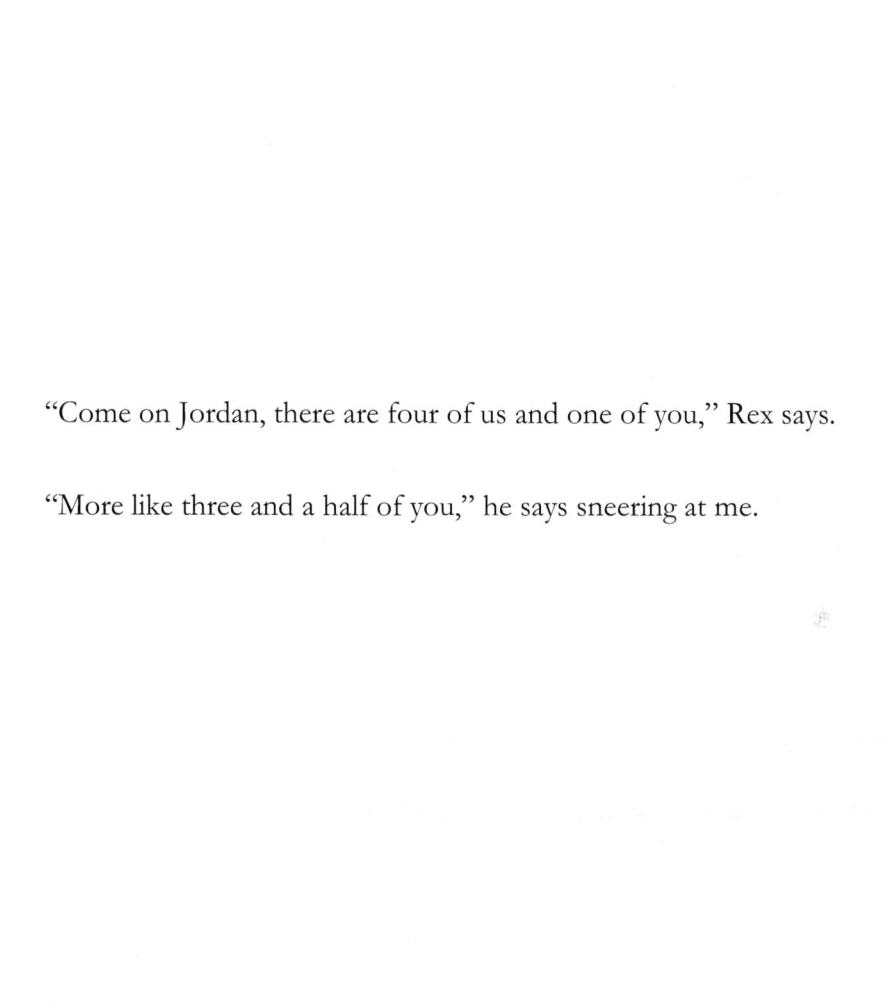

"Come on Jordan, there are four of us and one of you," Rex says.

"More like three and a half of you," he says sneering at me.

Chapter 20
RAIN

With each minute that passes my anxiety rises. I'm still sitting on the couch when I hear a commotion outside the living room door. I stand up just as Tyler and my brothers come barging through the door, followed by a pissed off looking Jordan.

"Rain," Tyler says, and I run into his arms. Being in his arms again brings me more comfort than I ever thought possible. The relief I feel is immediate and overwhelming.

"This isn't over," Jordan says. Tyler looks like he's going to kill him. My brothers obviously sense it too because they quickly circle the two of us before teleporting us back to my childhood home.

"That's awful, I feel like I just got off a carnival ride," Tyler says, leaning over bracing himself on his knees. His murderous intentions forgotten from a moment ago.

"You get used to it," I say. Tyler glares at me, already recovered.

"You," he says.

"What?" I ask.

"I told you to stay inside the cabin," he says. My brothers stand around us like they're watching a tennis match.

"Is that really what you're worried about? Do you think me being inside a wooden cabin would have stopped Jordan from getting to me?" I turn to my brothers "How did you find me so fast? And how did Jordan find me?" not that I'm not grateful for them.

"We figured it was Jordan who took you," Mathis says looking guilty "we might have mentioned where the cabin was," he says.

"Also, we have a tether on you," Rex says.

"What?" I had my suspicions that was the case.

"What's a tether?" Tyler asks.

"So how you were able to concentrate and feel our energy, if you concentrate the same way you'll be able to feel your own energy source. Getting connected to your own energy source and learning to manipulate it is where your chimera abilities come from. One of the things you'll be able to do is unravel a string of energy and attach it to someone else. Makes it so you know where they are and can keep tabs on them," Tanner explains.

"It's an invasion of my privacy," I say.

"Your safety trumps any privacy you think you should have," Mathis says.

"We can guide you on how to use your new powers," Tanner says to Tyler.

"Yeah, I'll take you up on that, but right now I need to take my mate home and deal with her disobedience," Tyler says.

"Disobedience? What do you mean disobedience?" I ask incredulously.

"And deal with her attitude," Tyler says turning towards me.

"Hey," I say, but before I can argue further, Tyler grabs me by the waist and throws me over his shoulder.

"Thanks for your help, I'll see you guys later," Tyler says walking to the front door.

"Put me down," I yell, squirming and hitting his back. I get one firm swat to my butt for my troubles, I can hear my brother's laughter all the way from the living room.

"Settle down," he says, carrying me outside and dropping me in the front seat of his car.

TYLER

Rain gives me the silent treatment while I drive. I can feel her anger pulsating off of her in waves, but underneath I can also feel relief and just a hint of residual fear. I'm finally getting a handle on my own anger from the entire ordeal.

"Hey, where are we going?" Rain asks, just now realizing that I wasn't taking the roads to take us back to the cabin.

"I didn't feel like the cabin was secure anymore. Also, I didn't want to have to leave you alone for as long as I did when I have to go to council meetings," I say.

"So, whose house is this?" she asks when I pull into the three-bedroom house, just a couple blocks away from my parents' house. It's a simple, but new, two-story house. It will feel big for just the two of us. It's also close to downtown.

"It's our house," I say.

"When did this happen?" I ask.

"It has been in the works since I turned eighteen. It has been ready for us, but I wasn't ready to take you out of seclusion yet," I explain.

"What about all of our stuff?" Rain asks.

"My dad had someone move everything for us, I messaged him before contacting your brothers to find you. I knew I wouldn't want to come back to the cabin," I say before getting out of the car. Rain follows me up to the front door, looking around inside when I let us in. I give her a brief tour that ends in the master bedroom. I close the door behind me before turning towards Rain.

"Strip," I say, folding my arms across my chest. Rain looks over at me surprised.

"Now," I add when she doesn't immediately comply. She puts her hands on her hips and glares at me.

"Your punishment is already going to be bad enough, do you really want to add to it?" I ask.

"I didn't do anything wrong," Rain says.

"What did I tell you before leaving the cabin?" I ask. Rain just continues to glare.

"Fine, don't say I didn't warn you," I say before stalking over to Rain. She tries to back up, but I grab her arm before she gets too far.

Chapter 21
RAIN

Tyler moved so quickly, my pants and underwear are down, and I'm face down across his lap while he sits on the bed before I know what happened. I know it's no use, but I struggle against him anyways.

"Let's try this again," Tyler says before giving my ass a sharp slap. "What did I tell you before leaving?" I sigh in response which earns me another slap.

"Stop that," I say.

"Answer the question Rain," Tyler says.

"You said don't leave the cabin," I say.

"And what did you do?" Tyler prompts.

"Hey, I didn't agree to your stupid rules Tyler," I say.

"Is that right? So, before I left when I told you not to leave the cabin, why didn't you tell me then that you had a problem with that rule?" Tyler asks.

"Because I didn't think it was a big deal," I say.

"You didn't think following the rule was a big deal?"

"Yes," I say.

"What happened that made you change your mind?" Tyler asks, rubbing my ass just a little too aggressively.

"I decided I wasn't going to just let you boss me around," I say.

"So, leaving the cabin was you proving you didn't have to follow my directions even though you didn't actually have a problem with my rule, you did it out of spite," he says.

"Well….."I say. Shit.

"You put yourself in danger to prove you didn't have to follow a rule you didn't actually have a problem following. Why didn't you just talk to me? Your mate," Tyler says, his hand stilled waiting for my answer.

"I don't know," I say a little more subdued.

"Do you understand why you earned this punishment?" Tyler asks.

"I guess," I say. Tyler resumes his rough groping.

"I want to hear that you understand and agree to being punished," he says.

"Fine. I understand why you think I deserve to get punished," I say.

"That's not what I said, and you know it," Tyler says, in a voice that tells me his patience is running out.

"I understand that I should've just talked to you, and I agree to being punished," I say as sincerely as I can.

"Good Girl," he says, and I hate myself for liking that so much.

"Ten swats with my hand, five with my belt," he says, and without further warning he starts spanking my butt. Five on each cheek, rapid fire. It didn't start to burn until after he was done. I feel him adjusting me so he can take off his belt.

"Are you doing okay?" he asks, his voice laced with concern.

"Yes," I say. Truthfully.

"This next part will be quick," he says. I hear the slice of the belt before I feel the sting on my ass. The second stripe came before I recovered from the first one. By the third my eyes were watering. The next two came in a blur. He drops the belt on the floor and gently massages my tender cheeks. It stings at first, but quickly morphs into a deeper burn.

"None of that," he says.

TYLER

I smell her arousal and I can't hide how hard I am with Rain on my lap. I help her to a sitting position and just hold her for a few minutes. When her breathing steadies out I gently glide her to her knees between my knees. She watches as I unbutton my pants and pull down my zipper, releasing myself. I grab the side of her face and force her to look in my eyes.

"I was so worried about you," I admit, stroking her face. "I was seconds away from killing Jordan," I say. She grins up at me. She grips my cock with her small hands and leans over to take me in her warm mouth. I groan when she makes contact. She gets the base of my cock slick, then pumps it up and down with her hands, in tandem with her mouth.

"Your mouth feels so good," I pant, brushing my fingers through her hair. Her hair was dark brown again, but with red highlights hidden underneath. It suits her. I pull on her hair, not hard, but enough to remind her I'm still in control and she groans in response. The added sensation almost pushes me over the edge. Only needing a few more pumps.

"I'm going to come," I warn, and she takes me deep, swallowing around me. I groan out my release, down the back of her throat. She slowly licks my penis until I pull myself away from her and zip back up my pants. I can smell how turned on she is, but she's still being punished. I gently push her hair out of her face.

"You are not allowed to touch yourself for the rest of the night. If you're good, I will let you come tomorrow," I say. She can't hide the disappointment on her face, but she doesn't argue.

"You want to take a more thorough tour of the house?" I ask to which Rain enthusiastically nods. I help her stand up. She looks thoughtful for a second.

"What would my punishment have been if I had immediately submitted to you?" Rain asks.

"I guess you'll never know, and I also guess you'll never find out in the future either," I say, which makes Rain grin. "Yeah, I don't see you immediately submitting to me anytime soon," I say, shaking my head laughing.

Chapter 22
RAIN

Despite how comfortable the brand-new bed was in our new home, I could barely sleep. It didn't help matters that Tyler found any excuse to put his large hands on me throughout the day yesterday. It was a slow torture that burned throughout the day. I really thought he would cave, but true to his word he didn't let me come the rest of the day. That didn't stop him from teasing me relentlessly most of the night. I'm not surprised I woke up grinding against his leg like a cat in heat.

Tyler was still dead to the world, so I decided to take matters into my own hands. Rolling onto my back, I snaked a hand down the front of my pants. A second ago I wanted him to wake up, but now I was moving as silently as I could. I needed a release, and I didn't think I could wait any longer. Not surprisingly, I found my warm center drenched. I closed my eyes, trying to keep my moans silent. I was almost over the edge when I felt Tyler's hand on my wrist stopping me. I let out a frustrated sigh, opening my eyes to see Tyler smirking at me.

"That was very naughty of you," he says. He maintains eye contact with me as he brings the hand, I was using to pleasure myself up to his mouth and licks my cream off my fingers.

"I was so close," I complain.

"I know," he says smugly.

"How long were you awake for?"

"It was hard to sleep through you humping my leg then almost bringing yourself to orgasm," he says.

I try to pull my arm away from him, but he just tightens his grip on my wrist before rolling me over and pinning me to the bed. He nuzzles himself between my legs, freeing himself from his boxers. He doesn't even bother taking off my sleep shorts, simply just pulling the thin fabric to the side. The groan he makes when he enters me is the picture of masculinity. Everything about Tyler is the picture of masculinity.

He brings both my arms above my head pinning me with his left hand, while he uses his right hand to find my clit, his movement restricted from my sleep shorts, but enough to give me the friction I needed. It doesn't take long to get back to the edge that I was so close to minutes ago. I don't hold back grinding my hips into him, as he kisses down my neck. My release crashes through me as I clamp down on Tyler's length. A few more thrusts and he finds his release too. When we both stop panting, he slowly eases out of me.

"Feel better?" he asks with a playful smile. I want to be sarcastic, but he earned his right to be smug.

"Yes, thank you," I say getting out of bed.

"I have another meeting today, but I arranged for your friend to come over," he says.

"Becca?" I ask not hiding my enthusiasm.

"Yes," he says.

"That's a good idea, she'll keep me out of trouble," I say with fake sincerity.

"Don't worry, I won't underestimate your ability to get into trouble again," Tyler says. Still sitting in the bed, he shuts his eyes and his face scrunches up like he is concentrating.

Chapter 23
TYLER

I focus on the energy inside of me and like Rain's brothers said I unravel a single thread of energy and extend it out to Rain. When it touches her energy, it feels like it snapped into place.

"What are you doing?" she asks. I open my eyes, then shut them again to see if the tether is still in place.

"Walk to the kitchen," I tell her. She sighs dramatically.

"You put a tether on me?" she asks. I stand up towering over her, slowly walking towards her, making her take a step back. I lean over to whisper in her ear.

"Do you have a problem with that?" I grab a lock of her red hair and give it a gentle tug.

"No," she says a little breathless.

"Then go to the kitchen, I want to see how well it works," I say. She scurries off without another word. After a minute I close my eyes again. I search for the tether and feel it as though it's a physical rope coming out of me. I follow along the path of energy that leads me to Rain standing in the kitchen. The image is a little distorted and out of focus but it's like looking through a telescope. Satisfied that the tether is properly in place I join Rain in the kitchen as she makes breakfast.

"Did it work?" she asks with a hint of annoyance.

"Yes. Rain I'm not letting something like yesterday happen again," I say.

"Fine," she says. Serving up two plates of scrambled egg. I know she wants to argue, but at the same time yesterday rattled her too.

"What time is Becca coming over?" she asks. I can tell she still wants to be mad at me, but the prospect of seeing her friend has her in better spirits.

"In around an hour," I say.

"That's perfect," Rain says.

"Is she part chimera?" I ask.

"That's not my information to disclose," Rain says. I appreciate her loyalty to her friend even if my curiosity goes unanswered. After breakfast, I clean the dishes and Rain goes upstairs to wash up. I find an odd sense of satisfaction just from performing such a domestic act. Becca arrives just as I finish getting ready and am about to leave.

"Both of you be good," I say.

"Sure," they both say at once.

"No leaving the house," I say.

"Got it Tyler," Rain says, pulling her friend along to give her a tour. I just shake my head before leaving, feeling a little better having the tether in place. I'll be checking in on her rather frequently after what happened yesterday.

RAIN

"I can't believe this is your house, you're such a grownup," Becca says as I give her a tour of the upstairs.

"I know, I'm not really used to it yet," I admit. Only the master bedroom has furniture, and even in there it's pretty sparce. I finish the tour in the living room, where thankfully we at least have a couch. The house has the essentials, but we'll have to decorate eventually.

"So, spill," Becca says, taking a seat on the couch.

"What have you heard?" I ask incredulously.

"Stop. Don't even pretend like you aren't sitting here claimed and don't act like I don't get updates on what's going on in Imperia. I heard Jordan took you," Becca says.

"How did you hear that?" I ask, but I already know. Our families have always been close.

"How do you think, your dad told my dad," she says.

"Do you know Jordan?" I ask.

"I know of him, but I've never met him personally, I heard he can be kind of a prick," Becca says, and I can't help but laugh. I give her a quick recount of being claimed and then being stolen by Jordan.

"That's terrible, I'm surprised Tyler didn't try to kill him," Becca says.

"Oh, he would have, my brothers got to him and teleported us back home before he had the chance," I say.

"Do you think Jordan is going to give up that easy?" she asks.

"I don't know. He wanted to be mated so he could run for something, said it would make people think he was more stable," I said rolling my eyes.

"I mean, by Chimera standards I guess he's average," she says giggling.

"Enough about my rollercoaster of a life, tell me what's new with you?"

"Well, nothing as exciting as you, I don't have multiple suitors fighting over me, but I did go on a date," Becca says, trying to hide her sly smile.

"What? Tell me everything," I say. Becca looks around as though someone could be listening before answering.

"I'm kind of dating Max," she practically whispers.

"Shut up, really?" I ask.

"After he apologized, we started talking and I don't know, we've been hanging out. It's nothing serious, it's just nice to be part of the popular crowd," she says.

"I'm happy for you," I say.

"I'm happy for you too," she says.

Chapter 24
TYLER

I've been following around my dad all day. The plan is for me to slowly takeover the day-to-day responsibilities of being alpha. So far, it's been an interesting combination of feeling like I was born for this role while also having no idea what I'm doing. He spends most of his day at the clubhouse, where pact members congregate, and it has been kind of nice to see some of my old friends from high school. I run into Max, just as I was leaving for the day.

"Hey Tyler, man it seemed like you dropped off the face of the planet. How is mated life treating you?" Max asks.

"It's better than I ever imagined it could be," I answer truthfully.

"Hell yeah, I'm so glad you mated Rain or else I wouldn't have really taken the time to get to know Becca," he says.

"Becca? Max you better not be messing with her," I say.

"No, of course not, how could you think that? Well, okay I could see how you'd think that, but no, we've been hanging out. I don't know, there's just something about her that I never noticed before. She has such a calming presence, I just really like being around her," Max says.

"Alright, just don't be an asshole to her. She's Rain's closest friend, and if you hurt her, I'll have to hurt you," I say.

"I'm really trying to be a better more mature version of myself, and Becca is helping me become it. I have to go but we should hang out some time," Max says.

"Absolutely, maybe we can go on a double date," I say before getting into my car and heading back home. The house is so close I really could have just walked. By the time I get home,

Becca has already left, and I find Rain in the kitchen making dinner. I wrap my arms around Rain's slim waist from behind. She's so much smaller than me I have to bend down to kiss the top of her head.

"Hi beautiful," I say. She turns around in my arms and stands on her toes to give me a real kiss.

"Hi," she says back.

"How was Becca?" I ask. "Seemed like you two stayed out of trouble," I say. I had checked in on her through the tether a few times. Each time was easier and clearer than the last.

"Becca is great. Thank you for arranging for her to come over, it was nice seeing her," she says.

"You're welcome," I say.

"It's nice our house is so close to her house, I can just walk over there," she says. Praxley is a small town, practically everybody lives close, but there's no way I'm letting her walk even a short distance on her own.

"I'll drive you over there if you ever want to visit," I offer.

"That's not really necessary," Rain says absentmindedly "I really should learn how to drive a car though."

"Absolutely not," I say. The surge of anger I had over the thought of Rain driving caught me off guard.

"I'm going to let you process all that emotion on your own," Rain says, returning her attention to cooking dinner.

"I'm serious Rain, I'm not going to allow you to drive," I say.

"And Tyler I'm serious when I say you need to learn how to reign in your chimera side all on your own. I don't want to have to fight a war with you every time I want to do something," she says.

"Then just do what I tell you and follow my rules and we won't have to fight," I say. Simple.

"Dinner's ready, which is good, maybe if you put something in your mouth, you'll stop saying stupid things," she says. I lean against her, caging her in against the countertop. I briefly get distracted kissing her neck over my claiming mark until I can smell a hint of her arousal.

"No Rain, I have something to put in your mouth to shut you up. Talk to me like that again and I'll shove my cock down your throat."

Chapter 25
RAIN

God why does that turn me on so much? What's wrong with me? I stop myself from grinding against his thigh, but there isn't much point, even I can smell my own arousal and know I'm wet.

"I'm sorry Tyler," I say, already forgetting what the argument was about. I'm left breathless when he pulls away. Slowly the fog of lust clears from my brain. I'm not capitulating so easily, but I need to regroup and come up with a better argument. I serve up the steak I made for Tyler and the vegetable stir fry I made myself. The rest of dinner was eaten in strained silence. I know he knows I'm not going to drop it.

Later, when we are getting ready for bed, I come out of the shower wearing a towel and find Tyler standing shirtless by the bed. The look on his face and his crossed arms made me hesitant to approach. When I come closer, I notice he has one of his belts wrapped around each post of the bed.

"Drop the towel and get on the bed," Tyler says.

"Why? What are you going to do?" I ask.

"Don't ask questions, just do what I tell you," he says in a tone that tells me I shouldn't argue. It's kind of pointless to be modest, but still, I feel weirdly exposed when I drop the towel. I get into bed as gracefully as I can.

"Lay on your back in the middle of the bed," Tyler says, and I follow his direction.

"Spread your legs," he says. He stares appreciatively at me when I comply.

"Your pussy is beautiful," he says. He caresses my foot before securing it to the bed post with his belt. He does the same with my other leg and then my arms, so I'm spread eagle for him.

"It takes all my willpower to not have you restrained like this all of the time. Do you know how many times I've fantasized about tying you up like this?" he asks, running a hand up the side of my breast. When I don't answer he pinches my nipple, hard. I cry out, my arms straining uselessly against the belts.

"No," I say.

"It's a thought I've had ever since getting you in the cabin," he says, returning to lightly caressing my stomach and between my breasts.

"Why?" I ask.

"Then I would know you were safe at all times," he says.

"Safe from what?" I ask, he pinches my nipple again, but this time he lowers his head and licks the pain he just caused away.

"I don't know, why did your family decide to hide among shifters when they're a group of predators?" he asks, looking up at me. I never really thought too in depth about it. He claims my mouth before I can answer him. When I try to grind into him as much as my restraints will allow, he slaps the inside of my thigh, and pulls away from the kiss.

"No, you're going to have to earn that," he says, crawling up my body. Holding himself up with one hand on the headboard, he uses the other to free his cock and lines it up with my mouth. He eases in gently, but I need more, I strain my neck to take as much of him as I can.

"Eager?" he asks, and I nod as much as I can. He pushes in as far as I can take him as I suck and twirl my tongue around him. I moan around his length, and I can tell he's close, but he pulls away before he finishes. I pout at being denied my prize. He crawls back down my body and nuzzles himself between my legs and lowers his mouth so that I can feel his warm breath on my core. His little kisses feel like butterflies up my inner thigh and on my lower lips. So desperately I want him to touch the one spot he's avoiding, I even try to close my legs to feel some pressure, but my restraints are too tight. Again, I feel weirdly exposed to Tyler.

Sweet relief floods my lower belly when he finally drops his mouth to my clit, devouring me. I'm so close to the edge when he stops moving. I was so close, but the pause brings me back from the ledge. I let out a frustrated sigh and when it's obvious my impending orgasm had sizzled out, Tyler returns to his ministrations, bringing me to the ledge again just to stop short of the goal.

"Please," I beg, strained.

"Please what?" Tyler asks, as though he isn't as desperate as I am.

"Please Tyler, let me come," he looks at me silently, as though he's thinking it over, while I writhe beneath him half delirious from lust. He nods and smiles before prowling up me again, but this time, he situated his hips between mine and almost immediately spears me with his length. Whatever reign he had over his self-control snapped, and he thrusts into me, finally with the vigor I needed to push me over the top.

"Come for me Rain," he says, his voice laced with lust and dominance. I didn't need to process what he said to follow his command, my orgasm hit me like a freight train after being built up and denied so many times. He thrusts through my orgasm, finding his own release shortly after. For a while, he just laid on top of me panting.

"We're probably going to have to wash the sheets after that," I say, and I feel his chuckle vibrate against me. He moves off me and I immediately miss his weight. With each belt he undoes to free me, he lovingly massages the skin underneath. When I'm completely unbound, he gets into bed and pulls me into his side, pulling the cover over both of us. He lightly strokes my back.

"If I let you learn how to drive, I would insist on you getting the safest car available," he says. I don't hide my grin. "You would need to take lessons and prove competent before being allowed to drive on your own," he continues.

"Okay," I agree.

"We'd have to have a tracker installed in the car," he says. I draw circles on his muscular chest.

"Why? You have a tether on me?" I ask.

"Tracker or no car," he says definitively.

"Fine, anything else?" I ask.

"Yeah, you need permission from me before going anywhere," he says.

"Yes, Tyler," my compliance seemed to smooth over his nerves, and I fall asleep in his arms.

Chapter 26
RAIN

"Bacon or sausage?" I ask looking at the dwindling contents of our fridge. We won't be getting food deliveries anymore, and we're at the end of the food that was supplied when we moved in. We'll have to start doing our own grocery shopping. One more reminder that we're a mated couple living on our own. That reality hits me in the face and I feel panic start to come on. It feels like I was slowly being pulled out to sea without noticing and now that I can't see land anymore and I might drown, I start to panic.

"Both," he says, before noticing my expression, "are you okay?" he asks.

"What? "Oh yeah, I'm fine," I say, placing the ingredients on the kitchen counter. Tyler wraps his strong arms around my waist from behind.

"Rain, you know I can feel your emotions now through the bond, why are you upset?" he asks. I don't really know how to articulate it to him.

"It just seemed like yesterday we were high school students, and I barely knew you. Today we're a mated couple who need to go grocery shopping," I say.

"I can go to the store if we need something," he says.

"No it's-" I turn to face him, "it's that I don't know how we got here so fast that when I stop and think about all that has changed it's overwhelming," I say.

"Yeah, the mating bond was no joke," he says and despite myself I laugh at him.

"Would it help if we had a mating ceremony?" he asks. Would it? Or would that make it worse?

"Maybe," I say, unsure.

"Or we can do whatever the chimera equivalent to a wedding is," he says.

"No thanks, it's kind of barbaric and antiquated," I say, returning my attention to making breakfast.

"Or we could have a kid?" he says.

"That's not even funny Tyler," I say, but by his grin I can tell he's joking.

"Okay no babies then, maybe a mating ceremony and we need to grocery shop. Got it," he says. "Oh, but grocery shopping will have to wait until later today, we both have plans today," he says.

"Oh? Is Becca coming over? We can go grocery shopping the two of us," I suggest, to get back at him for the baby comment.

"Absolutely not. No, Becca isn't coming over, you have an appointment with Mrs. Thomas today at noon," he says.

"Mrs. Thomas? Why?" I ask.

"She wanted help preserving her stories in some kind of format for the next generation to have and I volunteered you. If you don't want to, I can cancel and figure something else out," he says.

"No, I actually kind of love that idea," I say, already brainstorming ideas. I think having something to work on would be really great for me right now.

"I thought you might," Tyler says, obviously proud of himself. I serve both our breakfasts and sit down at our small dining room table to eat.

After eating and getting ready, Tyler dropped me off in front of the little cottage that Mrs. Thomas lived in. She used to have the younger kids stop by to tell them her stories. The frail looking lady ushers me into her cozy living room with her homemade quilts everywhere and her lazy pet cat sleeping in the window.

"Mrs. Thomas, I'm so excited to help you preserve our history," I say, taking the cup of tea she offers me.

"I knew you'd be Luna one day. You're exactly what was needed," she says. I fight off the same panic I had this morning.

"Thank you, Mrs. Thomas, I hope you're right," I say.

"Oh, I think your background is perfect for what's to come for the pack," she says.

"What do you mean?" I ask.

"I mean, you'll have to get the other part of your ancestor's history from your father," she says. I don't know how to respond.

"Don't worry, you'll know when it's time to disclose that part of yourself. I always figured one day shifters would have to learn how to work together with other beings," she says.

"Work together towards what?" I ask.

"Towards? Or against? I don't know," she says waving a hand dismissively.

"Is there other species stronger than shifters?" I ask, it seems like she knows about chimeras. Is there something else out there stronger than chimeras? I always assumed they were the top of the food chain.

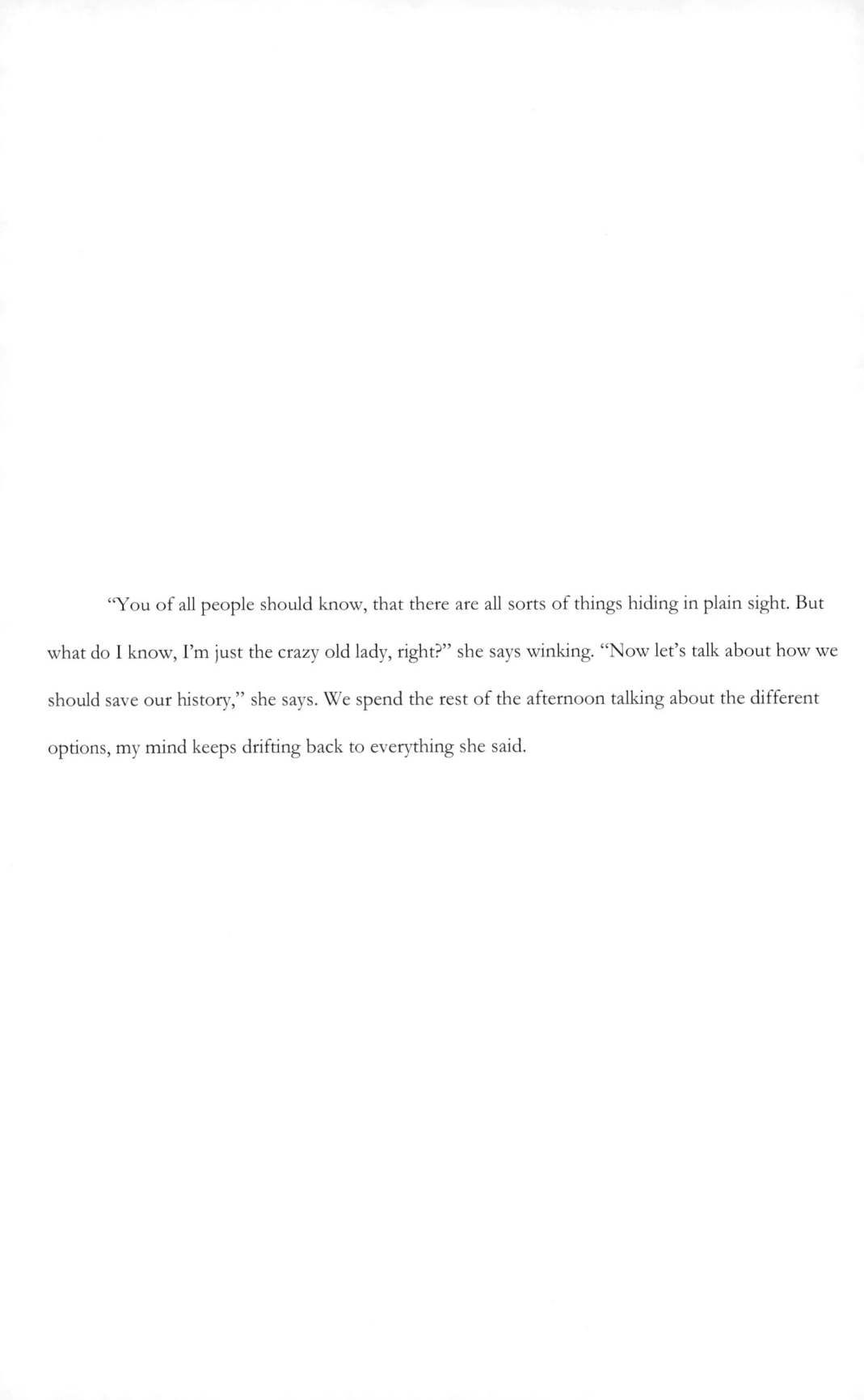

"You of all people should know, that there are all sorts of things hiding in plain sight. But what do I know, I'm just the crazy old lady, right?" she says winking. "Now let's talk about how we should save our history," she says. We spend the rest of the afternoon talking about the different options, my mind keeps drifting back to everything she said.

Chapter 27
TYLER

Rex is already waiting for me when I pull up to where we had planned on meeting, the heavily wooded area right outside of town. I've been all through these woods on all fours, so I knew exactly why he picked this location, there's a clearing far enough away from the road that we would be undetected.

Rex so far seems to be the friendliest of Rain's brothers, so when he offered to coach me on using my chimera strength, I accepted. He looks similar to Mathis and Tanner in build, but his hair is lighter like their mom's hair. Where Mathis and Tanner look slightly feral, Rex looks more controlled and civilized.

"You ready?" Rex asks, not waiting for a response before turning to walk in the direction of the clearing.

"I guess, each day I feel more acutely aware of the energy inside and around me, I'm starting to worry I'm going to blow something up by accident pretty soon," I say, following him through the overgrown path.

"You have better control than I expected you to have, but Rain's pixie and fae side are probably calming you," he says. It doesn't take long before I see the clearing up ahead.

"Alright, so the first thing I'm going to show you is how to throw energy," Rex says.

"Okay," I say.

"Shut your eyes, then feel your energy just like you did with the tether," he says.

"How did you know I put a tether on Rain?" I ask.

"You're her mate, of course you put a tether on her. Also, I can sense it. Now shut your eyes and focus, but instead of your energy unraveling like a piece of thread, it's going to collect in your fingertips," he says. I do as he instructs. It feels like little drops of water running from my chest down my arms to my fingertips.

"Now roll it up between your hands like a snowball," he says. I understand what he is asking, but when I try to manipulate the energy, it slips through my fingers and drops to the ground. I try a second time with the same results.

"What am I doing wrong?" I ask.

"You're holding it like you are afraid it's going to shock you," he says. I hadn't realized how tense and awkward my arms were until he mentioned it. I force my body to loosen and relax.

"Don't think about it as actually holding it, that was too literal. You hold tension with your mind, like a forcefield to keep the energy where you want it," Rex explains. I try again with a little bit more success.

"Why was the tether so much easier than this?" I ask.

"The tether is less energy you have to control so it's easier, also your energy is going to naturally seek out the energy of your mate. This time instead of just holding the energy in your hand you're going to throw it over to that tree over there," he says indicating the direction he wants me to aim.

I gather the ball of energy again. Muscle memory takes over and I pull my arm back to throw it like a football, but I didn't keep enough tension resulting in all the energy going in the opposite direction I was aiming for.

"Can we just pretend like that didn't happen?" I ask.

"Yeah, Tyler," Rex says, rubbing his forehead like he's fighting a headache. One entire afternoon, and several embarrassing slip ups later, I can consistently throw a baseball sized ball of energy in a general direction.

"Let's call it for today," Rex says.

"Can you show me how you would throw energy?" I ask. Without hesitation, Rex flicks his arm once and it was like five bullets hit the exact tree I had been aiming for and missing the past few hours. The little amount of pride I had from my progress today instantly evaporated.

"Holy shit," I say amazed.

"You'll get the hang of it," he says patting me on the shoulder before walking back to our cars.

Chapter 28
RAIN

"Are you okay? You look a little……..-drained. what were you doing today?" I ask Tyler when he picks me up.

"I'm fine. Rex was teaching me how to manipulate energy," he says. I didn't realize he had been with my brother.

"Oh. How did that go?" I ask, looking him over, he doesn't appear to be harmed.

"It's a work in progress," Tyler says with a tight jaw.

"That good, huh?" I ask, trying not to laugh.

"It's harder than it looks. Did you want to go grocery shopping before going home?"

"We have enough food for dinner but if you want to eat breakfast tomorrow, we better stop on the way home. Tyler, do we have money to go grocery shopping with?" I ask.

"Yeah, of course. I started getting paid as an alpha in training," Tyler says.

"I need to figure out what I'm going to do for work," I say.

"Your job is Luna," Tyler says.

"Unless that's a paid position, I'm going to need to figure something else out," I say, staring out the window when we pull into the parking lot of the grocery store. Tyler's silence doesn't go unnoticed.

"Do I get paid for being Luna?" I ask. Again, I'm met by silence. "Tyler?"

"What do you want money for? Tell me what you need, and I'll buy it," he says, avoiding the question.

"Tyler just tell me," I say.

"We get paid as a household. I decide how the money gets split. Which it won't be since we are not separate. It's our money," he says.

"That's fine, we can have a joint account as long as I have access to it," I say. Tyler glares at me.

"Rain, can you not just give me a little control over our situation? It's like you challenge my chimera side at every chance you get," Tyler says.

"How would your chimera side feel about me being stranded somewhere with no access to money?" I ask. I didn't need Tyler's answering growl to know he wasn't thrilled with the idea.

"I will never allow you to be in a situation where you could become stranded," Tyler said. I want to remind him of me being recently kidnapped, but that wouldn't help my cause, and having money in that situation wouldn't have helped.

"How about you give me access to our money, but I'll tell you first if I have to spend over fifty dollars. We can sit down and make a budget if you want," I say. I grew up with chimera males, I know how to negotiate with them.

"It's not that I don't trust you with money," he says.

"Then what are you worried about?" I ask.

"I don't want it to be easy for you to leave me," Tyer says.

"Tyler, Honey, that's a little unhinged," I say.

"No, it's not. You barely even tolerated me two weeks ago. Now my sanity is based on keeping you safe and with me," Tyler says.

"Things have changed. We're mated now and just like how I had to trust you when I let you claim me you have to trust me now. The bond won't let us stay apart. Can we go grocery shopping now? I'm kind of tired of sitting in this parking lot," I say, getting out of the car.

Chapter 29
TYLER

"You don't have to carry all the groceries inside in one trip," Rain says.

"Of course I do," I say. Shopping was a little tense after our discussion. Rain puts away all the food while I prepare dinner, roasted vegetables for Rain, roasted chicken for me. I watch her as she sets the table. All it takes is for her to lean over slightly to catch my attention. I can't help but appreciate the lines of her body. My body responds to her. It's drawn to her.

Our sex always seems so charged and intense, but I want to give her tender and loving too. It seems like every time we disagree, sex is the connection that brings up back together. Resets us. Gives me clarity to what matters and what doesn't. We have time before dinner will be ready, and I plan to use it wisely.

I walk up behind her and kiss her neck, wrapping my arm around her. She doesn't put up any resistance when I undo the button of her pants and pull them down. She turns to face me, and I peel her shirt off her too. Leaving her in her bra and underwear, I grab her by the hips and place her on the kitchen table and pull up a chair to sit in front of her. I don't have to tell her to spread her legs for me. She welcomes me all on her own. I cup my hands underneath her ass to pull her closer to me then trail kisses from her inner knee all the way up her inner thigh. I place a kiss right over her center, on top of her damp lace panties. She arches her back, seeking more pressure.

I debate tearing her lacy underwear right down the middle, but this was meant to be tender, so I hook my finger in the inside of her underwear pulling the thin material to the side instead. I blow cool air on her exposed warm center, making her shiver. I look up at her, but she has her eyes shut already.

"Look at me Rain," I demand. Her eyes pop open, and I slowly lower my mouth to her center. She grinds into my face, but I put my hands on her hips to hold her still. Even if it's tender, I'm still controlling the pace.

"Take your tits out," I say, before returning to her center. She goes to unclasp her bra, I slap the outside of her thigh in protest.

"I said take your tits out, I didn't say take off your bra," I say. This time she does what I want her to, pulling down her bra and propping up her full breasts nicely. Her nipples are already hard.

"Pinch them," I say. She lightly massages herself. I growl into her core, and she gets the message that she isn't pinching them hard enough. As she gets closer to orgasm, her eyes drift shut again, and her hands grow slack. Her nipples are red and elongated from her treatment to them.

"Keep your eyes open and keep pinching or I'm going to stop," I say. She gives a cute sigh of disappointment but watches me intently and returns to tugging on her nipples with more fervor, only stopping again when she called out her release. Once she recovers from the aftershocks, I stand and quickly free myself, and impale Rain on my erection. I can still feel her core fluttering around me from her orgasm, but I'm determined to wring one more out of her.

I pull back slowly and set a steady pace. I want her orgasm to build a little longer this time.

"Finger yourself," I say. I pull back so she has room between our bodies to find her clit.

"Come for me one more time," I say.

"Tyler I can't," she says.

"You don't get a choice," I growl into her ear. Despite her best effort, her body responds to my dominance. Her breathing becomes erratic, and I know her body is submitting to me. I kiss up the side of her neck, and she comes undone again. She grips me with her channel and her release sets off my own. After I catch my breath, I ease out and slide her underwear back in place and correct her bra. I want her sitting in our combined juices while she eats dinner, reminding her of what we just did. The timer on the oven sounds.

"Dinner's ready," I say. "Don't get dressed," I add. I plate up our food and take it to the table, placing both plates right in front of the chair I was just using. Rain looks at me confused, until I sit down and guide her onto my lap. She gives me a disapproving look but doesn't say anything. When I bring a fork with vegetables on it to her mouth she accepts without complaint. Rain even puts her arms around my neck and lets me feed her the entire dinner. Orgasms seem to make her compliant.

Chapter 30
RAIN

"Who would be knocking on our door this early?" Tyler asks groggily.

"Tyler it's like ten in the morning," I respond. I had been awake, reading in bed. I hadn't gotten dressed yet, but I had my house robe on.

"Maybe they'll just go away," Tyler says rolling over burying his face into the pillow as the pounding continues.

"I'll go see who it is," I say. I'm not surprised Tyler is exhausted today after learning to throw energy yesterday. It takes a lot out of even a veteran chimera. Then to top it off, we had sex after too.

"Hold on, I'm awake," Tyler says jumping out of bed and grabbing a pair of sweatpants and putting them on. I follow him downstairs, tying my robe. Tyler opens the door to my dad standing on the other side. He's wearing his leather jacket, jeans and sunglasses clipped on his shirt, a look that not many men his age could pull off.

"Good morning dad," I say. Tyler widens the door so he can come in.

"Good morning," he says giving my cheek a quick kiss.

"Did you come over to see the house?" I ask. He sighs.

"No, we have a problem," he says, taking a piece of paper out of his pocket and handing it to me.

"What is it?" Tyler asks.

"It's a challenge to forum," my dad says.

"What does that mean?" Tyler asks.

"From Jordan?" I ask.

"Yeah," my dad says.

"Can one of you please explain to me what's going on," Tyler says, earning a death glare from my father.

"Jordan is challenging you. It's called a forum. It's a series of three competitions, the winner gets my daughter as their mate," my dad explains.

"It's barbaric and archaic, I haven't heard of there being a forum in years. I thought he couldn't try to claim me after I've already been claimed," I say.

"Unfortunately, it's Jordan's legal right even if it isn't very common," my dad says.

"What type of competition?" Tyler asks.

"Can he just ignore it?" I ask.

"First of all, if he ignores it, he forfeits, and then Jordan would have a legal claim to you Rain," he says to me then turns to Tyler. "Second of all, would your chimera side let you ignore a challenge for your mate?" my dad asks.

"Hell no," he says without hesitation. "What do I have to do?"

"Forum takes place over three days, one competition each day. He challenged you, so you get to pick the first competition. Jordan picks the second competition, then our counsel of elders picks the third competition. I'll be honest, Jordan might not be overly liked, but the elders will be more likely to give the edge to a full-blooded chimera over a shifter. Whoever wins two or more wins," my dad explains.

"I don't want anything to do with Jordan," I say.

"I know Rain, but you know how it is, you have to let Tyler fight this one for you," my dad says.

"When is this happening?" Tyler asks.

"The first competition will be Wednesday, which means you have to decide what you will be challenging Jordan to by Tuesday."

"So, I have two days to decide. What the hell am I supposed to challenge him to?" Tyler asks.

"Historically, forum have been some kind of combat. Back in the day, it used to be a fight to the death on day one, but we've evolved. The past few forums that have happened have been more skill related. You need to really think about it and pick something you know you can beat Jordan at. The first day is your only advantage, and you need to make the most out of it. Jordan won't know what your challenge is until the day of, same with you when he chooses. I know you have been training with Rex, you don't want to overdue it and use up all your energy reserve before the competition even begins. Tyler, we support you fully and are here if you need anything," my dad gives me one more kiss on the cheek before leaving.

"Fantastic," Tyler mutters under his breath. I wrap my arms around his waist, laying my head on his chest.

"I'm sorry," I say.

"It's not your fault Jordan is insane," he says, kissing my forehead.

Chapter 31
TYLER

I keep going back and forth on what I should challenge Jordan too. On the one hand, I would love my shifter side to be the reason I beat him. On the other hand, I need to figure out something that he absolutely has no chance of winning by challenging him to something I've spent countless hours training for. Rain finds me pacing in the living room.

"How are you doing?" she asks.

"Mostly pissed off but also worried, anxious and nervous," I admit.

"If you lose, I'll kill Jordan myself," she says. It's adorable how serious she is.

"No way will I let him win, and Rain when I beat him, I want to celebrate by having an official mating ceremony," I say. I want there to be no question who she belongs to.

"Okay," she agrees without fighting which actually worries me a little bit about how serious my situation is.

I spent all Monday in aggressive indecision. Rain's hair was back to its original dark brown, which still looks beautiful on her, but I know it means she's worried. I'm also too worried to provide much comfort. On Tuesday, the speaker of the forum along with Rain's dad came by to get the details of my challenge. I tried to get as much sleep as I could under the circumstances.

Wednesday morning, Rain's parents and her three brothers meet us at our house, then all of us teleport to the stadium where the forum is held. It looks deceivingly normal. There's a medium sized crowd in the bleachers that came to watch. Rain and her family sit front row. The speaker of the forum was standing in the center of the stadium in front of a podium, that was between me and Jordan. Jordan has a smirk on his face like he has already won.

"Ladies and gentlemen, welcome to Imperia Stadium. Today for your enjoyment and entertainment, Jordan Forest has challenged Tyler Grant to a Forum for the legal mating rights to Rain Night. As customary, since Jordan is the challenger, Tyler gets to choose the first competition. Jordan, Tyler challenges you to throwing a football at a target," the speaker says.

"You've got to be kidding me," Jordan says, his smirk falling from his face, as he runs a hand through his perfectly styled blond hair. Rain said chimeras don't play sports.

"You'll each get five throws, if there's not a winner after five throws, you'll go head-to-head until one loses. Bring out the footballs and the target," the speaker says, and two people bring out a cart each filled with footballs, and a third person brings out what looks like a steel hula-hoop on a stand around twenty yards in front of us.

"First up is Jordan," the speaker says. Jordan grabs a football and it's obvious he has never held one before. He tries to throw it over his head like you would a basketball. I don't contain my laughter when it doesn't even make it halfway to the target.

"Next up, Tyler," the speaker says. My nerves are shot, but muscle memory takes over and I easily send the football right through the middle of the target. I can hear Rain's family cheer me on from the crowd.

"Jordan, your second throw," the speaker says. This time Jordan tries to copy how I threw the football, but his grip is awkward, and his second throw was just as clumsy as his first throw, bouncing on the ground not even halfway to the target.

"Tyler, your second throw," the speaker prompts. This time, all the jitters are gone, and I feel more confident. I don't hesitate and make it into the target just as easily. I spent all yesterday second guessing this decision, but I made the right call.

"Jordan, please take your third turn," the speaker says. I can see on his face how frustrated he is becoming. This time, he tries to throw the football with a little burst of energy, but it was too much, and the football explodes as soon as it leaves his hand.

"Tyler, if you make this shot, you'll have won today's competition," the speaker says. I gingerly throw the last ball directly in the middle of the target. A pissed off Jordan, angrily kicks the cart holding the footballs over and marches out of the stadium not saying another word. Rain and her family meet me on the field. Rain runs up to me and jumps into my open arms.

"That was a smart move," Rain's dad says, patting my back.

"Yeah, but how do I prepare for tomorrow though?" I ask.

"Your mate is on the line here, you'll figure it out," he says.

Chapter 32
RAIN

We spent the rest of the day lying in bed. I could feel Tyler's muscles tense beneath me, when I laid my head on his chest, drawing lazy circles on his abdomen. He's too in his head. I understand why, but it isn't helping the situation. Without being obvious, I trail my hand lower and lower with each circle I draw, until my fingertips grace the edge of his boxers. He grabs my hand to stop me before I get to my goal.

"I don't-"

"Tyler, you need to relax," I say, kissing his chest, "just lay back and let me do this for you," I say. This time he doesn't stop me, when I get to the band of his boxers and pull down to free his hardening cock. He watches me intently when I snake my right hand down my own pajama shorts and gather up the moisture from my own arousal, then lather it on his now fully erect cock to use as lube.

"I'm so wet because all I can think about is how you fought to keep me as your own," I say, sprinkling his chest with open mouth kisses. He groans as he thrusts into my hand. I slowly jack him off until his breathing becomes erratic, and his hips move in synch with my hand. His entire body tenses, before he shoots his load all over my hand and his lower abdomen. I lean over his body and quickly run my tongue up the side of his penis, tasting our combined arousal.

"Don't move I'll get a towel," I say. In the bathroom I wet a washcloth with warm water, then return to Tyler's side, slowly and reverently cleaning up his seed.

"Take off your clothes," he says.

"Don't worry about me, that was for you," I say.

"You have three seconds to start undressing or you're getting a spanking first," he says. I pull my pajama shirt over my head, and shimmy off my pajama shorts. He grabs my breast with his large hand and roughly squeezes. He positions himself in the middle of the bed.

"Come here," he says patting the spot by him. I kneel beside him.

"Now straddle me," he says, and I when I comply, he reaches under my thighs to cup my butt. I'm confused by what he's doing, until he pulls my body up, so my center is right in front of his mouth. I try to move off him and get a harsh smack to my left butt cheek for my efforts.

"Ouch," I say.

"Then do what I tell you, and put your hands on the headboard," he says. This time I don't hesitate, and I'm thankful I didn't because when he licks into me, I almost lose my balance. I can feel his deep chuckle vibrate through my core. I try to hover over him so I'm not suffocating him, but he pulls me closer anytime I try to pull away. It's not long until I'm lost to lust, and grind into his face with reckless abandon. He keeps a bruising grip on my hips, controlling the pleasure he gives me. He focuses all his attention on my clit. It's not long until I feel my orgasm building and call out my own release.

Once I recover, I roll off of him, and return to his side.

"You're right, I needed that," he says.

"I know," I say.

Chapter 33
TYLER

Day two of the competition is basically a repeat of day one, with the speaker at the podium between me and Jordan.

"Good afternoon, citizens of Imperia, welcome back to day two of Forum. For today's challenge, Jordan has challenged Tyler, to throw energy at a target. Same rules as yesterday, each opponent will get a total of five throws, if after five there isn't a clear winner, we'll go head-to-head. May the assistant please bring out the target," the speaker says.

The assistant brings out the same ring on a poll that was used yesterday. *Shit*.

"Tyler, you'll be first to begin, please take your throw," the speaker says. I try to remember everything Rex taught me. I pool the energy at my fingertips, and envision where I want it to go, I lift it and when I release, it goes in the right direction, but falls short of the target.

"Jordan, please take your first turn," the speaker says. Jordan doesn't even break a sweat, without hesitation, he flings his hand in the direction of the target, and a burst of energy flies through the target dead center. He turns at me and smirks.

"Tyler, your second throw," the speaker says. This time I focus so hard it hurts, and I make it closer to the target, but still don't make it in.

"Jordan, your second throw," the speaker prompts. Again, Jordan makes hit shot effortlessly.

"Tyler, your third throw," the speaker says into his microphone. I close my eyes and center myself. I gather the energy at my fingertips, and this time I don't give it an option to not do what I want it to. My throw isn't as graceful as Jordan's, but this time, I make it into the target. I can hear Rain's family cheer me on from the stands.

"Jordan, your third throw," the speaker says. He looks pissed, but I guess I didn't rattle him, he makes his shot just as easily as his first two.

"Tyler, your fourth throw," the speaker says, and I do exactly what I just did. Just barely, I make my target a second time.

"Jordan, please take your fourth throw. Jordan if you make this shot, you'll be the winner of today's competition," the speaker says. Not surprising, Jordan makes his fourth shot. I expected it, but I'm still a little crushed. I don't even want to face Rain.

"Hey if you want to forfeit now, I'll take Rain off your hands for you," Jordan taunts.

"You'll literally have to kill me first," I say.

"We'll see," he says, before leaving.

RAIN

The entire rest of the day Tyler locked himself in the bedroom, not letting me in. Even when there was a knock on our front door and I answered it myself, he didn't leave the bedroom. When I open the door Becca rushes me, squeezing me in a hug that I didn't know I desperately needed. I didn't realize how stressed I was until comparing it to Becca's calming presence.

"My dad just told me today that Jordan challenged Tyler to forum. I had no idea, or I would've insisted on coming. How are you holding up?" she asks, looking at me with her warm hazel eyes that always seemed just a little too big for her face. With her long wavy blond hair and petite frame, I always thought she looked like a porcelain doll.

"Tyler won the first challenge, Jordan the second one. Tomorrow is the final competition. We're both nervous," I say.

"It's going to be okay," she says.

"I hope so," I say. We sit together on the couch.

"Your brothers would never let Jordan have you," she says.

"That's true," I say. She just holds my hand and sits with me.

"I'm so glad you came over Becca, I was losing my mind," I say. She rubs my back in a comforting circle.

"Anytime," she says. Becca stays with me the rest of the night. When I come to bed Tyler had locked himself in the bathroom, and he didn't come to bed until after I had fallen asleep.

Chapter 34
TYLER

Just like the last two days of the competition, the speaker of the forum was standing at his usual podium, Jordan and I on either side. Today's crowd was larger than yesterday and the day before. I at least slept last night and feel a little less stressed. Either I'm ready or my body is just done, I'm not really sure which. I feel bad about avoiding Rain last night, but I felt like I didn't deserve her.

Jordan looks distracted today instead of his typical collected self. I see him staring at where Rain is sitting in the bleachers. The speaker is talking, but neither of us are listening. It happens so fast I would have missed it if I hadn't been studying him. Jordan growls then bolts straight to the bleachers where Rain is sitting. I'm a second behind him. If he thinks he's going to just steal Rain again he has another thing coming.

Rain's brothers were watching too and formed a protective shield around her. But Jordan runs right past her to where Becca is sitting, grabs her throwing her over his shoulder then turning to the speaker.

"I forfeit," Jordan yells, before teleporting away with Becca in tow.

"Becca," Rain yells, "you can't just let him take her like that," Rain pleads, turning to Becca's dad.

"I wasn't expecting that," Becca's dad says.

"You have to go after her," Rain says.

"Rain, I'm not thrilled with it, but Jordan is obviously Becca's mate," Becca's dad says.

"Give them a couple days and we'll check in on them like we did with you," Mathis says.

"He's such a prick though," Rain says.

"Yeah, but it appears being mated to an amazing woman can turn even the biggest idiots around," I say, holding onto Rain. She sighs into me.

"I guess," she says.

"It's over, we can plan our mating ceremony now," I say.

"I feel like a terrible friend, Becca has always been there for me and now I feel like I'm letting her down when she needs me," Rain says.

"Rain, you know a chimera would never hurt their fated mate, that even includes Jordan," Rain's father says.

"You promise to check in on her in a couple of days? And do something if she isn't happy?" Rain asks her brothers.

"Of course, you know we were fully prepared to take Tyler out for you," Tanner says.

"Thanks," I mutter.

"Do not for a second think that's not a standing threat Tyler, she says the word and I'll happily take you out," Mathis adds. I would be mad at their threat if they didn't obviously love Rain as much as I do.

Chapter 35
BECCA

12 hours previous

"I have to go tomorrow, she's my best friend," I plead. I really can't believe he didn't tell me sooner.

"I knew I should've waited to tell you," my dad says, rubbing his temples like I'm giving him a headache. I don't care though; I'm not backing down from this one.

"You should've told me two days ago," I say.

"Forum has become more civilized over the years, but there's still a very real risk involved. I don't want you to see anything you can't unsee," he says.

"Yeah, but Rain's going to be watching her mate. Anything that'll potentially be upsetting for me is going to be exponentially worse for her," I say.

"You are a-" my dad struggles to find the word he wants to use "-kinder soul than Rain is," my dad says.

"Are you saying Rain isn't nice?" I accuse.

"I didn't say that, I love Rain like a daughter and I think she's a wonderful strong personality," my dad says.

"Well, I'm going, so you can either take me yourself, or I'll get Rex to take me," I say. My dad surprises me by laughing.

"Did you really just stomp your foot at me Becca?" he asks.

"Well…" I can feel my face blush, okay that was a little childish.

"Becca, if I didn't want you going that would be the end of the discussion and you wouldn't be going. But, probably against my better judgment, I'll take you tomorrow to support your friend," he says.

"Thank you, Daddy," I say standing on my tippy toes to wrap my arms around his neck.

"But if I say we're leaving, we're leaving, and I want you by my side the entire time," he says.

"Deal, I promise" I say.

PRESENT DAY

Not what I expected. All the stories I've heard about Jordan made him out to be a pompous jerk so in my head, he was an ugly caricature of a man. But I knew he was a chimera, so I should've realized he would look like Adonis reincarnated. I've never seen an ugly chimera male. Taking center stage in the stadium made him look even more like an ancient warrior. He has a defined back and muscular butt I can't help but look at. Shit, he turns towards my direction, and I think he caught me checking him out.

We meet each other's gaze and it's weirdly intense. I feel like a fangirl, but I can't seem to force myself to look away. The moment seems surreal, one second, we are looking at each other, next second he's charging towards the stands with Tyler close behind him. There's a blurry of commotion all around me as Rain's brothers try to protect her. But all the men being focused on Rain gave Jordan the opportunity to come straight for me and hoist me over his shoulder with ease.

"I forfeit," he yells. I can't see what's going on, but I can feel that he's teleporting me somewhere. I'm used to teleporting but doing it upside down is making me woozy. It's over as quickly as it started though. That's when the reality of my situation hits me. Jordan just kidnapped me.

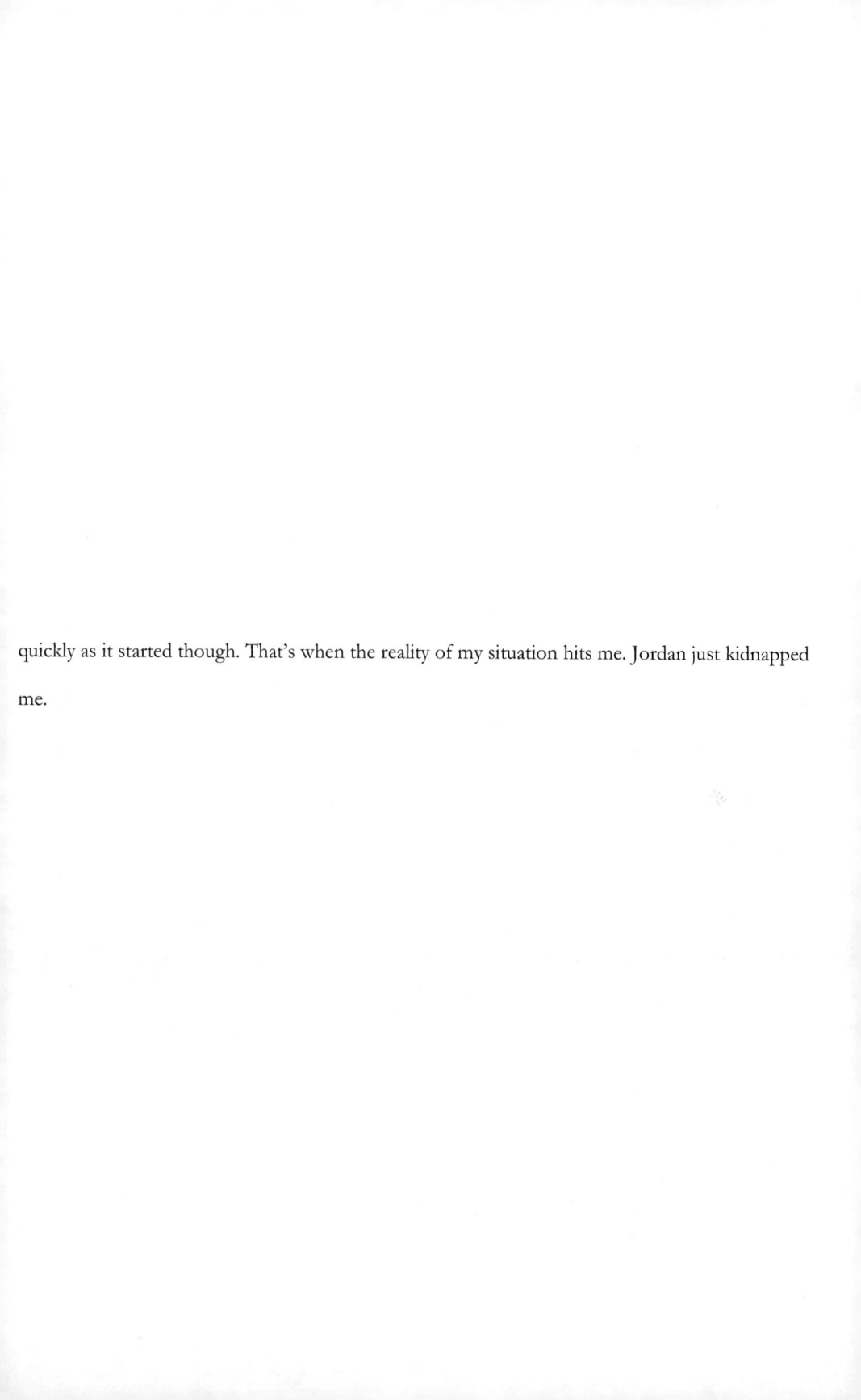

Chapter 36

JORDAN

"Put me down," the little slip of a girl currently over my shoulder says, while trying her hardest to pound on my back.

"What exactly are you trying to accomplish?" I ask.

"What exactly are you trying to accomplish?" she throws back at me. I let her slide down my body, but before her feet touch the floor, I sweep her up into my arms to carry her bridal style. Fitting really.

"Where are we?" she asks now that she can take a look around.

"My bedroom, well, our bedroom," I say. "You smell amazing."

I gently lower her onto the oversized bed in the middle of the room, nuzzling her neck and inhaling deeply before letting go.

"Take me back Jordan," she says.

"What's your name Pet?" I ask.

"I'm not your Pet, and it's none of your business, take me home before my father comes and destroys you," she says. Feisty little thing.

"Your father? The same man that stood by and let me take you not even a minute ago?" I feel slightly bad for saying it when her expression changes to one of betrayal.

"He…."

"He recognized that you're my mate," I say. Her impossibly large hazel eyes grow wider. There's something strangely ethereal about her. "What are you?" I ask.

"My mate?" she says, now all the fire's gone from her veins.

"Answer my questions," I say.

"What?" she barks at me, the fire returning.

"What's your name and what are you?" I ask.

"Take me home and I'll tell you," she says. I lean over her, putting both my hands on either side of her on the bed. Her translucent skin contrasts with the black satin sheets beneath her. The majority of the bedroom is black and red. It will be interesting to see how our two worlds merge together. Because even though she's fighting me right now, I have a feeling her default disposition is much kinder under most circumstances.

"Pet, you're not in a position to negotiate and you know I'm not letting you leave," I say.

"Stop calling me Pet," she says. I grab her chin to force her to look me in the eyes.

"Then tell me your name," I say.

BECCA

"Becca," the answer falls out of my mouth, and I can't force myself to look away from his eyes.

"What are you?" he asks. It feels like something is slithering over my skin forcing me to answer.

"My father is a shifter turned chimera like Tyler and my mother's half water sprite and half succubus," I say.

"Interesting combination, how did that happen?" he asks and I'm still transfixed under whatever spell he has me under.

"My mother's father is a water sprite. He met my mother's mom, who is a succubus, when she was bathing in a lake," I say. He nods, dropping eye contact, and it's like the spell is broken.

"What are you?" I ask unsure if this is really happening or I'm stuck in some kind of vivid dream. I look around his dimly lit room, with dark almost gothic décor, dominantly red and black. It's a strange choice for a chimera male, they usually prefer lots of natural light. I've never experienced anything like what Jordan just did to me either.

"I'm going to have fun with you," he says, giving me a wicked smile.

Chapter 37
TYLER

"She's going to be fine," I say, massaging Rain's tense shoulders as she sits in front of me on the bed. Rain barely ate any dinner, even when I insisted on feeding her. I can feel her guilt radiating off of her, she blames herself for Becca getting taken. I can also feel that she's just a tiny bit relieved that forum is over, and I think that's making her feel even worse about herself.

"You don't know either one of them as well as I do," she says. True.

"Becca's so kind and gentle, I know Jordan isn't going to think twice about taking advantage of her," she says.

"Think about all the mated couples you know. Is there a single one where the man takes advantage or in any other way oppresses his partner? Or doesn't look out for her best interest?" I ask.

"Well, no. But Jordan's such a prick," she says.

"Yeah, I agree, and he most likely will continue to be one to everybody who isn't Becca, but she's his fated mate and the bond will make him want to devote his entire being to her. Wait, how does chimera mating work?" The thought just occurred to me.

"What do you mean?" she asks, she groans as I work a particularly hard knot on her back.

"Well, my chimera genes weren't activated yet when we mated, is a chimera's fated mate similar to a shifter's? They turn eighteen and know their mate by scent? None of your brothers are mated right? How do chimeras claim their mate?" I ask.

"It's not exactly the same. Males know their mate by scent, but not necessarily at eighteen, it's random and can happen younger or older than eighteen. None of my brothers are mated yet. Claiming's the same," she says.

"Interesting, there's so much chimera history I don't know about" I say.

"Huh," Rain says.

"What?"

"Well, you know the project I've been working on with Mrs. Thomas?"

"Yeah, how's it coming along?"

"It's a process, I want to make sure I capture the stories the way she envisions them, but maybe I should be doing the same thing for chimera history too," she says.

"I think it's a great idea, do you think that's something you could share with shifters?"

"I'd have to talk to my parents before doing that, still I think it would be worth doing," she says.

"We've got one more thing to talk about, the claiming ceremony," I say, kissing her neck over my claiming mark.

"I can't plan it without Becca," she says.

"How about we start planning it now, but we won't have it until the Becca situation is a little more……..settled," I say.

"I guess," she says.

"Alright, now I'm going to help you forget everything that's happened the past few days, by screwing your brains out," I say kissing her forehead. I can feel her body vibrate when she chuckles in response.

"Oh yeah? Well, you'll have to catch me first," she tries to bolt, but she doesn't make it off the bed before I catch her around the waist and pull her back on the bed. She giggles as I hover over her and proceed to make good on my promises. Now that I feel like I'm worthy of her again, I plan to make up for lost time.

Chapter 38
RAIN

We decided both to take a couple days off after forum to regroup and reconnect. Tyler's parents understood, they were both nervous wrecks not being able to attend forum. They understood their latent genes weren't enough to grant them access to Imperia. We had a late morning after a very active night, all night. It was a great distraction, but it didn't erase my guilt. I know Tyler's right, and fated mates have a way of working themselves out, but I won't feel better until I see Becca happy. I heard someone knock on the door while I was reading in the living room. Tyler was upstairs in the shower and must not have heard it, or he wouldn't have let me answer.

"Max?" Of all the people I expected to be there when I answered the door, he was the one I expected the least, "Can I help you?" I ask unsure, taking in his worried demeanor.

"Sorry to bother you, I was wondering if you'd heard from Becca or knew where she was?" he asked. *Shit.* What can I tell him?

"I heard from her yesterday, I'm sure she's fine. Becca sometimes does this thing where she needs to take a break from being social and doesn't respond to any of my messages," I say. It's the best excuse I can think of on the spot. He's not convinced.

"We were supposed to have dinner last night, but Becca never showed. I've been trying to call and text her but she's not responding. I went by her house this morning, but her dad pretty much told me to piss off," he says.

"Yeah, he covers for her because he knows how she is, just give it some time," I say.

"Has she……..talked to you about me?" he asks, his expression is so raw, that it hurts me a little knowing that they were never meant to be. I debate which would hurt less, telling him the truth, or lying and telling him she never talked about him. I never in my life thought I would be trying to spare Max's feelings, of all people.

"Not really," I say, deciding to go with a vague noncommittal answer.

"Oh," he says, looking defeated.

"If I hear from her, I'll tell her to call you, but trust me, the more you try and contact her the longer her self-isolation is going to last," I say.

"Thanks," he nods like a sad puppy, before leaving.

JORDAN

Not exactly how I thought this would go, but then again, I never thought I'd have a fated mate, so I guess I can't say I really had any expectations. Becca looks so angelic when she sleeps, it's hard to reconcile this image of her with the little hellcat that tried to claw my eyes out when I told her we'd be sharing a bed together, no negotiations. Which is why I'm still a little confused on how I ended up sleeping on the couch in my room last night instead of the bed that Becca is currently sleeping in. I could've used compulsion on her, it would've been easier, but I had a feeling that would've been the wrong move. I'm not used to considering how other people will perceive my actions. It's a little exhausting.

She looks so tiny in my large bed. I could've slept in the bed without even touching her. No, that's probably not true, I would've tried to touch her. I've been watching her for a while, so I notice when her breathing pattern changes. Cute. She thinks she can hide from me.

"I know you're awake Pet," I say.

"I'm not your Pet," she says, not even a little sleepy.

"Debatable," I say. She huffs out a breath in response.

"You know, I would really like to have a shower and change into some clean clothes," she says sitting up on the bed. I gave her one of my shirts last night to wear, but she refused it and slept in her clothes instead.

"You're welcome to use my shower, I'll even help you wash off if you'd like," I say, and she pins me with a death glare.

"No thank you," she says with fake politeness, "I don't have any clothes here".

"Well, what do you want then?" I ask.

"To go home," she says.

"No. We can go shopping and buy you some new clothes," I say as a compromise.

"Jordan, I have a life, you can't just keep me in your house like this," she says.

"What's more important than being my mate?" I ask.

"For starters, I have friends back home. I'm starting college classes soon. My phone is dead, and I can't charge it," she says.

"Your cell phone isn't going to work here anyways, I'll get you one you can use to communicate with people from your old home," I say.

"Praxley is my current home," she says adamantly. She reminds me a little bit like a caged wild animal that might attack if startled.

"Well, luckily I can teleport, so the commute will be inconsequential," I say, and that seems to be the right thing to say.

"So, you'll take me back to Praxley?" she asks.

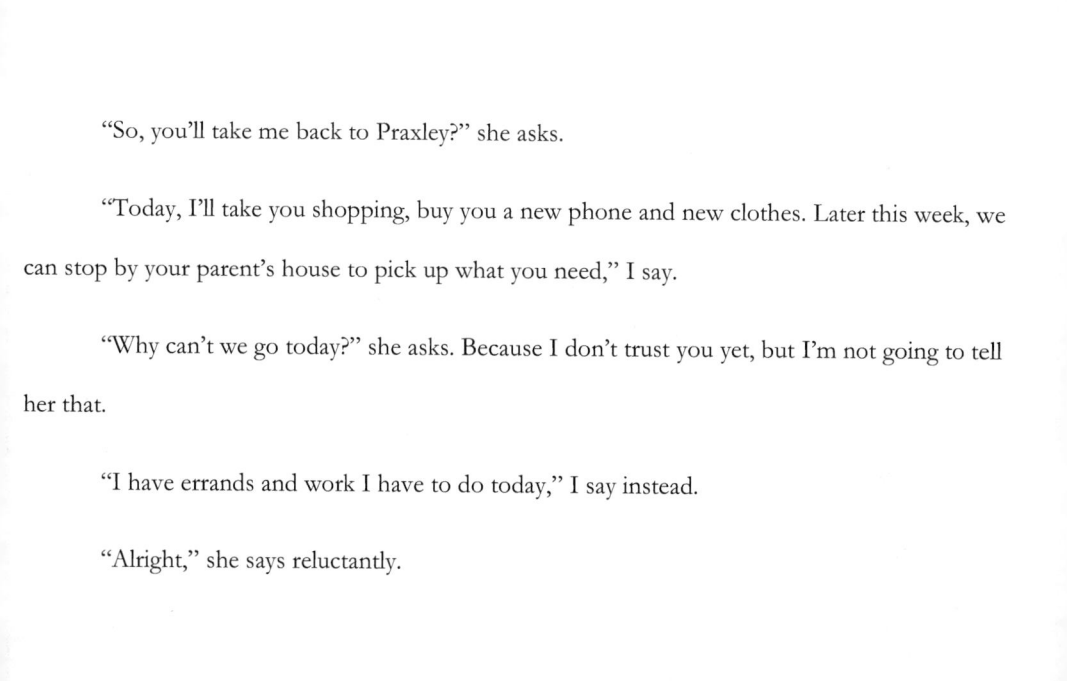

"Today, I'll take you shopping, buy you a new phone and new clothes. Later this week, we can stop by your parent's house to pick up what you need," I say.

"Why can't we go today?" she asks. Because I don't trust you yet, but I'm not going to tell her that.

"I have errands and work I have to do today," I say instead.

"Alright," she says reluctantly.

Chapter 39

RAIN

"You said a couple of days, it's been a couple of days," I say. I won't be able to stop thinking about Becca until I lay my eyes on her.

"I also said that I'd go and check on her, I didn't mention anything about taking you with me," Mathis says.

"I need to see her for myself, I'm not really sure why you're arguing with me right now when you know the end result will be you taking me with you," I say.

"Wow, okay Brat, as long as your mate is okay with you going, we can go check on Becca," he says.

"He said it was fine," I glance out the back window. Rex is working with Tyler in the backyard practicing manipulating energy together, while Mathis and Tanner were visiting in the living room. Tanner and Mathis are both off work for the next two weeks and have been staying at our childhood home like they usually do. It's unusual for their time off to line up that way though. In the back of mind, I recognize that means the mating ceremony needs to happen in that time frame for them both to be able to go. But I can't think about that right now.

"Alright fine, let's go," Mathis says.

"Alright, I'm coming with you," Tanner says, before the three of us teleport to Jordan's house. After knocking on his front door, it takes a couple of minutes before Jordan answers. I don't have great memories of this house, and seeing it makes my guilt over Becca being here escalate even more.

"What do you want?" Jordan asks, not fully opening the door.

"We're here to check on Becca," Tanner says.

"She's fine," Jordan says before trying to shut the door, but Tanner slides his foot in to prevent it from closing.

"Then you won't mind letting her talk to us," Tanner says.

"Jordan, she's my best friends, I need to know she's okay," I plead. He stares at me emotionlessly, but then sighs.

"Fine, stay out there though," he says, before slamming the door shut.

BECCA

"Becca," I hear Jordan call out. I had been reading in his library. It quickly became my favorite room in the house. It's the only room with any natural light. I find Jordan's choice in color schemes a little depressing, but the library has more gold and red than black. Most of the other rooms are overwhelmingly black with little hints of red and gold.

"Yes?" I say, putting down the romance book I was reading. I was pleasantly surprised to find an entire collection of romance books in Jordan's possession.

"You have visitors," he says. Interesting. I follow Jordan to the front door.

"Rain," I run out and hug her like I haven't seen her in months. She holds me out at arm's length, looking me over.

"Are you okay?" she asks.

"I'm adjusting," I say looking over at Jordan. He leans against his front door with his arms across his chest. He certainly is easy on the eyes at least.

"Like I said, she's fine," Jordan says.

"Jordan be nice," I say. He looks at me like he can't believe what I just said.

"Wow, I really hope my mate is less bratty than you two women are," Mathis says.

"I hope whoever gets the misfortune of being your mate has a spine of steel," Rain says.

"Becca are you really okay?" Tanner asks.

"Yes, Jordan and I are trying to work out our differences," I say.

"Try to take her from me and see what happens to you," Jordan challenges, but his body language remains relaxed.

"That's really not necessary," I say.

"So, you're not being held prisoner against your will?" Rain asks.

"No Jordan isn't holding me hostage, right Jordan? You said it would be fine for me to visit Praxley," I say.

"Yes, as long as you recognize your home is here with me in Imperia," Jordan says.

"So, she can come visit me tomorrow?" Rain asks. Jordan rolls his eyes, but nods.

"Alright, you've seen her, she says she's fine, you may all leave now," Jordan says. Rain gives me one more hug before leaving with her brothers.

JORDAN

I escort my little mate back inside.

"Were you serious about letting me see Rain tomorrow?" Becca asks, looking back at me.

"Of course, I have no intention of lying to you," I say.

"Thank you," she smiles hesitantly at me. She's been slow to warm up to me, and I'm not used to caring about what other people think about me. It's been challenging.

"If you would like to properly thank me, you'll accept my invitation to go out on a date tonight," I say.

"Where to?" she asks.

"Dinner, the black cocktail dress I bought you would be appropriate for where I plan on taking you," I say. I want to take her to a nice fancy restaurant; I think she is getting tired of being stuck inside the house all day.

"Go get ready, we leave in an hour," I say. We've been sharing the master bedroom, although I've still been banished to the couch. Any attempts at intimacy so far have been swiftly declined. It's frustrating when I know Becca finds me just as attractive as I find her, we're fated mates, there should be nothing in our way. Becca told me about how Tyler and Rain were practically enemies. We don't have that negative shared history that they had, but she's still distant with me.

TYLER

"You make it look so easy," I say. Today Rex taught me how to catch an object with energy. I feel like I've mastered throwing energy, and I do feel like each new skill I learn is a little bit easier than the previous.

"You make it look painful," Rex says. Okay, maybe not that much easier.

"Thanks," I say.

"You'll get the hang of it, and it'll be second nature for you. I've had a lifetime of practice. Once you come into your own, there'll probably be things you can do that I can't," Rex says.

"Really?" I can't tell if he is just trying to hype me up.

"Yeah, there are certain things that all chimera males can do to varying degrees, but everyone's a little bit different in what they can do and what their strengths are. Ready to call it a day?" Rex asks.

"Yeah, I've had enough," Rex pats my back before we both head inside.

"I wonder where everyone went?" Rex asks, just as Rain, Tanner and Mathis teleport back into the living room. I've seen people teleport several times now, but it still catches me off guard.

"Where were you guys?" I ask.

"Visiting Becca, your mate said you approved of her going," Mathis says, before sitting on the couch and propping his feet up on the coffee table.

"I did not approve of her going," I say, glaring at Rain.

"It's a good thing I don't answer to you then," rain challenges.

"We'll see," I promise.

Chapter 40
BECCA

"Is the food the same here? I'm not really sure where Imperia is," I admit. Jordan looks even more devastatingly handsome in a suit, with his just a little too long hair, he looks like a CEO that rides a motorcycle on the weekends.

"Imperia is just one of the many chimera communities," he explains, looking over his menu.

"But where are we, are we still on earth?" I ask. Jordan laughs in response.

"Yes Becca, Imperia is on earth. The original chimera set up locations all over the earth that non chimeras wouldn't be able to get to. There's a forcefield around Imperia. Most of the chimera communities are in remote locations, islands, places that would be otherwise unlivable to humans due to extreme weather," Jordan explains.

"What happens if a human stumbles on a chimera community?" I ask.

"Nothing happens, it's like how I can teleport, the same energy that allows me to do that is what creates the forcefield, so if a human was to stumble upon a chimera community, they would walk into the energy that would transport them out the other side, they wouldn't even notice what had happened. If the remoteness of the locations didn't deter them, the energy the forcefield gives off does. They don't know why they don't like the spot, but their subconscious tells them to stay away. A lot of times when people say that a forest is haunted, it's because they unwittingly stumbled onto a chimera community," Jordan explains.

The waiter comes and quickly takes our order, I order the vegetable stir fry, and Jordan orders the steak rare.

"So do most people live here full time then?" I ask. It was hard to tell, it didn't really look like Jordan had any neighbors.

"Most of the people who live here full time are the people who work for our government, like me. There are also people who commute to Imperia for work. Usually families don't settle here, because Imperia was set up for people who could teleport, that's why there isn't any kind of roads, and since only men can teleport, usually mated chimera males leave Imperia to settle down. Imperia is where all the government headquarters are located, it's like the capital. There are businesses here, but mostly cater to people who work for the government. Then there are people like Tanner and Mathis that commute to all the different chimera communities," he says.

"What do you do exactly?" I ask.

"Well as you can imagine, we can use a lot of our talents to have an unfair advantage over humans. Problem is that they outnumber us greatly, and anytime they get a whiff that we aren't exactly normal, mob mentality takes over and presents a real threat. I work for the sector that specifically deals with keeping us unknown and making sure we stay that way. I started out as an enforcer, so when a chimera broke a law related to keeping our species secret, I would catch them and bring them to our prison for trial. But now I work for the department that actually maintains our laws. With technological advances, our laws have to reflect the changes that are happening around us. So, I help write laws that go up for vote," he says.

"So, you're a politician," I say.

"What? No," he says. "I'm more like a protector," he says. Alright, not going to argue that.

"What position were you trying to get that you needed a mate for?" I ask.

"The position I currently hold is a lower position on the totem pole. The position I'm trying to get, is a position that gets a vote and more say on what laws get proposed," he says. I take a sip of my drink as the waiter comes and sets down our dinner.

"This is what you think rare is? There's no way this would fit any sane person's definition of rare, take it back and bring me back something closer to what I asked for," Jordan says.

"Sorry Sir, right away," the waiter says before scurrying off. It's strange seeing a chimera male cower, but Jordan's dominance is hard to question. That doesn't stop me though.

"Jordan, you can't talk to waiters that way," I admonish.

"What do you mean?" He looks at me genuinely confused.

"You can't be mean to waiters Jordan," I say. He looks over his shoulder in the direction the waiter went.

"He's living is he not?" he asks.

"Are you being serious right now?"

"Are you being serious right now?" he asks.

"You made him feel bad," I said.

"He messed up, he should feel bad," he says.

"Apologize when he comes back or I am walking out of this restaurant," I say.

"Now that would be rude," he says. The waiter returns with a new steak, rare this time.

"Sorry, sir, here's your correct order," the waiter says, not making eye contact. Jordan looks at me.

JORDAN

"I'm …sorry. Even though you messed up, it was rude of me to point it out?" I look to Becca to see if that was sufficient.

"Jordan's sorry for how he spoke to you, it was uncalled for and not that big of a deal. Right Jordan," Becca asks, smiling at me sweetly.

"Right, sorry," I say.

"Thank you, Sir," the waiter bows before leaving us again. I make a mental note to be nice to waiters in the future.

"Why waiters?" I ask, cutting into my steak.

"What do you mean?" Becca asks.

"Why do I have to be nice to waiters?" I ask.

"No Jordan, you have to be nice to everyone," Becca.

"Come on, you have to see how unreasonable that is," I say. She doesn't respond, just stares at me.

"Okay, I'm going to really try to be nicer to people, but it isn't exactly in my nature, and it's new for me, but for you I will make a conscious effort," I say.

"Thank you, I appreciate that," she says and some of the tension leaves her shoulders.

"What exactly is a water sprite?" I ask. We hadn't really discussed it. I didn't ask because I didn't want her to ask questions about myself.

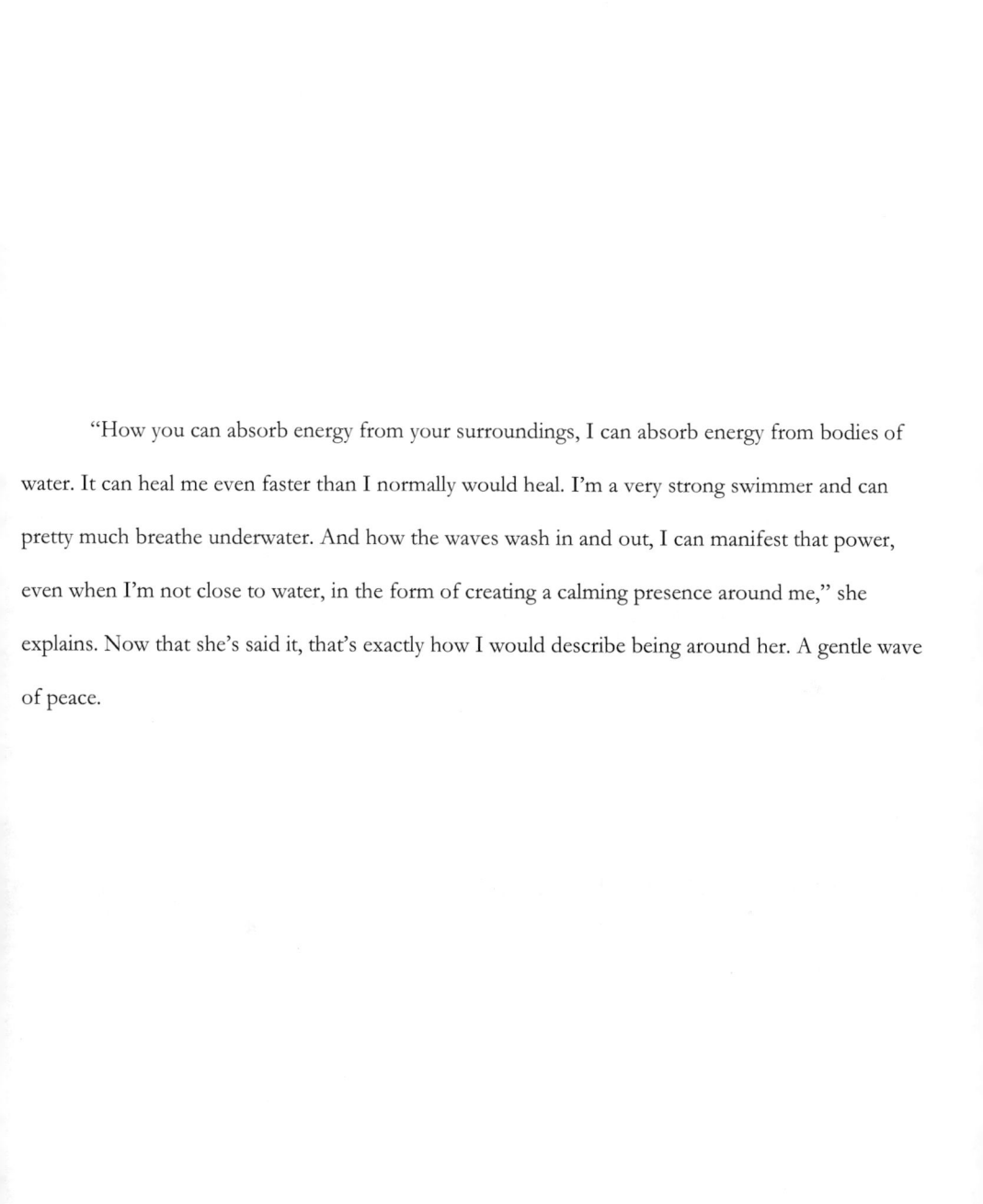

"How you can absorb energy from your surroundings, I can absorb energy from bodies of water. It can heal me even faster than I normally would heal. I'm a very strong swimmer and can pretty much breathe underwater. And how the waves wash in and out, I can manifest that power, even when I'm not close to water, in the form of creating a calming presence around me," she explains. Now that she's said it, that's exactly how I would describe being around her. A gentle wave of peace.

Chapter 41

RAIN

"You honestly don't see a problem with what you did?" Tyler asked. The drive home was silent and tense, and Tyler seems contemplative, like he's trying to be careful with how he expresses himself. I'm the opposite, I would rather say something without hesitation, get everything out in the open. Dump the mess on the floor, then work together to clean it up.

"Problem with what?" I ask, but I know what he's upset about.

"I was literally in what could've resulted in a fight to the death with Jordan days ago and you really thought it was okay to go to his house without me?" he asks. I hate when he makes his irrational behavior sound reasonable.

"You know I felt responsible for him taking Becca, I needed to see her," I say.

"I would've gone with you," he says.

"I didn't think you'd want to have to see Jordan, and I wasn't going to let it go, and I'm sorry, but I'll never ask for your permission before going somewhere," I say.

"It's not about asking for my permission; I just want you safe. Rain, even if I completely disagreed with you, I wouldn't stop you from doing something you thought was important. But you have to realize that you're not single anymore and your actions impact me. I'm just asking for the common courtesy of you telling me what your plans are, at least give me the chance to fight in your corner," he says.

"I'm sorry, you're right," I say. He steps closer, running a finger through my hair, slightly tugging on it when he gets to the end. It's still dark fire engine red, with shades of dark brown. The same brown as Tyler's hair. He's overdue for a haircut, but I kind of like the slightly longer haired look on him.

"If you want to prove how sorry you are, you'll let me take you upstairs, spank you, then fuck you," he says I can't get words to come out, so I just nod. That's all the permission he needs, he hoists me over his shoulder and quickly climbs the stairs, then slides me down his body when we get to the bedroom.

TYLER

She seems so close to getting it sometimes. It's not that I want a cowering submissive wife, I'm not looking to overshadow and consume her. I want our strengths to come together accumulatively. She's so strong, but I want her to be able to rely on my strength too. I'll happily shoulder that burden for her.

"Strip, then nose in the corner with your ass sticking out," I say. She quickly complies, I come up behind her and lovingly rub her luscious bottom. I give a tentative smack, and her ass gives a satisfying bounce. The air is thick with her arousal. It almost makes me dizzy. It's a lesson in self-discipline, to not immediately sink into her warm center. But Rain is giving herself over to me and deserves my full attention and for me to be completely in control of myself.

I smack her other cheek, and a lovely light pink is already blooming across her bottom. I alternate back and forth, until the light pink turns to a darker red, and she starts shifting her weight on her feet. What I imagine started as a light sting, should be a deep burn by now. I give two more solid smacks to each cheek, then unzip my pants pulling out my shaft. I put one hand on the middle of her back to keep her in the position I want her in, then use my other hand to guide my penis in her wet center.

I have to bend my knees a little to get the angle right. When I've impaled her on myself, I hook my arms under her knees and hoist her up so I can stand up fully. I slide her up and down while I thrust into her.

"Touch yourself," I say, my voice rough with lust. She keeps her left hand braced on the wall in front of her and snakes her right hand down to find her clit. I see her rub herself vigorously, and the sight alone is almost enough to push me over, but I grind my teeth and hold off until she finds her release. I kiss her back, up to her neck, licking over my claiming mark. That's all it takes.

"I'm coming," she calls out her release and I feel her channel clamping down on me. I lose hold of whatever self-control I had left and pound into her until I shout out my own release. After a minute of heavy breathing, I gently ease out of her, and place her back on the ground.

"Are we good?" she asks, breathlessly, and I have to chuckle.

"Yeah Rain, we're good," I say. I grab Rain's hand and guide her over to the bed. She lays down, and I get a warm towel to wash up our combined fluids from between her legs. She lets out a small gasp when I slide the towel over her clitoris, but I don't linger. I throw the towel in the hamper then get into bed and pull Rain to my side, kissing her forehead.

"So, I know we have a lot going on right now, but I was thinking that you might be interested in taking a couple of classes at Praxley College. I looked into it, you have a couple weeks left to register, and there are all sorts of classes, like creative writing and drawing, even a painting course," I say.

"I'd have to learn how to drive and get a car, but I really like that idea," she says, kissing my chest.

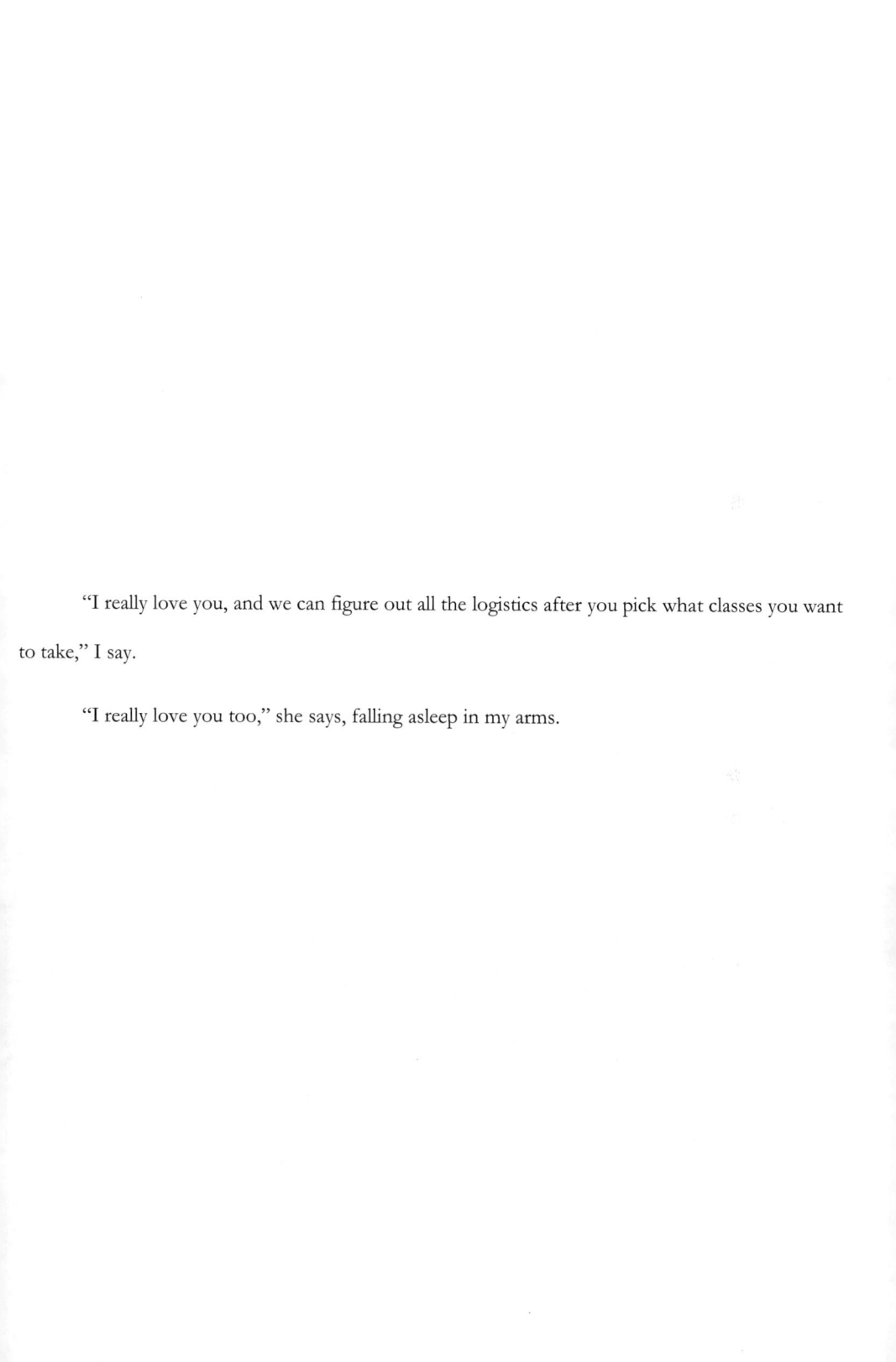

"I really love you, and we can figure out all the logistics after you pick what classes you want to take," I say.

"I really love you too," she says, falling asleep in my arms.

Chapter 42
RAIN

"I'm so glad you're here," I say hugging Becca tighter than necessary. Tyler stands behind me eying Jordan but saying nothing.

"I'll be back in an hour to pick you up," Jordan says to Becca.

"That's not enough time, I'll call you when I'm ready to be picked up," Becca states. I'm glad she's standing up to him. They both just stare at each other, until Jordan relinquishes with a small nod before teleporting away. Tyler satisfied that Jordan was gone, goes back upstairs. He made one of the spare bedrooms into an office for himself that he's been using to do whatever an alpha of a pack does in.

"So, tell me everything," I say, pulling her to the living room couch to sit down.

"Honestly, there isn't much to tell," Becca says.

"You're really okay?" I ask.

"Oddly enough, Jordan has been respectful of my boundaries, and I haven't given him an inch," she says.

"What do you think of him?" I ask. Becca sighs, and I rub her arms.

"I obviously hate how he treated you, both when he kidnapped you and when he challenged Tyler. I feel guilty that because I'm connected to Jordan, it means that you and Tyler are going to have to tolerate being around him," she says.

"What? No Becca, I don't care about that at all. I mean, yeah, he's not my favorite person, but I wouldn't want our past to stand in the way of you being happy with your mate. For you I can forget what happened. This entire time I've been feeling so guilty that I was the reason you two met," I say.

"Well, they always say fated mates find each other eventually, if not for you he still would've found me somehow," Becca says.

"Do you think he's someone you can be happy with?" I ask.

"In his own weird way, I think he's trying. I don't know, I'm just seeing where things go at this point, I mean we're supposed to be destined for each other," she says.

"Well, speaking of potential suitors, Max has been asking for you nonstop, each time he comes by he's progressively more unhinged," I say.

"Yeah, about that," Becca shifts her position.

"What?" I ask.

"I was going to try to meet up with Max. Jordan got me a new phone that could work in Imperia, but I kept the same number, so I've been getting all of Max's texts, but I didn't know what to say to him and felt like I needed to talk to him in person," Becca says.

"Do you need me to do anything?" I ask.

"I told Max I'd meet him at the park in an hour to talk, do you think Tyler can drive me to drop me off? And pick me up after, before I call Jordan?" she asks.

"Yeah, of course," I say.

"Great, now we need to plan this mating ceremony that's happening in less than two weeks," the reminder makes me groan.

"I think I'm going to recruit my mom and Tyler's mom, although they're at totally opposite ends of the spectrum. His mom has her junk drawer organized by color, my mom believes if she was meant to find something it would just magically appear in front of her, if not it wasn't meant to be," I say. Becca laughs since she knows my mom just as well as I do.

"So, what can we work on today?" Becca asks.

"You really don't have to help, I know you have enough to worry about right now," I insist.

"I need the distraction," she says.

"Could you help me with the seating arrangements? Just thinking about them gives me a headache," I say.

"Of course," Becca grins, and I bring out all my mating ceremony plans so far, including the layout of the tables in the hall we'll be using, the same place council meetings are held.

"I made sticky notes with all the guest names so I could move people around, there's just so much drama and pack dynamics," I say. Becca silently gets to work rearranging what I've already done. Of course, her arrangement makes a hundred times more sense than mine did.

"Are you seriously inviting Heather?" Becca asks. I cringe.

"Yeah, unfortunately, I don't have a choice. She's still part of the pack, she by default gets invited to anything publicly hosted by the alpha," I say.

"Okay, well, let's just put her somewhere in the back then," Becca says. She picks up a name, and sighs. I know whose name is on it before she sets it down. I take the sticky note with Max's name on it from her.

"Do you know what you are going to tell him?" I ask.

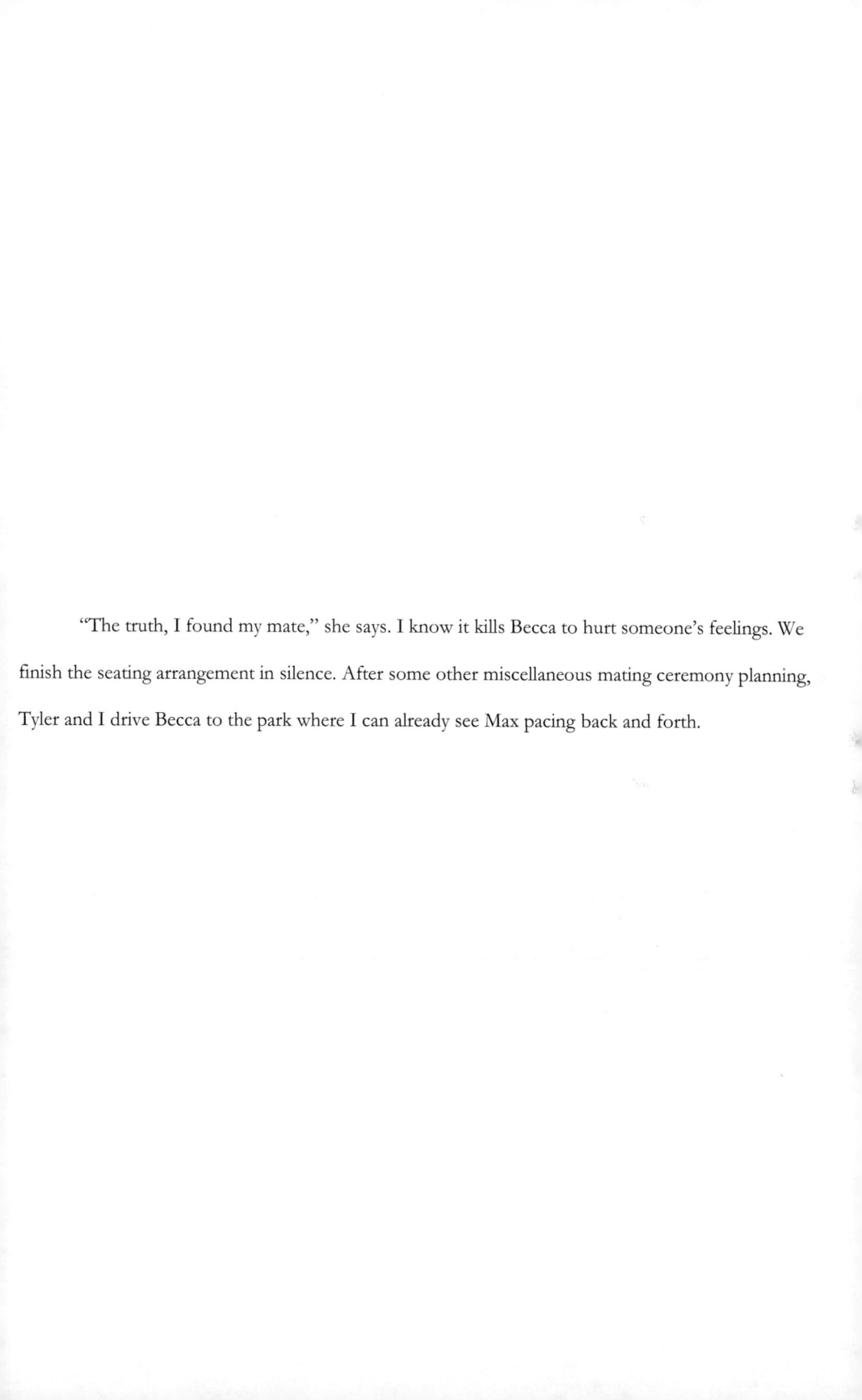

"The truth, I found my mate," she says. I know it kills Becca to hurt someone's feelings. We finish the seating arrangement in silence. After some other miscellaneous mating ceremony planning, Tyler and I drive Becca to the park where I can already see Max pacing back and forth.

Chapter 43
BECCA

"Oh my god Becca," Max says, grabbing me frantically. Rain wasn't kidding, he looks like he's falling apart. I knew it was a risk that if he spent too much time around my succubus side, he could possibly become infatuated, I just figured it would've taken a lot more exposure, and actually being intimate with each other, which we never did. Luckily, the park was empty besides the two of us. We take a seat at an empty picnic table.

"Max, are you okay?" I ask. His usually perfectly imperfect hair was a mess and his clothes rumpled like he hadn't changed them in a couple of days.

"I was so worried about you, you weren't answering my calls, your parents weren't telling me anything. What did I do wrong Becca?" he asks, and it kills me to see how much pain I've caused him. I should've never let him get this close to me. It just felt so nice being part of the popular crowd, and after spending time with Max, I found out he was actually a pretty nice person.

"Nothing Max, you've been so kind, and I'm glad I got the chance to know you better," I say, wishing I knew how to make this better. A year ago, I wouldn't even believe it if someone said Max and I became friends, let alone that Max would be upset about me breaking up with him.

"So, we can go back to dating?" he asks hopefully.

"Max, it wouldn't be fair to you for me to lead you on, so I'm not going to do that. I found my fated mate," I say.

"What?" he asks, the look he gives me is pure devastation.

"I'm sorry," I say.

"What the hell is going on here Becca?" Jordan asks. *Shit*. I didn't see him teleport behind us, but he must have.

"Nothing, Jordan," I say, standing between the two of them. I'm not letting Max get hurt because of me, but of course, Max must have felt the need to defend me, because he tries to stand in front of me. I see Jordan's nostrils flare when Max puts a hand on my arm.

"Don't fucking touch her," Jordan says, with deadly intent. Max must sense the real threat Jordan presents because he immediately drops his hands.

"Hey man, I don't want any trouble," he says, putting his hands up in surrender.

"Then don't touch my property," Jordan says.

"I am not your property, Jordan," I say, stomping my foot. For a second Jordan looks at me like he wants to laugh but doesn't.

"Not now Becca," he says.

"Jordan, this is Max, he's just a friend. Max, this is my mate Jordan," I say.

JORDAN

Bullshit, just a friend. I had a feeling Becca was lying to me, I wasn't expecting her to be meeting up with some boy though.

"Come here, Becca," I say, trying to contain my rage. The second she's at my side, touching me I feel instantly calmer. She has that power over me.

"Please don't hurt Max, I was just telling him that the reason I wasn't able to hang out with him anymore is because I'm mated to you," she says. Dammit, I really want to hurt him. I decide on the next best thing though. Slowly walking up to Max, making sure I don't spook him, I roughly grab him by the chin and force him to look me in the eyes. He's a shifter, so he's a good size, but still a foot shorter than me.

"Max, you're going to stay away from Becca, whatever feelings you think you have for her are over now, and you're going to forget about ever meeting me," I say, my voice laced with heavy compulsion. Max nods, I let go, his eyes still in an unfocused trance.

"What did you just do?" Becca asks me suspiciously.

"Let's go," I say grabbing her arm and teleporting her back to our bedroom.

"Jordan, what did you just do to Max?"

"Becca, not now," I say.

"No, what are you? And how did you know where I was?" she asks, furious, like an angry kitten.

"When I gave you that phone, I made sure I was able to access it remotely to be able to go through your texts. When I left you with Rain, I had the sense you were lying, so I went through all your recent texts, and found the one with Max. I also have a tether on you, that's how I knew you went to that park," I admit.

"Jordan, that's not okay," she says.

"No, Becca," I say stalking towards her "what isn't okay is you lying to me about where you were to meet up with some boy who obviously has a crush on you," I say. I notice with great satisfaction that she doesn't try to back away from me if anything she leans in closer.

"Tell me Becca, did you ever kiss that boy?" I ask, pushing a lock of her curly hair behind her right ear.

She hesitates before answering, "No," she says.

"No?" I question.

"Maybe just a goodnight kiss," she admits, her cheeks blushing. I claim her mouth. Possess her, and she doesn't stop me. I capture her groan, holding the back of her neck in my large palm. I can hear her pulse quicken. We're both breathless when I pull away from the kiss.

"What did you do to him?" she asks. Her concern for the boy grating on my nerves.

"I used compulsion on him," I say.

"Compulsion? What does that mean?" she asks. I had been avoiding the question. Deep down I know I was afraid of how she was going to react to what I am.

"It means I can force him to do what I tell him to do," I explain.

"Have you done that to me?" she asks, but she already knows.

"Just that one time, when you wouldn't tell me what you were," I say.

BECCA

"But I did tell you, so why won't you tell me what you are?" I ask. If we're going to be mated, I would really like to know what I'm signing up for first.

"I'm a chimera," he says. Well obviously.

"Chimera mixed with what?" I ask.

"My mom's a vampire," he says. What the hell?

"What does that mean?" I ask. I've never heard of actual vampires. I knew there were other beings I was ignorant of, but not vampires.

"My chimera genes are dominant, so for the most part I'm chimera," he says.

"So, do you……suck blood?" I feel silly even asking.

"I can," he says. That thought really shouldn't turn me on as much as it does. By Jordan's smirk, he can smell my own arousal and knows how much that thought turns me on. He leans down to whisper in my ear.

"Do you like that idea?" he asks, his warm breath on my neck causing goosebumps.

"No," but we both know that's a lie.

"Tsk, tsk Pet, that's the third time you've lied to me today," Jordan says.

"Sorry," I offer up lamely. He gently caresses my cheek and I lean into his touch.

"Now what kind of mate would I be, if I ignored the fact that my Pet was in obvious need of some discipline," he says. His voice deep and smooth like aged whiskey.

"Jordan…..I…..." concerned by how fast this is escalating.

"Hey, look at me," he says softly. I look up into his dark blue eyes. "I would never give you more than you can handle. If something is too intense or if we're moving too fast just tell me, and we can talk about it," he says, reassuring all my worries. I surprise myself with how comfortable I am with Jordan.

Jordan sits down on the bed, silently guiding me between his legs. Out of reflex, I stop Jordan when he puts his hands on my pant button. He stills and looks up at me, although with him sitting we are s+close to the same height. I drop my hands, and he continues, undoing my jeans and pulling them down. He keeps my underwear in place though. The lacy material offers little protection, other than a little modesty.

With his hands helping me, he puts me over his knee with my butt up in the air. Without warning, he administers a solid smack to one cheek. The underwear helps less than I thought it would.

"You okay?" he asks before proceeding. I nod.

"Use words, I want to hear you," he says.

"I'm okay," I say. Jordan resumes the task at hand, alternating between cheeks, this time not stopping until the light sting turned into a deep burn. I couldn't help but think about why I was laying here across his lap, including how upset Max was. The combination of my guilt and the pain from the spanking was overwhelming and surprisingly cathartic. I felt the tears run down my face before I even registered that I was crying. It was a minute before I realized Jordan had stopped.

He helped me up to a sitting position on his lap, and I winced when my punished backside came into contact with the harsh fabric of his jeans. Jordan chuckled in response. This time, I started the kiss, a much gentler version, my lips wet from my tears. As I deepen the kiss, I grind into Jordan, but I'm surprised when he stills my hips with his strong hands.

"Don't you want to……."

"More than anything," he says with conviction, "but you are emotionally raw right now, and I want you to be one hundred percent sure before we take this further," he says. I nod in agreement. I feel needy, but I know he's right.

"Just don't lie to me anymore he says," kissing me again before helping me up and pulling back up my pants.

Chapter 44
JORDAN

It's physically painful to pull away from Becca's warm soft body, but I know taking this any further would be the wrong choice. Possibly.

"Are you okay?" I ask, looking into her face for any signs of unease.

"Yeah, I'm fine," she says with a shy smile.

"Alright, I'm going to take a shower before bed," I say. There's no point in hiding my erection, she must have felt it when she was over my lap. I leave Becca in my bed. While the shower heats up, I take off my clothes throwing them in the hamper. I took a shower this morning already, but that's not what this is about. If I don't relieve myself, I'm going to end up doing something I'm not sure Becca is ready for.

The warm water works some of the tension out of the muscles of my back. I widen my stance and grip the base of my cock. It's already slippery from the water, but I add a squirt of body wash to my hand just for extra lubrication. I start out slow, but steady, running my hand up and down the length of my cock. It gets washed away, but I can feel the bead of precum gathering at the tip. I'm so lost to what I'm doing, I'm caught off guard when I hear a gentle moan. My eyes snap open, and Becca is standing at the bathroom door, squeezing her legs together like she's desperately looking for some friction.

"Awww, Little Pet, did I leave you wanting?" I ask, still gently stroking myself up and down. She blushes, then looks away, but gives a slight nod.

"Say it out loud," I say. That makes her look back at me.

"Tell me what you want," I say.

"I …. Don't know what I want," she says.

"Do you want to watch me come?" I ask. Her blush deepens but this time she nods enthusiastically. I don't hide my own amusement. Not to disappoint, I return to a more serious pace. Her hazel eyes stay transfixed, watching each stroke with undivided attention. I watch her watching me.

"Take off your clothes and come here," I say gently. I search her face for any hint of hesitation but am assured when she immediately rips off her top and pants, followed by her underwear and bra. I take in the sight of her fully naked. She's a vision of perfection. She has a soft tapered stomach, with wide hips and a perfect handful perky breast. She looks up at me, stepping into the shower. She places her small hands on my lower abdomen tracing the ridges of my muscles.

I let her replace my hand with her own. She lightly strokes my length, watching for my reaction, speeding up and applying more pressure. I slowly lower my head to her pebbled nipple, looking up to her for permission before I take her into my mouth. She pushes her breasts into my face, and I accept the green light, sucking on her gently. I was already close before I started, and despite my efforts to prolong this moment, I can't hold off any longer.

"I'm going to come," I warn, a second before spilling my seed all over the shower floor. She watches with interest.

"Now Pet, let's take care of you. Normally I wouldn't let you orgasm after a punishment, but I think you deserve it," I say, pushing damp hair out of her face.

"Would you like that?" I ask.

"Yes," she says, her voice heavy with lust. I guide her to turn around so her back is to my chest, and I wrap my arm around her lower waist, finding her wet center. I start with slow wide circles around her clitoris. I keep my pace steady though; I don't want her orgasming just yet. She tries to grind into my hand to apply more pressure. I push her up against the shower wall, so I can brace her with my hips and stop her movements.

"No Pet, I decide how much pleasure you get," I whisper into her ear. I tease her, until she is panting in desperation. She makes the cutest little whimper when I stop fingering her. Her pupils are dilated when I turn her around.

Luckily, I have tall ceilings for what I'm about to do. I bend down and hoist Becca onto my shoulders, so my face is between her spread legs. I lick into her folds, gripping her hips to move her in rhythm to my ministrations. I teased her long enough that it doesn't take long to get her back to the edge, this time I don't pull back until she finds her release, with her hands lightly pulling my hair. Her shapely thighs squeeze me as she rides out her orgasm. I wait until the last aftershock is finished, and slowly let her slide down the shower wall. Leaning down, I capture her mouth with my own. Possessing her. Staking my claim, and it's more than gratifying that she lets me.

"Come on, I'll help you dry off," I say, before shutting off the shower.

Chapter 45
JORDAN

Sitting at my desk trying to work, I can't stop replaying the scene from yesterday. Watching Becca's round bottom turn a pretty blush under the weight of my hand, followed by what we did in the shower. After, she let me sleep in the bed with her. Very few times in my life have I felt so at peace as when I was holding her in my arms. Just the two of us.

I try to concentrate on the documents sitting in front of me, the ones I should be reviewing, but my motivation is nonexistent. I can't help to think back to my original plan. I was going to force Rain to be my mate. I was neutral to the thought; it was simply a means to an end. I needed to be mated to level up to a position where I can push my agenda easier. I can compel people, but it has its limitations. I'll have far more power if I can have direct access to the people who pass our laws. Sure, I'll have my own vote, but it'll also be significantly easier to only have to compel a small group of high-power officials instead of the more indirect methods I'm currently using.

When I used to think about mating Rain, I didn't care either way. She's beautiful but I didn't have any real feelings towards her. The idea of mating Becca on the other hand, stirs emotions I didn't know I was capable of. It works out that my professional agenda lines up so well with my personal agenda. The more I think about having a mating ceremony, the more solid of a plan it becomes until I know I have to act on it. I know just what to do too.

"Jordan," the familiar voice answers on the phone.

"Hello mother," I say.

"How are you son, I miss you, are you going to visit me soon?" she asks. Now that I think about it, it has been a while since I've visited. It's hard to make up excuses when you can teleport.

"I need your help," I say.

"Sure, what do you need?" she asks warmly.

"Can you help me plan a mating ceremony," I say. The line is silent for so long I think we've been disconnected.

"I'm sorry, Jordan I must have misheard, I thought you said help you plan a mating ceremony," she says.

"Yes, that's exactly what I said. A mating ceremony between me and my fated mate," I say.

"Jordan," my mom squeals, "you found your mate? Why didn't you tell me? What's she like? When can I meet her?" She's so excited she doesn't pause between words.

"I hadn't really thought about it," I say.

"How about tonight?" she says hopefully.

"I'll talk to her and let you know," I say. I realize now they would have met sooner or later regardless, but I usually like my life to be more compartmentalized, and the thought of them mixing is slightly unsettling. It shouldn't be though. My mother and Becca are the two nicest people I know.

"Well, tell me about her," my mom demands.

"Her name is Becca, and she's absolute perfection," I answer truthfully.

"I'm so happy for you Jordan, and I'd love to plan a mating ceremony for you. Do you have a timeline?" she asks.

"As soon as possible," I say.

"Alight, I'll get started, but it would be helpful for us to meet," she says.

"Fine, we'll be there for dinner tonight," I say. I have to pull the phone away from my ear, my mom squeals so loud.

"Mother, please, don't overwhelm her," I say.

"Of course not," she says, "I have so much to do, I'll see you tonight," she says, hanging up the phone before I answer.

Chapter 46
BECCA

There's not much to do here. That's my excuse anyways. If I had a distraction, I wouldn't be incessantly replaying our shower activities from last night in my mind. So, I can't really be held responsible for seeking relief at my own hands. Not that I'm any stranger to finding pleasure by my own hands, because I'm definitely not. It's just that it still feels like Jordan's house, and masturbating in someone else's bed just seems, wrong. Apparently not wrong enough to stop me though.

I hide under the blanket. The problem with being mated to someone who can teleport is that there's no warning when they just show up. It's fine though, I can be discreet, keep myself covered and keep my clothes on. I snake my hand down my front, squeezing it into my jeans, and sliding it in my underwear. I'm not surprised to find myself wet, thinking about all the things Jordan did to me.

Of course, it's like me thinking about Jordan summons him here. I had just got started too when Jordan appears out of thin air.

"What are you doing Pet?" Jordan asks, grabbing the head of the bed with one hand to lean over me, his face hovering over mine.

"Nothing," I say, acting innocent. He firmly grabs my wrist, slowly bringing my fingers to his mouth, gently sucking on the fingers still smeared in my own arousal. I feel him chuckling around my fingers before biting down on my hand, just hard enough to cause a tinge of actual pain but light enough it quickly dissipates when he releases.

"Tastes familiar," he says. "Although I'd love to get second helpings directly from the source," he says, dropping my wrist and grabbing my mound through my jeans, squeezing roughly "we don't have time for me to enjoy it properly. Get ready, we're going to dinner. I'll pick you something out to wear," he says.

"Oh, and Becca, you're not allowed to masturbate without my permission. Your pleasure belongs to me, and I get to decide if you orgasm," he says. God, why does that turn me on?

JORDAN

I have more discipline than I'd have given myself credit for. I'd love nothing more than to make good on my promises, and delve face first into Becca's delicate petals, but I don't want to keep my mom waiting. I do feel bad for not visiting lately, and for not telling her about Becca right away. My mother has just always been such a compassionate person, and I've always felt guilty about not being capable of reciprocating.

At least I can give her a compassionate daughter-in-law, who'll in turn give her compassionate grandchildren. Children. No that's something I've never thought about before, not positively at least. With Becca, that thought doesn't seem so far-fetched. She'd look sexy pregnant too.

She comes out wearing the dark green dress I left for her. I love that she doesn't fight me when I pick out her clothes for her. I like having any control she'll let me exert over her. The green of the dress compliments her eyes, making them seem even larger than they are. Adds to the other worldliness quality that Becca has about her. It's like she's a goddess sent from another planet.

"Are we going to go to dinner? Or were you just going to stare?" she asks.

"Brat," I say. I hoist her up by her waist throwing her over my shoulder, giving her ass a solid smack before teleporting to my mom's front porch. She doesn't live in Imperia, although she has enough chimera genes that she's able to get in. My parents prefer living in a human community. Their house is secluded, hidden in the woods with no close neighbors, so being seen teleporting isn't a concern.

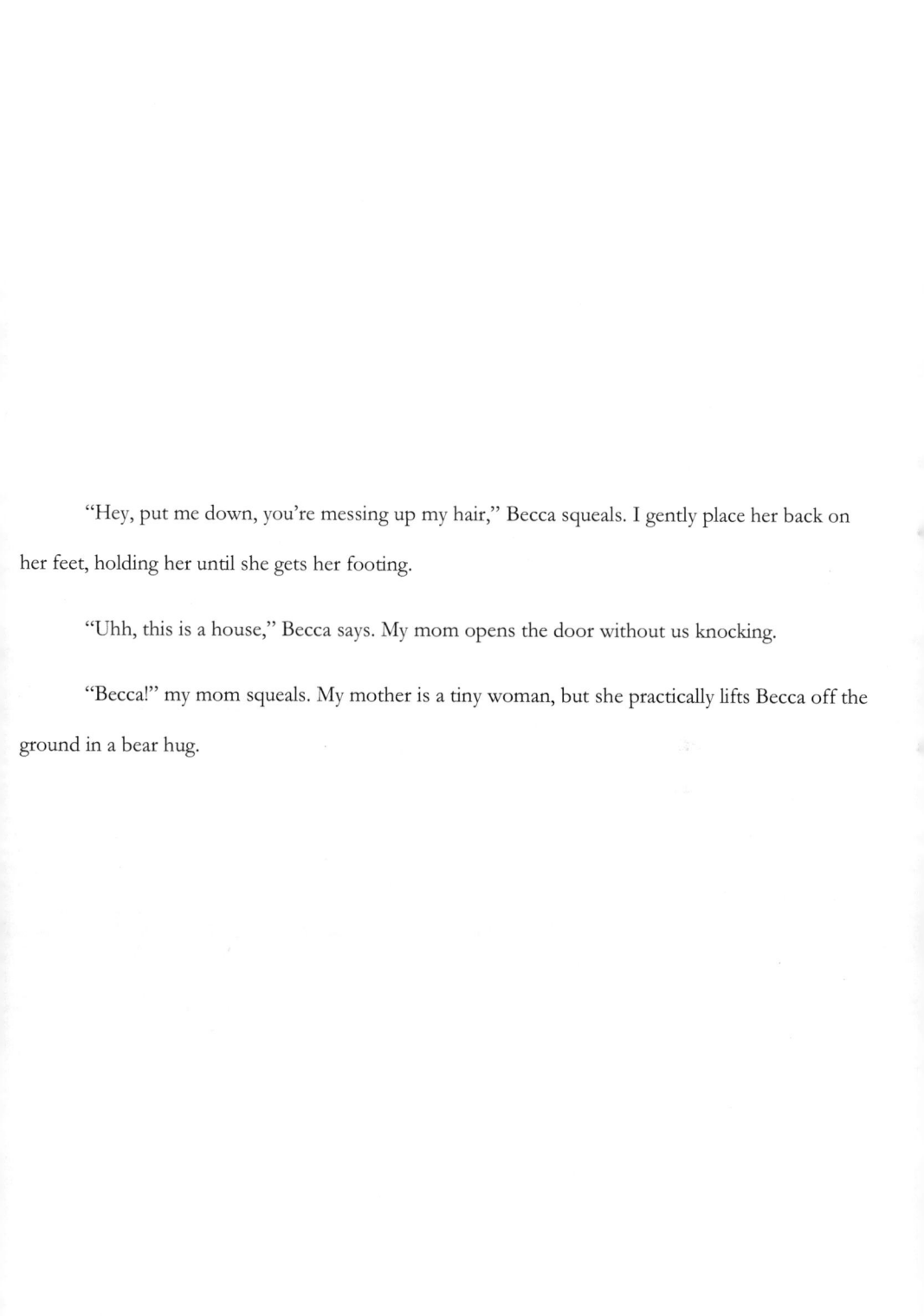

"Hey, put me down, you're messing up my hair," Becca squeals. I gently place her back on her feet, holding her until she gets her footing.

"Uhh, this is a house," Becca says. My mom opens the door without us knocking.

"Becca!" my mom squeals. My mother is a tiny woman, but she practically lifts Becca off the ground in a bear hug.

Chapter 47
BECCA

What's happening? A browned haired woman, about my size has me in a death grip. I look at Jordan for an explanation of what's happening.

"Hello Mother," Jordan says. Mother. What?

"Jordan, you didn't tell me you were taking me to meet your mom," I say accusingly. I return the hug as much as her tight grip will allow me.

"Oh Jordan, what's wrong with you?" his mom says. It's such a startling dichotomy, the stoic and powerful Jordan side by side with this expressive petite woman who I'm having a hard time picturing as his mom.

"Well come on in you two," his mom ushers us inside, "we're having a drink in the living room, Becca, do you drink, can I get you a wine?" his mom asks warmly.

"I could use a wine," I say, shooting daggers at Jordan. Not that I mind meeting his family, he could've given me a heads up though. In the living room, an older brute of a man, stands up in greeting, this must be Jordan's father. Now he makes sense, his dad looks just like him.

"Becca, my name is Foster, I'm Jordan's father, and you met my wife," Foster says, extending his hand for a firm handshake.

"Oh, what's wrong with me, I didn't even introduce myself. My name is Hayley, you can call me Mom though," Jordan's mom says, squeezing my upper arm affectionately. She pours me a glass of wine from a wet bar they have in the living room.

The last person in the room, is a younger woman with short straight black hair and light blue eyes. She stands to greet me.

"Hi, I'm Lucy, Jordan's little sister," she says smiling, "my condolences on being mated to my brother," she says, giggling. I'm not sure what I was expecting Jordan's family to be like, but this isn't it. Honestly, once he said vampire, I was expecting coffins, emotionless creatures of the night.

"Hey, watch yourself kid," Jordan says to his sister.

"I'm inclined to agree with her," Hayley says, "you didn't even warn her that she was meeting us," she says.

"I told her we were going to dinner," Jordan says in his defense.

"Yeah, but not with your family," Hayley says.

"So?" Jordan asks.

"I was just a little caught off guard, I'm so happy to meet you though," I say honestly.

"Of course, Dear. I am so excited to be planning your mating ceremony," Hayley says. I take a big gulp of wine.

"Mating ceremony? What mating ceremony?" I ask, looking at Jordan.

"Jordan, you are your father's son, that's for sure," Hayley says.

"Of course, I am, who else's son would I be?" Jordan asks. Looking at Jordan's parents I see why we were mated together. We're just like his parents. I guess we're supposed to balance each other out. Despite being thrown into this situation, it's reassuring to see how happy of a family they are. That could be our future together.

Chapter 48

JORDAN

"We didn't talk about a mating ceremony," Becca says. She's upset but I can't understand why.

"Of course we're having one, I didn't talk to you about it because there's nothing to discuss," I say exasperated. "I thought we were on the same page, especially after what we did last night," I say. Becca's large eyes open even wider, and a beautiful blush creeps up her cheeks.

"Jordan," she squeals, lightly slapping my arm.

"What?" I ask confused.

"Not in front of your parents," she whispers.

"Why? You're my mate, they know I'm going to fuck you," I say.

"Jordan, Darling, I'll put the plans on hold, that'll give the two of you a chance to talk about it first, I can resume whenever the two of you are ready," my mom says.

"No need for that, we're mates, there's no other possible outcome than us becoming mated. I want it officially announced," I say. Becca eyes me suspiciously.

"I think your mom is right, and we should talk about this in private later," Becca says.

"How about we have some dinner?" my mom suggests. I'm frustrated, but let it go, for now.

"Fine," I say. I escort Becca to the dining room, where my mom has laid out several covered dishes of various foods.

"Becca, I didn't know what you ate, so I made a selection of different things," my mom says.

"Oh, you didn't have to do that, I could have just eaten whatever," Becca says, taking the seat next to me. My parents take their usual seats at the head of the table.

"You drink blood?" Lucy asks jokingly, sitting across from Becca.

"Oh, uh…..right," Becca stammers.

"Lucy don't make Becca feel uncomfortable" I warn.

"Sure, it seems like you do a good enough job of that all on your own Jordan," Lucy counters. I glare at my sister but leave it be. I love her but she can be annoying.

"Becca, I made several vegetable dishes and meat dishes. I figured you probably ate plant based though," my mom says.

"Thank you, you're right, I'm a vegetarian," Becca says, accepting the plate of vegetables my mom hands her.

Chapter 49
BECCA

I really wish Jordan had warned me that we were having dinner with his family. I should have asked him more questions about them being vampires and what that actually entailed. I don't want to ask questions that will offend them, but I'm very curious about their diet. I relax a little when Hayley uncovers a tray of steaks. That makes sense, I've seen Jordan eat mostly steaks.

The rest of dinner passes, with comfortable small talk of safer more neutral topics and despite being initially annoyed by Jordan for several reasons, I did enjoy meeting his family. Before we leave, his mom and sister both hug me and insist I come back for dinner regularly.

"I can't believe you Jordan," I say, as soon as we return to his bedroom.

"What?" he asks.

"First of all-" I start, but Jordan cuts me off.

"There's more than one issue?" he asks. Seriously?

"Yeah, Jordan, there are several," I say. I'm momentarily distracted when he starts undressing, pulling off the shirt he was wearing. I shake my head to clear it. Where was I? Oh right.

"First of all, you didn't warn me that I was meeting your family," I say. Jordan steps closer to me, close enough his scent overwhelms me a little.

"Did you not like them?" he asks, playing with a piece of my hair.

"Of course, I liked them," I said.

"Then what's the problem?" he asks.

"I had never even met vampires before, if I had known I was meeting your parents I would've asked you a bunch of questions first, so that I wouldn't inadvertently embarrass myself or offend them," I say.

"Did you really expect not to meet my family? And you didn't say anything offensive or embarrassing, so that fear was unfounded," he says.

"Secondly, you started planning a mating ceremony when you haven't even claimed me yet," I say.

"Oh? Are you ready for me to claim you?" he asks, with a predatory smile, bending down to grab my ass, squeezing playfully. I swat him away. God this man is distracting.

"You should've talked to me about it first," I say.

"Okay I'm seeing a reoccurring theme here," Jordan says, running a hand through his slightly too long blond hair.

"That you need to communicate with me better," I say.

"I'm sorry, I'm not used to explaining myself or caring what other people think of me or how other people feel. This is all new to me," Jordan says.

"Why do you want a mating ceremony so soon?" I ask.

"Why not?" he asks.

"You challenged Tyler to forum, in order to claim Rain," I say.

"Are you jealous? I never actually cared about Rain," he says.

"I know and that's exactly why I'm suspicious. There was a reason you wanted to be mated so badly," I say.

"I told you, so I could move up at work," he says.

"No, I know, but why? Why is it so important to you?" I ask. Jordan sighs, not making eye contact and I know he's about to lie to me.

"No reason," he says.

"I know that's not the truth, I would really rather you say you don't want to discuss it instead of lying to me. I'm going to give you the benefit of the doubt and trust that your plans aren't nefarious, and you'll tell me when you're ready," I say. Gently, he leans down and kisses my forehead.

"I'll tell my mother to start planning the mating ceremony," Jordan says.

"It's going to have to wait until after Rain and Tyler's ceremony," I say.

"Why?" Jordan asks.

"Jordan, I swear you have the emotional IQ of a cucumber," I say exasperated, turning towards the bathroom to get ready for bed. Jordan follows right behind me.

"What's that supposed to mean?" he asks. Like he doesn't already know. I turn towards him, leaning back on the bathroom counter.

"Rain's getting mated before us, in a little over a week from now. We'll be attending her ceremony. It'd be rude for us to have our ceremony before her or right after it," I explain.

"How long do we have to wait then?" Jordan asks.

"I don't know, a few weeks at least, we can start planning it after Rain's, assuming I even agree to it," I add.

"It's cute you think you have a choice," Jordan says, grabbing my hips and placing me on the counter. The bathroom is one of the few rooms in his house decorated in light colors, the countertop light gray, and the shower tiles white with gold accents on the vanity.

"It's cute that you think you can tell me what to do," I counter.

"Oh, but Pet, you already know that I can," he runs his finger down the valley between my breasts. "You know I'm much bigger than you and much stronger, but I don't really need all that when I can just compel you," he says seductively.

"I don't think you'll compel me though," I say, and I believe that.

"No?" he asks, kissing my neck.

"I know you wouldn't," I state firmly. He pulls back to look me in the eyes, considering his words before he speaks again.

"I wouldn't want to have to force you, and you should know that before you I wouldn't think twice about using compulsion to my advantage, but I'm not willing to let you ever leave me and realistically I can only resist the urge to claim you for so long," Jordan says.

"Yeah?" I ask, processing what he's saying.

"Yeah, but I'm not worried. I'm confident I can win you over and have you begging me to claim you before I'd ever have to force you," he says.

"You're pretty sure of yourself," I say.

"Yeah, I am. Now I want you to get ready for sleep, then I want you in bed. I want to watch you finish what you started," he says.

"Finish what?" I ask, he stares at me until I realize he means touching myself from earlier. I can feel my cheeks blush. I nod, and he leaves me in the bathroom. I quickly brush my teeth and change out of my dress to my pajamas and join him in bed. He's already changed into the sleep pants he wears to bed, laying down on his side propped up on one arm, patting the middle of the bed with the covers pulled back.

I lay on my back, nervous for a minute. I close my eyes pretending like he isn't there. Just like earlier, I snake my hand down the front of my pajama shorts and inside my underwear. I let out a small moan when I make contact with my center. He trails down my neck with open mouth kisses, pulling down my top to expose my nipples for his attack. He sucks one into his mouth roughly while pinching the other between his fingers. I arch up into his skillful mouth, while quickening my pace. I'm teetering close to edge when Jordan puts his large hand over mine, stopping me.

"What?" I mutter frustrated from being denied my release.

"I told you, I control your pleasure, not you," he says, claiming my mouth with his own. I feel his hand replace my own, and he slowly circles around my clitoris, quickly pulling me back to the ledge, before aggressively pushing me over. I call out my release. I ride the waves of my aftershocks, grinding into his hand.

Once my breathing even outs again, I look down at Jordan's prominent tent in his pants. I tentatively place my hand over his erection, but he stops me before I reach my goal.

"I expect you to ask permission," he says.

JORDAN

She acts surprised, but I can tell she reacts to my dominance. I can tell how turned on she is.

"May I touch it?" she asks sweetly. I trace my fingers down her arm.

"Touch what?" I ask. I'm going to make her say it.

"Your penis," she says. Her large eyes are all pupils, she's so aroused.

"Touch it with what?" I ask. She looks like she's seriously considering all her options before answering.

"With my mouth," she says, surprising me. I roll on my back, placing my hands behind my head.

"Yes, you may," I say. As though I'd ever stop her from sucking me off. She pulls down my sleep pants, I bridge my hips to help her, causing my erection to spring free. She positions herself on her knees before grabbing me with her small hands. She looks up at me, maintaining eye contact as she lowers her head, taking me into her warm mouth.

She swirls her tongue around my tip, before taking me as far back in her mouth as she can. She uses her hands in tandem with her mouth. The thought briefly enters my mind that she's too good at this for this to be her first time, but I push that thought away. I'm not going to ruin this moment. I bring one of my hands down to cradle the back of her head, guiding her. Her mouth feels amazing. Sooner than I would like, I feel the familiar sensation at the base of my spine, warning me of my impending orgasm.

"That feels so good, I'm going to come," I warn. She doesn't attempt to pull away. She doubles down on her effort and that is my undoing. I shoot warm ropes of seed down the back of her throat and she swallows with no complaint; she even licks me clean. I pull her up to me after, kissing her reverently this time. At times I will claim and possess her, other times I will worship her.

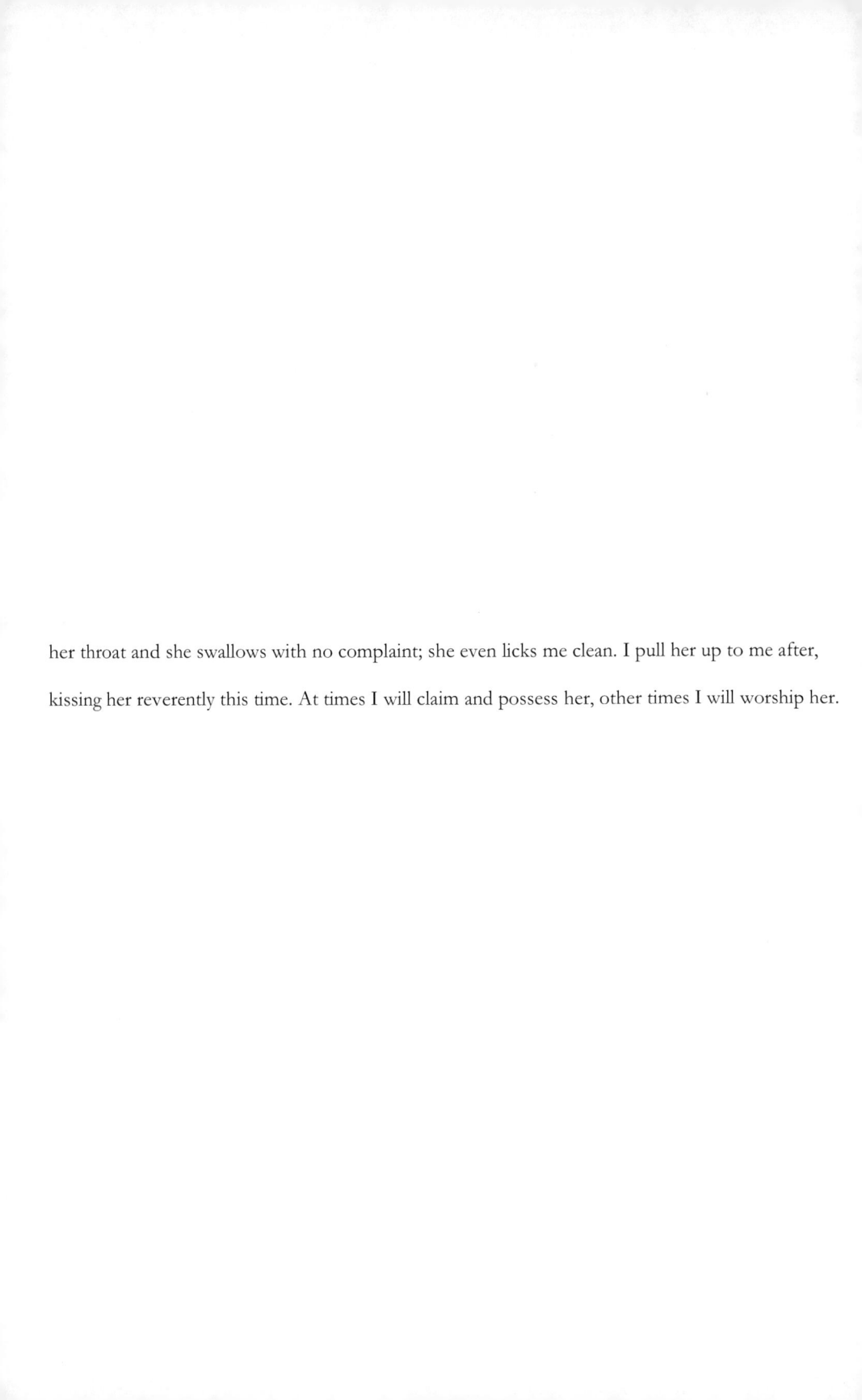

Chapter 50
RAIN

"Shit, Tyler, do you have to practice teleporting into rooms I'm in without giving any warning?" I ask. You'd think I'd be used to it, growing up with a household of men who could teleport. Although I'm very proud of how fast Tyler has been learning chimera skills lately, he's been startling me nonstop the past few days.

"Sorry, he says," but his smirk tells me he isn't really "what are you doing? How's the planning going? Do you need me to do anything?" he asks.

I look over the various documents, lists, brochures I have scattered in front of me on my desk. When I suggested to Tyler that I'd probably need an office space, I was thinking the second spare bedroom. However, that day, Tyler went out and bought a second desk and put it in the room he was using as an office. So far, us sharing an office has worked out, but we'll see how we do when I start the classes I signed up for in a couple of weeks. I decided to just test the waters, so enrolled in a creative writing class and a drawing class to begin with.

"Actually, everything's pretty much planned at this point. Which is kind of ridiculous considering we just started planning a few days ago. Your mom doesn't mess around. We made a list of what had to be done, and she recruited volunteers from the pack and divided everything up and delegated it," I say.

"That's good as long as it's how you want it to be," he says.

"I kind of like the idea of having all the local influences being the inspiration," I say. A mating ceremony isn't something I ever thought about. I used to picture myself fighting dragons as a little girl, not planning out my mating ceremony. Tyler places his hand on the desk leaning over me, looking at what I'm working on.

"I'm just finishing up approving the playlist," I explain. Absentmindedly, he rubs his thumb up and down my arm, looking at the list over my shoulder.

"So, there's one detail that we haven't really discussed," Tyler says. I'd believe it, I'm kind of just winging it here.

"Oh yeah?" I ask.

"Yeah," he says, kissing my neck, "I want to talk about consummating our mating ceremony," he says seductively, whispering in my ear before gently biting it. The heat from his breath gives me goosebumps up and down my neck.

"What do you suggest?" I ask.

"How do you feel about me using alpha commands on you in the bedroom? I know the last time I used an alpha command on you, you were upset by it, but things have changed between us," he says.

TYLER

I still remember how mad she was when I unintentionally used an alpha command on her, but that was before I had gained her trust. That was before she even liked me.

"What did you have in mind?" she asks, turning her chair around to look at me. I place my hands on the arms of her chair, caging her in.

"Do you like the idea of surrendering completely to me? Being completely under my control, following my commands?" I ask. My intention was to arouse her, but I think my words are turning myself on even more.

"What would you make me do?" she asks, lust lacing her words. I lean over kissing her cheek.

"I guess you'll just have to wait and find out, won't you?" I ask. "That's if you agree," I add. This isn't something I'd push her to do if she wasn't completely on board, but by the look in her eyes, and the scent of her arousal heavy in the air, I think we're on the same page here.

"I trust you," she bites her lip, looking thoughtful, "can we have a safe word though?" she asks, looking up at me, with her dark blue eyes.

"Of course, I'd only want to do this if you were completely comfortable with it," I say, searching her face for any hesitation, not finding any.

"I trust you," she says, which is more than gratifying. I don't deserve Rain, but no way I'd ever give her up.

"What do you want your safe word to be?" I ask.

"Barnacle," she says, without hesitation.

"Barnacle? Really?" I ask.

"Yeah, why not? It's not something I'd ever say during sex," she says. Reasonable. Our conversation gets cut short by the doorbell ringing.

RAIN

"Are you expecting anyone?" I ask. Tyler turns toward the hallway, as though he could see through the walls and tell who was there.

"No, I'll go find out who it is," he says. I follow him downstairs. Tyler opens the door to find Heather standing on our front porch.

"Can we help you?" Tyler asks suspiciously. She sighs before talking.

"Yeah, I wanted to talk to you two," she says. Fidgeting under Tyler's glare.

"Then talk," he says.

"I just wanted to apologize, for everything, to both of you. The things I did were childish and at times borderline irrational," she says, looking contrite.

"Borderline?" Tyler says accusingly.

"Okay, the things I did were full blown irrational and I'm very sorry I did them. I know you only invited me to your mating ceremony because I'm part of the pack and you had to, but I did want to attend and I didn't want it to be awkward or have you feel like I was there trying to ruin your day, so I wanted to clear the air," she says.

"Rain, what are your thoughts?" Tyler asks.

"I forgive you, and am okay with you attending our mating ceremony," I say. She's always going to be part of the pack, and I don't want this animosity between us forever.

"Thank you. That means a lot to me," she says sincerely.

"Heather, I want to believe you and am willing to give you the benefit of the doubt, but absolutely know, if you pull any of your shit at our mating ceremony, you'll be banished from our pack permanently," Tyler says. "Do you understand?" he asks.

"Yes, I understand. Thank you, and sorry again," Heather says, before turning and leaving. Tyler turns to me after shutting the door.

"Are you okay with that?" he asks.

"Yeah, I'd rather bury the hatchet. She's not going anywhere and if she's going to be at events that we attend, I'd rather it not be awkward. I mean, I don't think we'll ever be friends, but I would settle for a neutral truce," I say.

"You're the most compassionate, amazing person I've ever met," Tyler says, holding the back of my neck, kissing me.

"I just hope, that wasn't the wrong decision though, I'll be beyond livid if she tries to pull something to ruin our day," Tyler says. I wrap my arms around his waist, laying my head on his chest.

"There's absolutely nothing she could do that I'd allow ruin our day," I say.

"Alright, but I'm serious, she's at her final warning. She pulls anything and I'll banish her," Tyler says.

"It'll be fine. Maybe I'll have your mom assign someone to watch over her though," I say smirking.

Chapter 51
BECCA

"This is it, this is the one," I clap my hands together, and let out a little squeal.

"Becca, you've said that about every dress I've tried on," Rain says, "but this time I think you might be right," Rain says, twirling in front of the three-fold mirror, standing on a small podium. She's mostly tried on shorter dresses, she seems to like fitted strapless gowns, that flare out into what looks like a long punk rock tutu. The one she currently has on is a soft violet, strapless, corset back with dark purple tulle that hits just at the knees. It fits her perfectly.

"I can't help it, they all look so good on you, you're going to be so beautiful," I say, trying to hold back tears.

"Thank you, Becca. Are you sure you don't want to try on some dresses too?" Rain asks. We already have my dress for her mating ceremony picked out, I'll be standing next to her the day of. My dress is dark blue, a simple but elegant strapless dress.

"I'm sure, can you believe we both are mated," I say, fixing the tulle so it lays perfectly.

"No, I really can't, I get so caught up in the day to day and then out of nowhere the thought that I'm a mated woman hits me like a bag of bricks," Rain says.

"You're happy though, right?" I've never seen her look so happy before, but I know Rain, and she's very stoic. She's so strong and never lets anything get to her. Growing up she was always the one to fearlessly stand up for me.

"I really am, how about you? You know my brothers will deal with Jordan if you want them to," Rain says, smiling. My father is a little more traditional and would never think of going against a fated mating. Rain's brothers, on the other hand, are not so opposed to using violence to send a message when they feel it's warranted.

"I know they would, but no, he's oddly charming in his own way," I say.

"He's different with you, you're good for him," Rain says. I hold up two different veils against the dress, to compare which one looks better.

"How are you doing your hair?" I ask.

"I'm thinking no veil, and for the color," she turns from the mirror to look at me, "birds of paradise," she shakes her hair out, turning it streaks of vibrant blue and deep orange, and a hint of green. It's perfect with the color of the dress. This time I can't hold back the tears and start bawling.

"You look so perfect," I say between sobs, and even Rain's eyes tear a little bit. I wrap my arms around Rain, being careful not to get my tears on her dress.

"What's going on?" Jordan practically shouts, barging into the dressing area, with Tanner and Mathis trying to hold him back.

"Jordan?" I exclaim.

"Why are you crying?" he asks, grabbing the sides of my face in his large hands, making me look up at him, while checking me over like he's looking for injuries.

"You look beautiful Rain," Mathis says, leaning down to kiss his sister on the cheek.

"Are you hurt?" Jordan asks looking confused, Tanner looks at him like he's an idiot.

"No, I'm just happy," I say.

"You're crying" Jordan looks lost in thought, "because you are happy?" he continues like he's trying to process the words still.

"Come on, Jordan, Rex isn't going to be able to hold Tyler back much longer, and I'm sure Rain doesn't want him seeing her yet," Mathis says.

"Why, he knows what she looks like?" Jordan asks confused, but still releases me, and lets Tanner pull him out of the dressing room.

TYLER

The only thing holding me back is the fact I don't want to upset Rain by seeing her in her dress, that and Rex physically holding me back. She was very resistant to the idea of us being here at the bridal shop at the same time, her main concern was me seeing her. I promised up and down that I would stay on the men's side, where we're all getting our tuxes.

I wasn't thrilled when I found out Jordan was coming, but I get it, he's Becca's mate now so he's going to be around, and if Rain can forgive Heather, then I can forgive Jordan. Really, he's not that bad when he isn't trying to steal my mate and he seems to genuinely adore Becca, which is good because if he hurt her, I'd have to hurt him. Although, I'd have to stand in line behind Rex, Mathis, and Tanner for that privilege. They all talk about Becca like a second little sister.

"She's fine," Jordan says returning to the dressing room.

"You didn't see Rain changing, did you?" I don't know what made me ask.

"I don't think so, I was only focused on Becca," Jordan says.

"Rain was completely dressed and looked amazing, so you better pull out all the stops," Mathis says.

"No matter what I do, she's still going to look like she's out of my league," I admit. This was our final fitting, we all came in and got measured a couple of days ago, picked a color, and a few days later, here we all are in our perfect fitting suits. It's humbling how everyone came together to make our mating ceremony happen so quickly, which is good because our mating ceremony is days away.

"Everything looks good, lets wrap this up so we can get out of here," I say.

Chapter 52
MATHIS

It's so surreal that my baby sister is having her mating ceremony today. She'll always be a little kid in my mind, albeit a strong, determined, brave and stubborn little kid, a kid, nonetheless. A small part of me just wants to grab her, throw her over my shoulder and run. Lock her away in our attic and never face the fact that she's growing up.

The only thing stopping me is the fact that I don't hate Tyler, and I do believe he'll do everything in his power to take care of and protect my little sister. He wasn't even that mad at mine and Tanner's involvement of what resulted in Jordan kidnapping Rain. Granted, we didn't actually expect for him to kidnap her and then challenge Tyler to forum. Tyler definitely proved himself and gained our respect though.

Looking over at Tyler, there isn't even a hint of doubt, in fact I haven't ever seen him this relaxed and happy. Tyler, Tanner, Rex, Jordan, Max and a couple other guys that are friends with Tyler are all sitting around the lounge in the back of the hall where council meetings are held. We're all dressed in our suits, and honestly, we dress up pretty nicely. Tanner busted out the whiskey as soon as we all got here, and we've all had a few. Shifters and chimeras metabolize alcohol likes it's water though, so none of us are anything more than a little buzzed.

There seems to be some tension between Jordan and Max. Max keeps eyeing Jordan suspiciously like he's trying to put together a puzzle. It's not unusual for pureblooded shifters to feel uneasy around chimeras though, and Jordan is particularly menacing.

"You guys ready?" my dad asks, coming in the lounge. Him and Tyler's dad had got ready with us, but then went out to the hall to greet people as they arrived. He walks over to the open whiskey bottle and takes a generous swig.

"How you holding up?" I ask, patting my dad on his broad shoulders.

"I can't believe my baby is old enough to be mated," he says, the expression on his face reflects my own feelings, a mixture of sadness and pride. Next, he approaches Tyler.

"Tyler, welcome to the family son, don't make me have to hurt you," he says.

"Understood," Tyler says. We've all threatened him quite a bit today, I think he gets the message.

RAIN

This morning has been a flutter of activity and chaos. I feel like a ship at the center of a storm and am glad I have the support I need to make this day perfect. Now that hair and makeup are complete and we're all dressed, it feels like we have a minute to breathe. Becca, my mom and Tyler's mom all got ready in the lounge on the opposite side of the council hall from where Tyler and the guys are getting ready. My brothers and father periodically checked in with us throughout the morning. Making sure I didn't have any last second doubts, even though we're already mated, and this ceremony is mostly a formality.

I could hear the beginning of commotion as guest arrived out in the hall, telling us it was almost go time. The moms went out to help greet people, leaving just me and Becca in our dressing room. My dad is going to come get me when it's time to walk down the aisle.

"Rain, are you ready?" my dad says coming into the dressing room. I look over at him and he looks like he's about to cry, which is something I've never seen before.

"Yeah, dad I'm ready," I say. Trying to keep my emotions in check, I don't want to ruin the hours of makeup I just sat through. My dad pulls me into his arms, kissing my forehead like he used to do when I was a little kid.

"You look beautiful," he says, his voice laced with emotion.

"Thank you," I say.

"Are you sure you want to do this?" he asks, which makes me laugh. Each one of my brothers has already asked.

"Yes, I'm sure, Tyler's my future and I couldn't change that even if I wanted to," I say. He nods in agreement.

"He's okay," he says, smirking. He would never think anybody was good enough for me. Becca walks out before me. I wait with my dad until it's my turn, grasping his arm for support. The hall is packed. It's overwhelming how many people showed up, but the moment I enter the room, my eyes find Tyler and the expression on his face is pure happiness. I focus only on him and block out everyone else. At the end of the aisle, my dad gives me a quick kiss, then puts my hands in Tyler's then goes to sit with my mother.

Tyler's dad stands in front of us at the podium, Becca on one side, my brothers and Tyler's friends on the other. As pack alpha, Tyler's dad is performing our ceremony.

"Thank you all for attending the mating ceremony between Rain and Tyler. Mating ceremonies are fundamental to the stability of our pack, but today's ceremony is even more meaningful to me on a personal level. I'm so happy to see my son find his mate, someone to cherish, love and support. The legend says fated mates are destined to be the perfect complement, two halves of a whole, ying to a yang, balance and harmony. Time and time again, this has been proven without a shadow of a doubt. Destiny brought you two together. Destiny made you the perfect companions. Destiny gave you the qualities you'll need in each other," he says before turning to Tyler.

"Tyler, do you take Rain as your mate? To love and protect for the rest of your life?"

"I do," Tyler says. He then turns to me.

"Rain, do you take Tyler as your mate? To love and support for the rest of your life?"

"I do," I say without hesitation or reservation.

"Please, everyone give your congratulations to the future alpha and luna of our pack, you may kiss your bride," he says.

Tyler's mouth descends on mine before his dad has even finished his sentence. We are met with a chorus of whoops and cheers throughout the crowd.

"We did it," I say elated when we break away from the kiss.

"We'll be doing it the second I get you alone," Tyler whispers in my ear, with a seductive smirk.

Chapter 53
JORDAN

The mating ceremony was always an abstract concept, nothing more than a means to an end for me, but now that I'm experiencing one and it's real, it stirs emotions I didn't know I had. Looking up at Rain and Tyler, I imagine Becca and I taking their place. Although Becca looks beautiful today, it's hard not to imagine what she would look like in a mating ceremony gown of her own, walking down the aisle towards me, taking my hand, devoting herself to me.

The oversized hall is divided up into an area where the ceremony occurred, and an area with tables and an open dance floor where dinner will be served, and the celebration will take place. I didn't expect to enjoy myself tonight and was only here because it was important to Becca to be here for Rain. I was especially upset when I found out Max was going to be here.

I used compulsion on him, which he shouldn't be able to fight. Compulsion is strong, even stronger than an alpha command. Where an alpha command feels like pressure to do something, compulsion causes immediate compliance without thought. Someone can fight an alpha command, especially if they're strong willed. It might be uncomfortable for them, and the pressure will feel like it's increasing, but they have a chance to fight it. Compulsion, they act first and question why they acted second.

When the ceremony was over, Becca slipped her tiny hand inside of mine as we found our seats next to the head table. It's strange considering I'd have literally killed Tyler not long ago, now I'm sitting here celebrating his mating. I realize now how shortsighted I was at the time. I'm thankful I didn't succeed in mating Rain. It would've been an even more complicated situation if I hadn't met Becca until after I mated Rain. The mating bond is powerful, but it can only overcome so much. I don't dwell on the thought of having two mates at the same time.

"You looked beautiful up there, I can't wait until it's our mating ceremony though," I say, bending down kissing her cheek. I catch Max staring daggers my way. I might need to reinforce his compulsion. He shouldn't remember who I am, and his wolf should recognize me as a threat on a subconscious level and want to avoid me.

"Thank you, you look pretty good yourself," she says smiling up at me. At least Max isn't sitting with us. We're at a table with Rain's brothers and parents. I wonder if they're tasked with keeping me in line. I'd never cause any problems here, but I can see how they'd think that I would. I'm not offended by them taking precautions to make sure their ceremony is perfect.

"Can we dance?" Becca asks excitedly, practically bouncing in her seat.

"I don't think I know how to dance," I say. In fact, I know I can't dance. The pout on Becca's face would be upsetting if it wasn't so cute. I run my thumb over her lip. That rewards me a smile.

"I'll dance with you Becca," Tanner offers.

"Yeah, me too," Rex adds.

"Same," Mathis says, looking off in the distance like he's preoccupied. I know they don't mean any harm, but the idea of any of them touching Becca pisses me off, I don't stop the possessive growl I make at the thought. To which, all three start to laugh. Becca giggles at the interaction.

"Back off and don't touch what's mine," I warn.

"Excuse me," Becca says, placing her tiny hands on her hips. I bet if she was standing, she'd be stomping her little foot.

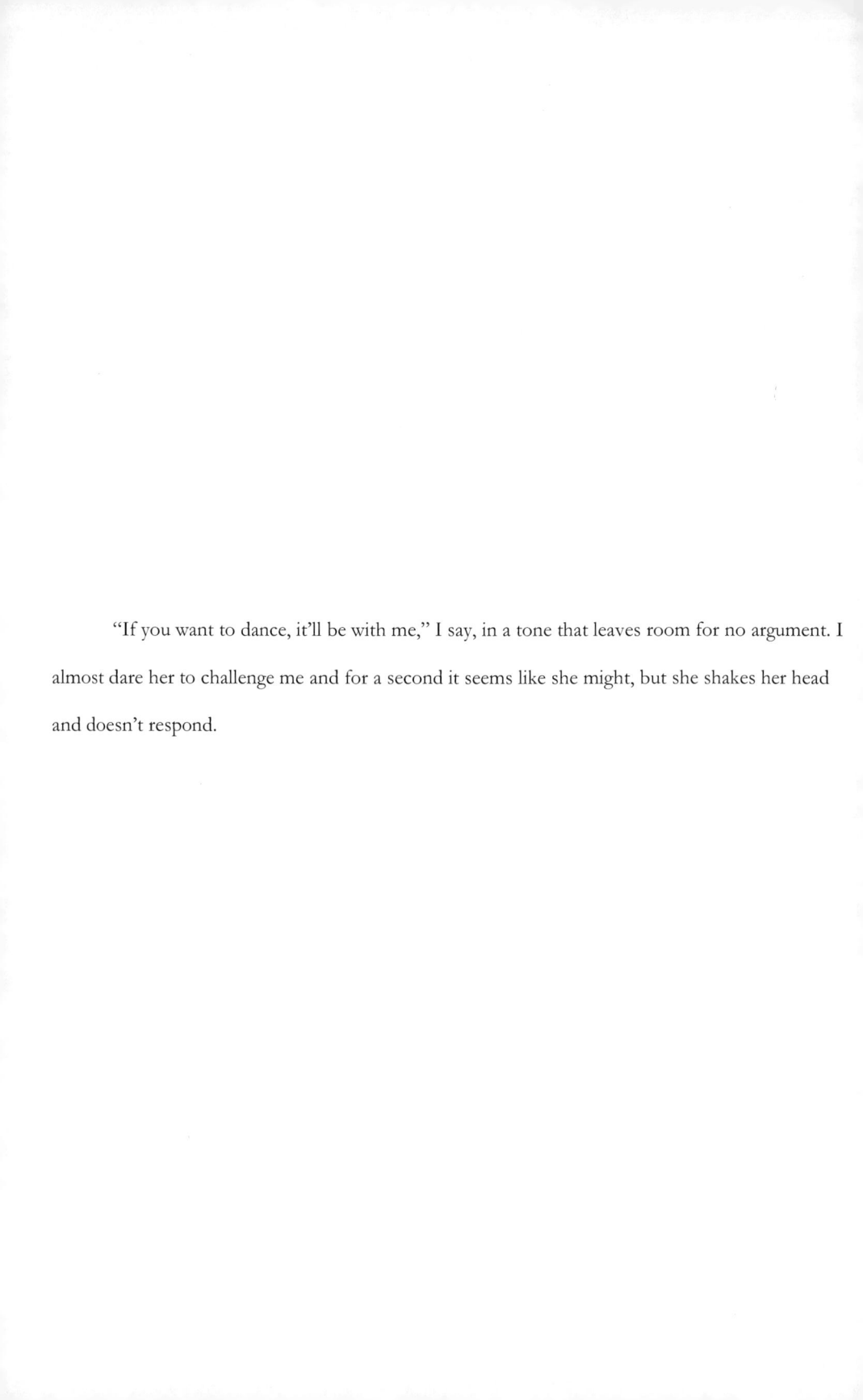

"If you want to dance, it'll be with me," I say, in a tone that leaves room for no argument. I almost dare her to challenge me and for a second it seems like she might, but she shakes her head and doesn't respond.

Chapter 54
BECCA

I've grown up around enough chimera males, including the three sitting at this table, to know when to pick my battles. Although Tanner, Rex and Mathis see me as a little sister, and dancing with any one of them would be like dancing with a brother, Jordan's not going to accept that. I know they're just trying to get him going too. It's in a chimera male's nature to challenge each other like that, even when they don't really mean it.

"It's okay Jordan, I can lead," I say, smirking, when all the guys at the table fail to hold back their laughter. It's hard to not cower under Jordan's intense glare, but I know this man will never let any real harm come to me, especially at his own hands. Jordan slowly leans down, quickly kissing my neck before whispering in my ear.

"I can see you need a reminder of who's in charge here, Pet" he says, in his deep voice that seems to make my core vibrate.

"Yes, Sir," I whisper back. He pulls back, looking at me with surprise, before a predatory smile creeps across his face. I'm not sure I can handle what I just potentially started, but I can't quite stop myself. We haven't taken our relationship to the next step yet, and I know Jordan wants to, but he's been respectful not to pressure me. Maybe even a little too respectful. Although, when Jordan, does finally let go of his self-control, I might regret pushing him. Only one way to find out though.

Dinner is a buffet, and after there are speeches and toasts from various members of the pack. The crowd gets louder as the night goes on and more drinks are poured. The entire dinner, Jordan has been drawing light circles on the back of my neck. Such an innocent act has me practically panting, and he absolutely knows what he's doing. True to his word, Jordan dances with me, well attempts to dance, he mostly just holds my waist as he sways back and forth. Which I guess counts.

Maybe I should see if he'll take lessons before our own mating ceremony. I wonder where ours will even be. Jordan isn't a member of the pack, so it won't be here. That thought's kind of sobering. I guess our mating ceremony will be a smaller affair, which I don't hate the idea of. I never really imagined what mine would be like, even recently I pushed it to the back of my mind to focus on Rain, but after tonight there won't be an excuse to delay it any longer.

I guess we could have our mating ceremony in Imperia, everyone I would invite could make it there. That is, everyone but Max, and I don't think Jordan would let him anyways. It's sad thinking about losing him as a friend. I know he was pushing for us to be more and was taking our relationship more serious than I was, but he was still someone I enjoyed hanging out with. I'm not even sure he remembers that we were friend with Jordan's compulsion. It hasn't escaped my notice that he's been eyeing us all night. Rain was always going to be my best friend, but Max was different, being friends with him was a much-needed confidence boost, the first time I experienced being part of the in crowd.

"What's the matter, Little One, you look sad," Jordan says.

"Oh nothing," I say.

"You wouldn't be lying, would you?" he asks, with a warning in his voice, narrowing his eyes.

"Just trying to figure out the logistics of our mating ceremony," I say.

"Oh, don't worry about that, my mother has been planning it since I was a kid," Jordan says.

"Okay," I say, smiling at the thought.

Chapter 55
MATHIS

All night my skin has felt tight and prickly like there are ants crawling all over it. What I originally brushed off as simply being unsettled by having to face the indisputable proof that my baby sister is growing up, has magnified as the night progresses. Deep down I know I'm happy for her, so I don't understand all the turmoil. I'm practically buzzing with anxious energy and I'm not sure why.

Sitting at the table by myself, I watch as my brothers clumsily hit on women from our pack. Normally I'd be right there with them, even right now, there are several pretty women giving me sly looks and seductive smiles. Shifter males avoid us, because they can sense the threat we pose to them. They can tell we are a more dangerous predator. Shifter females, however, recognize us on a subconscious level as the fiercest possible mates. The most capable of protecting them and they instinctually want to seek out the most worthy mate.

My body forces me to stand before my brain processes what I'm doing, something's pulling me, physically pulling me, to the back of the hall. Finally, it all makes sense. Sitting at a table all by herself, is the image of perfection, an athletic woman with light brown hair and deep brown eyes. She's sitting with her toned arms crossed in front of her chest. Even sitting down, I can tell she's tall for a woman shifter. She's toned, but thin, maybe a cheerleader, or something similar?

"Can I help you?" she asks me with an edge to her voice. I always thought my mate would be meek and submissive, but I can now finally see the merits of a feisty brat that I get to punish.

"What's your name?" I ask.

"Why do you want to know?" she asks, eyeing me suspiciously.

"You're at my sister's mating ceremony, I just want to know who you are," I say. With that some of her ice melts a little.

"Look, I was invited and I'm not here to cause any problems," she says, putting her hands up in surrender. Okay, now I'm interested. More interested.

"Just answer my question, and tell me who you are," I say.

"Heather," she says. *Fuck*.

HEATHER

"So, you're the Heather who has bullied my baby sister for all these years?" he asks, looking disappointed.

I thought this might be a mistake coming here tonight, but I so desperately don't want to be the person I've watched myself become over the past few years. I nod, not meeting the menacing stranger's eyes. I've seen one of Rain's brothers before, maybe at a pack event, but the younger one, not the one currently standing in front of me, practically seething.

There's an apology on the tip of my tongue, but I stop myself. I didn't do anything to this man, and he isn't going to make me feel more guilty than I already am. That guilt belongs to Rain and Tyler, not him. I don't owe him anything.

"That's not really any of your business," I say, holding my chin high.

"Yeah?" he laughs, like this is some kind of joke to him.

"I'm not apologizing to you. I'm not here to start drama, so if that's what you want, I welcome you to walk away from me," I say, turning my chair so I'm no longer staring at this menacing, albeit gorgeous man. He just stands there staring at me in silence before he lets out a deep chuckle.

"I look forward to fixing that little attitude problem you have," he says, narrowing his eyes at me.

"Excuse me?" I say, outraged by his audacity, and even more upset that this random stranger was able to so quickly rile me up.

"You heard me," he says.

"I really don't think I did, either that or you're delusional," I say, we stare at each other in intense silence. Rain comes up from behind me, startling me as she approaches.

RAIN

I'm not sure what I just interrupted here, but I can hardly breathe there's so much tension in the air. I didn't really want to interact with Heather, but Tyler and I were about to leave, and I wanted to say bye to my brothers and family.

"Rain, you looked absolutely gorgeous today, congratulations," Heather says with a level of sincerity that I'm not used to from her.

"Thank you, and thank you for coming Heather," I say, she gives me a shy smile, before I turn to Mathis, looking like a statue he's so tense.

"Mathis," I say, but he doesn't take his eyes off Heather. Shit, I've seen that look before, but I'm not going to unpack that right now. I don't want any drama spoiling my perfect day.

"Mathis," I say again, this time I approach him, putting my hand on his shoulder, finally getting his attention.

"Tyler and I are leaving, I wanted to say goodnight, and thank you," he leans down so I can give him a kiss on his cheek.

"Of course, I love you Rain," he says, "tell Tyler to keep his hands off you," he says.

"It's a little too late for that," I say, turning and leaving. I already said goodnight to Becca, who is slow dancing with Jordan. The party is still very much alive and will most likely keep going until late into the night. I find Tyler at the entrance with a lost looking Max. I didn't really have the option to not invite Max, since he's Tyler's friend. I tried to come up with a solution to minimize how awkward it would be for Becca to see him here, but she brushed off the concern and told me not to worry. She didn't think it would be a problem.

Tyler opens his arms to me when he sees me, and I walk into his embrace.

"You ready to go home?" he asks with a seductive grin. I fake yawn.

"Oh yeah, I'm so exhausted, I'm ready for some sleep," I tease. Tyler's answering growl makes me laugh harder.

"Don't worry, I'll take you right to bed then," he says, before scooping me up in his arms, bridal style, which seems appropriate, carrying me out to our car.

Chapter 56
JORDAN

My mate looks exhausted. I really wasn't looking forward to tonight, but honestly, it's been a revelation. The crowd has thinned a little, but the party is still very much alive.

"Are you ready to go back home, Pet?" I ask. Becca looks up at me giving me a sleepy smile.

"Just one more dance," she says, and I know it'll be a battle to ever deny her anything she wants.

"Okay," I say, holding her chin as I lean down to kiss her.

"Who the fuck are you?" A disgruntled Max approaches us, encroaching in our space.

"Max?" Becca squeals surprised, but he ignores her.

"I'm Jordan, how do you not know that. I've practically spent most of the day with you," I say. "Calm down," I say with compulsion.

"Stop it," he screams, everyone around us looks over. He grabs his head like his brain is exploding.

"You're not right, there's something very wrong about you. I can't sense your wolf, you're messing with my mind," he rages like a lunatic, I look around at the crowd forming around us.

"Max, maybe you should lay off the booze," I say.

"Max, calm down," Becca says.

"Becca, you're okay with whatever he is?" Max says, grabbing her wrist, and I see red, I charge him, picking him up and throwing him across the hall, with a surge of energy. The music cuts off, and we have the entire hall's attention now. It's too many people to use compulsion on at once.

"Becca, time to go," I say, hoisting her over my shoulder, making a quick dash to the exit, as soon as we're in private, I teleport us back home.

MATHIS

The crowd goes from completely silent, to hushed whispers. It's hard to tell how much of that people actually saw. It happened quickly, but there was an obvious burst of energy that came directly from Jordan. Max looks disoriented, but otherwise fine, when I approach him. I see my dad, Tanner and Rex, fanning out through the crowd. They'll get a handle on what was seen and what needs to be contained.

All of us have experience in this type of situation. People want a reasonable explanation, most of the time they come up with their own excuses for anything abnormal they've seen, even if it means suppressing what they actually know.

"You okay? That Jordan is a strong dude," I say.

"There's something wrong with him," he says.

"Yeah, he's always been kind of a jerk, you want me to get you another drink?" I ask, motioning to the bartender to bring another round.

"It's more than that, there's something different about him," Max says.

"No Max. Jordan's just a very strong guy and you touched his mate. You know how territorial shifters are, especially when they have a mate that they haven't claimed yet. That's all that happened. But don't feel bad, not many people could have taken him on," I say.

"Maybe," he says, the bartender drops off our rounds, and I hand him a glass of amber liquid that he quickly drinks. I hand him mine which he also accepts. The music starts again, and people start dancing again. I notice my brothers encouraging people to drink too.

Seems like the situation is contained. I look around to try and find Heather, but she's nowhere to be found. Luckily, I put a tether on her before she left. I close my eyes to follow it to her and see she's at home. That's a shame I didn't get to talk to her more. All in good time though. At least Rain and Tyler left before the incident between Jordan and Max, I would've hated for that to ruin their night. Speaking of which, I can't imagine Rain being thrilled with Heather being my mate. It's okay, I have every intention of keeping her in line.

Chapter 57
TYLER

"Welcome home, Luna Rain Grant," I say, carrying Rain over the threshold of our house bridal style. I look down at her and she has her face all scrunched up.

"Nope, I don't like that," she says.

"Too late for takebacks," I tease, carrying her up the stairs and into our bedroom.

"I've been waiting all night to unwrap this colorful present," I say, gently placing her feet on the ground turning her around so I can unlace her corset. She looks absolutely stunning, and so quintessentially Rain that I can't help but smile, but I want her naked. I lightly graze the back of my hand over the soft skin of her shoulder, before helping her step out of her dress. She's wearing no bra, and white crotchless lace panties.

"God, if I knew this was what was hiding under this dress," I say cupping her mound," I don't think I would've made it through the ceremony".

I start at her shoulder, and trace my fingertips down to her wrist, gently cupping both of them before lifting them up into the air above her head, crossing them at the wrist.

"Keep them here," I say with an alpha command.

"Yes, Tyler," Rain says with a smirk.

"You can call me Sir," I suggest.

"You have to earn that title," she says. I love her fire.

"I'll see what I can do," I tease, leaning her against the bed post, then dropping to my knees in front of her so I'm at eye level with her glistening, plump lips.

"I like these," I say, sliding a finger in the side of the of panties. They are practically just straps with a tiny bit of lace "I might insist you always wear them".

"I don't know, they're sexy, but the entire night I went from feeling exposed when they were in place, to incredibly turned on when the strap would accidentally move between my lips," she say. Turning me on even more with that visual.

She gasps as I pull both the edges of her panties in between her lips, rubbing them against her clit. "Like this?" I ask.

"Yes," she nods with both her hands up in the air.

"I don't have a problem with that" I say.

RAIN

I'm forgetting why I had a problem with it too. The panties definitely made me feel sexy, especially only wearing a dress on top of them.

"Look at me," Tyler says, and I instantly comply, even without him using an alpha command. He pulls the drenched lace from my pussy lips and replaces it with his warm mouth. I wish I could run my fingers through his hair, but it's painful when I try to move them, it feels like pressure in my brain when I try to go against an alpha command.

I whimper in disappointment when Tyler takes his mouth off me. He's still fully dressed in his black pants and dress shirt.

"Pinch your nipples," he says with an alpha command. I grab my nipples between my thumb and my fingers, pulling on them, enough to get them hard but not enough to hurt.

"Harder," he says, hooking my right leg over his shoulder, before returning his mouth to my center. His dress shirt feels rough against the soft skin of my thigh. I would lose my balance if he wasn't tightly gripping my hips, keeping me in place. I pinch my own nipples until I whimper out in pain. I grind my hips into Tyler's face, looking for more friction and pressure. He pulls away again, to give another alpha command "stop moving your hips," he says sternly.

The look on his face is evil, but I'm into his games. He digs his fingers into the flesh of my butt and returns to devouring me. This time, he doesn't stop until my body seizes in orgasm. I'm still pinching my nipples, riding out my orgasm. He stills, giving me a chance to recover.

"You can drop your hands," he says with another alpha command, I sigh in relief, letting go of my punished, swollen nipples. He stands, and takes one red peak into his mouth, suckling gently, easing the pain on one then the other.

"Get on the bed, on all fours with your ass up in the air and your face in the mattress," he says with another alpha command. At this point, I don't need them to immediately comply. I hear him undressing behind me, I still have the crotchless panties on, not that they cover much. I feel his weight behind me, and he runs the head of his penis through my slippery folds, covering himself with my arousal. The tissue is still sensitive from my recent orgasm, but I'm already panting for more. He rubs the tip past my entry a few times, teasing me, making me needy.

"Please Tyler," I plead, desperate for him to impale me.

"No, you have to earn my dick," he says, throwing my words back at me and I know exactly what he wants to hear.

"Please, Sir, I need your cock inside me," I say, I can practically feel him smile behind me. Without any more hesitation, he slams into me, we both groan out together. This position is a different sensation, hits different spots inside of me. Feels deeper. He braces his weight on one of his forearms, and I get a perfect view of him flexing his arm in front of my face. I feel his other arm snake in front of me, pulling the straps on my panties back between my lips, rubbing against my clit, giving me the extra friction I needed. His thrusts are the perfect rhythm to send me over the edge. He's so in tune with my body and knows exactly what it needs.

"Be my Good Girl and milk my cock for me, I want to feel you spasm around me," he growls. His dirty words push me over the top, and I grip down on his girth, setting off his own orgasm. In perfect synch. We ride out our pleasure together. Even our breathing is in synch with each other. I feel him softening before pulling out.

"Relax," he says, before retrieving a warm washcloth from the bathroom. He pulls down my drenched panties and throws them in the hamper, before reverently cleaning me up with the washcloth. After, we get into bed together and he pulls me to his side.

"Goodnight, Luna Grant," he says kissing my forehead.

"I at least want to hyphenate," I say. I feel his deep chuckle vibrate against me.

"I'll think about it," he says.

Chapter 58
HEATHER

"Where the fuck were you last night?" my dad asks, already slurring his words from his morning whiskey, even though it isn't even past noon yet.

"At a pack event," I say, trying to keep my tone neutral.

"Sure, you were you little slut, why do you reek of alcohol then?" my dad asks with unfocused eyes. Alcohol usually doesn't impact shifters much, but decades of alcohol abuse has taken its toll on my father. I'm not even sure he can still shift to be honest.

"So, why is it?" he prompts.

"Why is what?" I ask, I can't tell if I'm not paying attention or if he isn't making sense, probably both.

"Why do you smell like liquor?" he arches a brow, almost stumbling over his own feet even when standing still. I want to scream you're smelling yourself you idiot, but I know better.

"Dad, I have to go to work," I say, not waiting for him to respond before heading out the front door. I miss being in school. It was easier to ignore my shitty life when I was away from home eight hours a day. Now all I have is a minimum wage part time job at a coffee shop to get me out of the house. It's part of the reason I wanted to make amends with Tyler and Rain. I want to be able to attend pack events and I can't do that if he banishes me from them. Also, every day I see a little bit more of my dad's cruel personality when I look at myself in the mirror, and I just couldn't live with myself if I turned out like him.

Pack life has always been survival of the fittest, so conveniently enough, things like alcohol abuse and being an unstable parent get swept under the rug and ignored. Our community is tightknit, but it's just not built to support social issues like that.

The coffee shop is a five-minute walk from my house, which is great because we don't have a working car. We have a car, it's just so old that it's impossible to keep running, and the few times we're able to start it, my dad has already blown all the gas money on booze. I also have an old bike I sometimes ride instead, but I almost always want to walk. Anything to keep me out of the house as much as possible.

The smell of freshly ground coffee hits me when I open the front door to the little coffee shop. I love that smell. It's one of my few comforts. I grab my apron from behind the counter, and quickly fasten it around my waist.

"Good morning, Sue," I greet the owner.

"Good morning, Heather," she greets warmly. I've worked with Sue for a few months now and she treats me like I'm her own daughter. Being around her really highlighted how much I craved that type of parental affection. I get lost in my workday, taking orders, making coffee, and cleaning with any downtime I get. There aren't that many places in Praxley, so the coffee shop stays pretty busy.

"How did you like the mating ceremony last night? Wasn't it just perfect? Rain is such a lovely girl," Sue gushes after the midday rush is over, and the coffee shop has settled down a bit.

"I'll be honest, she's better than we deserve," I say, remembering all the times Rain has given people the benefit of the doubt and has shown forgiveness. I look over at Sue conspiratorially "I think she might even be out of Tyler's league," I say, Sue treats me to fer full-bodied laugh in response.

"Did you see the fight? I had already left, but I heard Max got into a fight with one of the out of towners," she says.

"I snuck out just as it started, I didn't really see much. Were they both okay?" I ask. I don't mention the intense stranger I met. Mathis, that's what Rain called him anyways, he never actually gave me his name. It was a cowardly move to duck out when all the commotion started. I don't know why I did it, he was just so overwhelming. It's a shame. He was incredibly attractive, but I could tell from a mile away he was trouble that I absolutely do not need.

"Of course, they were both fine," Sue says, waving her hands dismissively, "you know how it is with shifter males, especially after they've had a few drinks, it turns into a pissing contest," Sue says, making me laugh.

Chapter 59
JORDAN

"Why are you still so worried?" I ask, running a thumb across the worry lines in her forehead, trying to ease her tension. An unpalatable thought crosses my mind.

"You're not worried about that shifter boy, are you?" I ask. She's been in a closed off mood ever since last night. She even tossed and turned in her sleep, and she's usually out like the dead.

"No, I know he didn't get hurt. I just feel guilty, I knew there was a risk spending too much time with him, but I just liked having friends," she says.

"You didn't do anything wrong," I say.

"Should I be worried about what will happen to you?" she asks. My Becca, always so worried about everybody but herself.

"For throwing energy in front of shifters? I'm not sure. Thankfully, Mathis and Tanner were there and would know how to deal with the situation," I say. I probably should've stayed and helped sort out the mess Max created for me, but my only concern was getting Becca away from the situation. I know I'll eventually have to answer for my actions, but I don't want Becca to worry more than she already is.

"Can you get in trouble for that? Isn't your entire division devoted to keeping things like that from happening?" she asks.

"Yes, it is, and I'll probably have to face a summons but there's a big difference in using energy to defend your mate once and blatantly flaunting it around," I explain.

"Okay," she says, but she still looks worried.

"I want to show you something," I say reaching out for her hand. I assist her off the couch when she places her delicate hands in mine.

"What?" she asks.

"You'll see," I say. I guide her outside, to the wooded area behind my house. It's similar to the house I grew up in, which was the main reason I chose to live in this particular neighborhood. I love feeling secluded, surrounded by nature.

BECCA

Jordan leads me through a mostly overgrown path. A path so narrow he has to walk in front of me since there isn't room to walk side by side. It's kind of comical that he doesn't even duck or anything, to try and avoid the underbrush and branches sticking out, he just plows right through them, so I have a clear path in his wake.

It's moments like this that make me realize how much of a stranger Jordan is. I mean, I wouldn't follow any other man into the forest like this, especially one I just met. I almost run into Jordan's back when he quickly stops in front of me.

"You okay?' Jordan asks, turning around to look back at me.

"Yeah, fine," I say.

"I felt your fear, you were afraid of something," he says.

"It's nothing, I was just thinking about the fact I'm walking through the forest with a man I barely know," I say. He steps closer towering over me.

"You're right to be concerned, remember I bite," he says, leaning down to nip at my neck playfully. I swat him away.

"You're so cheesy," I say. He turns to continue walking, and I dutifully follow behind him. After about ten minutes of walking, I start to sense where he's taking me. My suspicions are confirmed when the trail opens up to a clearing, with a crystal-clear lake with a small waterfall.

"What do you think Jordan asks?" looking at me hopefully.

"It's beautiful," I say.

"It certainly is," Jordan says, not taking his eyes off of me. "So, do you want to go swimming?" he asks.

"I don't have a swimsuit," I say.

"I won't tell," he smirks.

"You just want to get me naked," I say laughing.

"Did it work?" Jordan asks, arching a brow. I rip off my shirt in response, throwing it at him before turning towards the water. I quickly pull off my pants and run into the cool water in my bra and underwear. It's so clear I can see the bottom. It's just deep enough that my feet barely touch the ground. Water has always been restorative for me, and I welcome it thoroughly.

Jordan gets completely naked before coming into the water. He's so much taller than me that it barely comes up to his waist. He dives under the water, swimming around me, reemerging behind me, pulling me into his muscular chest.

"Do you really need this bra on?" he asks, dragging his finger under the strap on my right arm, gently kissing my shoulder before pulling it down. Next, he pulls down the left bra strap too, before unhooking it in the back and pulling it off completely and throwing it on top of our other clothes, scattered on the ground.

My nipples are already hard from a combination of the comfortably cool water and my arousal. Jordan spreads his large hand out on my belly, his other hands grabs an exposed breast, kneading it. His hand on my belly creeps down to the top of my underwear, clinging to my body now that they're wet.

"It's cute that you thought these would actually protect you from me," he says, I feel his deep chuckle behind me.

"Maybe I didn't want to be protected from you," I say.

"What was it that you called me yesterday, you know that I liked so much?" he asks. I kind of love playful Jordan.

"I think it was Sir," I say.

"Yeah, that was it," he says, and I can feel his smile. I'm disappointed when he suddenly pulls away from me.

"Come on, I want to show you something," he says, and I follow him with more trust this time. He pulls me over to the small waterfall. It's really just a stream flowing down a high rock. The water gets shallow again the closer we get.

"What did you want to show me?" I ask, stepping out of the water, onto a bed of rocks.

"Nothing, I just wanted to fuck you against, that wall of rocks," he says before capturing my mouth with his own. I hear the tear of fabric before I register him shredding my underwear with his hands. I grab his shoulders, tracing my nails over his skin. Just when I start panting, he pulls back again.

"Shit," he mumbles.

"What?" I asked worried. He runs his hands through his long wet blond hair.

"I really wasn't planning on this, I didn't bring a condom," he says, looking at me with regret. "I mean, I would love to pump you full with my children, but I have a feeling you are not ready for that yet," he says.

"I'm on birth control," I say.

"I've never seen you take birth control," he says. I hold up my arm and point to where I have my implant.

"I have a birth control implant in my arm," I say. As soon as the words are out of my mouth, he's passionately kissing me again. He grabs both my legs, under my thighs and lifts me up in the air, my back against the stone wall. He rubs his penis back and forth over my clit until I'm wet enough for him to slide right in. He takes me excruciatingly slow. I feel every inch of him stretching me. Claiming me. He leans his forehead on mine when he's fully seated, and we both just enjoy the connection. I try to grind against him, but he holds me still.

"Please," I say, needing him to move. He doesn't make me wait long, he pulls back and slams back into me. I let out a loud groan. He's the perfect fit, hitting all the places I need him to. He rubs against my clit with his pubic bone and it's all the friction I need.

"Do not come yet," he says.

"I can't stop it," I say, out of breath. I've never been able to control my orgasms and now is no exception. I clamp down on his length and call out my release.

JORDAN

Such a naughty little Pet. I wish I could pretend to be mad, but watching her orgasm is the most erotic thing I've ever witnessed. The scenic background just adds to her already ethereal beauty.

"I said not to come," I say, accenting each word with a thrust.

"I'm not sorry, not even a little bit," she says. Her honesty makes me laugh. Or it would if I wasn't consumed with lust. I feel the familiar sensation of my impending orgasm. A few more powerful thrusts and I growl out my release. In the back of my mind, I know I'm gripping her thighs too tightly and they'll probably bruise, but I can't bring myself to care.

I lower my head to Becca's slim neck that she's offered to me, and I take my claiming bite. It's like the bond that was already forming solidified in place completely. It's like the moment I claimed her, her peace flowed through me freely. I realize now I was only feeling a small fraction of her calming powers, but now that we are connected, I feel it at full force. It almost knocks me on my ass. It's humbling. This tiny slip of a woman holds so much power in that little body of hers.

Once we both recover, I pull out and we swim back to the other side of the lake, to find our clothes. The thought of her putting on pants with no underwear has me semi hard again. Her coy smile tells me she knows what I was thinking.

"Now remind me Becca, did I give you permission to come?" I ask. She groans in answer.

"Jordan, I have no control over my orgasm. Even if I did, I'm not sure I'd be willing to stop it," she says, putting back on her shirt, leaving off her wet bra.

"Okay, you are going to face punishment for disobeying then," I say, sliding on my pants.

"Can't you just give me permission now to orgasm whenever I need?" she asks.

"No," I say.

"Do you have to ask for permission to orgasm?" she asks.

"No," I say.

"Why not?" she asks, as we retrace the trail we took.

"You know why, in this relationship I'm the leader. I'm the one in control and I get to decide the rules, and your pleasure and your discipline both belong to me," I say.

Chapter 60
MATHIS

She's so painfully beautiful even in her ugly apron and with her hair in a messy bun at the top of her head. It's hard to reconcile the woman standing in front of me, well standing inside the coffee shop in front of me while I watch her from my car, with the woman that Rain has told me about.

I haven't figured out the best plan of approach yet. I have to tell Rain. I don't want her to find out through someone else. I took off the next two weeks from work, so at least I have some time to make and execute a plan. I feel bad dropping this on Rain, since her mating ceremony was just yesterday, but I have to let her know before I approach Heather. Rain is one of the most forgiving people I know, but if she found out I was mated to one of her former bullies from anyone other than me, I wouldn't even try asking for forgiveness, because I don't think I would deserve it.

It's hard to leave Heather, but I need to talk to Rain before I take this any further and that conversation should happen face to face. I'm not going to come over unannounced the day after her mating ceremony though, so decided to call first. I take it as a good sign when Rain picks up the phone after the first ring. It's middle of the day, she should be up by now, even if she had a long night. I try not to think of those implications.

"Hey," she answers.

"Hey, how are you doing today? Recovered from last night?" I ask.

"As recovered as I'll ever be," she says.

"I know your mating ceremony was yesterday, and it's not great timing but can I come by and talk to you?" I ask.

"Is it about Heather?" she asks. Of course, she would know. I close my eyes, leaning my head back against the headrest.

"Yeah," no point in lying.

"Mathis, if she's your mate, then I'm not going to question whatever little role in destiny we've each been chosen to play. She came to apologize to me before the mating ceremony, and I think she truly meant it," she says.

"Really?" I ask, that surprises me. The two of them reconciling makes this a lot easier. It's probably still going to be a little awkward, but it would be a lot worse if they still hated each other.

"Yeah. You can come over if you want to talk about it, but I imagine you're stalking her in some sort of capacity at the moment," she says.

"You are such a brat," I say lovingly. Rain bursts out in laughter on the other end of the phone.

"No Mathis, you're about to experience what dealing with a true brat is actually like," she says. I have a feeling she's right.

"I'm sorry, Rain, she isn't who I would have chosen," I say.

"Mathis, I'm not going to make this hard for you, Heather and I agreed to starting over with a clean slate, and I stand by that, and I'll talk to Tyler too, but I'm sure he'll agree," she says. I can't stop the possessive growl that comes from my chest. I completely forgot she was Tyler's ex-girlfriend. I despise that thought. Rain burst out laughing a second time.

"Get over it, because you're not fighting my mate over this," Rain says.

"I know, I'm sorry," I say.

"It's okay. Good luck Mathis, let me know how it goes," she says.

"Alright, thank you Rain," I say, before hanging up. Well, that was easier than I thought it would be. I should've known; Rain was always the most levelheaded sibling.

HEATHER

"You work too hard," Sue admonishes me like she always does, because I was cleaning the counters between customers.

"You're my boss, shouldn't you want me to work too hard," I tease. My shift was almost over, but there still was a couple hours until closing. It didn't matter what time it was in the evening; the coffee shop always has a steady stream of customers.

Oddly, before I even looked up, I knew exactly who it was when the bell above the door jingled as it opened and closed. I could smell him over the heavy scents of the coffee. I almost bolted to the back of the shop to hide, but it was too late. I look up, and Mathis is standing in front of me.

"What can I get you?" I ask with fake sweetness. I know the general location of where Rain's family lives and it's close to town, but I've never seen Mathis here before. Considering yesterday was the first time I ever met him, I don't believe it's a coincidence that he's here now. But how could he know where I worked? He must've asked someone that knew at the mating ceremony last night.

"Coffee," he says. I don't bother asking a size, I grab a cup fill it with black coffee and hand it to him.

"Two dollars," I say. He smirks as he pulls out his wallet throwing a five on the table.

"Keep the change," he says.

"Thank you," I say, without sincerity. Him being here feels intrusive. He makes me feel nervous, and I'm never nervous. I hate the feeling.

"When's your shift over?" he asks.

"That's not really any of your business," I say.

"I'll just wait if you don't tell me. I'm actually going to wait either way," he shrugs.

"Sorry, there's a no loitering policy, you stay more than 20 minutes and I call the cops," I say. Something instinctual inside of me pushes me to challenge this man.

"I'll take my chances," he says, sipping from his black coffee, taking a seat in front of the counter, angling his chair so he can watch me. I ignore him, helping the next customers in line.

When the end of my shift comes, Mathis is still sitting in the same spot, his mostly untouched coffee sitting in front of him. There's a back exit, only for employees, I plan to sneak out of. I don't think he notices when I slip out the back to quickly gather my stuff and head out the exit. I round the side of the shop, to start my walk home, and run directly in a wall of muscle.

MATHIS

"Watch yourself," I say. I had a feeling she was going to make a run for it. It's easy enough to keep tabs on someone when they are tethered though. She grunts in frustration.

"Excuse you," she says, trying to walk around me. But I grab her arm to stop her.

"I just want to talk," I say. Around the side of a coffee shop isn't really where I want to have this conversation, but at least we're alone.

"Talk then," she says, trying to pull her arm out of my grasp, folding her arms over her chest when I do let her go.

"Heather, you're a shifter, do you really not recognize what I am to you?" I ask.

"Yeah, my stalker," she says. I growl and her body immediately responds to it. She looks dazed for a second, before she processes what just happened, her eyes grow wide the moment she puts it together.

"No," she says.

"You're my mate, Heather," I say.

"Mathis, right? You know you never did give me your name," she says, accusingly.

"Yes, my name is Mathis," I confirm.

"This just really doesn't work for me, I'm going to have to pass," she says, again trying to walk around me, I turn to follow her to the sidewalk heading in the direction that she lives.

"You're joking. You know better, that's not how this works," I say.

"What did you expect? For me to immediately lay down and let you claim me?" she asks. She glares at me when I laugh.

"I'm going to have so much fun fixing your attitude," I say, smiling. She scoffs with indignation.

"Don't be a creep," she says halfheartedly. I recognize this for what it is, a female shifter wanting her mate to prove himself to her my asserting his dominance, I speed up in front of her to cut her off, putting my hands on her forearms to stop her. She's wearing short sleeves, and the exposed skin is unbelievably soft, especially compared to my rough hands. She's tall, but I still tower over her, crowding her.

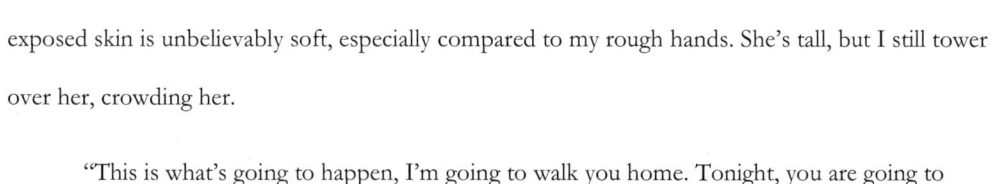

"This is what's going to happen, I'm going to walk you home. Tonight, you are going to pack a bag, assume you'll be gone for at least a week. Sleep well tonight, I'm going to pick you up in the morning," I say.

"Fine," she says flippantly, she shrugs out of my hold and takes off in the direction of her house. I know she's just agreeing because she wants to get away from me, but that's fine, I have ways of dealing with an errant little mate.

Chapter 61
HEATHER

As soon as Mathis leaves, I try to come up with a plan to avoid him. I always knew there was a possibility of me finding my fated mate. I dreaded the day though. My dad was long passed knocked out by the time I got home, sleeping on the couch with an empty whiskey bottle on the ground in front of him. I try to be quiet, even though a parade wouldn't be loud enough to wake him up. Still, I don't take any chances.

It's a visual reminder of why I can't be claimed. Looking at him sleeping, I see a glimpse of the man I remember from my childhood, the man he used to be before my mom passed away. That's the power a fated mate has over someone. Not someone, that's the power mates have over each other. I was only six when my mother died unexpectedly in a car crash, too young for the fierce independence I had to learn to survive so that my father could wallow away for the next twelve year in self-pity.

Before going to my bedroom, I check on my younger brother, Matt, the only reason I haven't moved out yet. I knock on his bedroom door, but as usual he doesn't answer. I crack the door open a little.

"Matt," I say.

"Hey, I'm decent," he says, laughing. I open the door a little wider as he takes his headphones off, the video game he was playing paused on the screen.

"Did you eat dinner?" I ask. I had premade a meatloaf for him, all he had to do was heat it up.

"Yeah, mom, I ate," he says rolling his eyes at me. He jokes, because I'm only two years older than him, but I'm the closest thing he'll ever have to a parent.

"Did dad eat?" I ask.

"No, and I'm not his babysitter," he says. I sigh, it means he's going to be in a shit mood tomorrow morning. He's always pissy when he's more hungover. The amount of alcohol he drinks is usually consistent, but the nights he doesn't eat anything makes for a rough morning.

"I know," I say.

"And I swear, if he gets up in my face again, I'm going to knock him out. In his mind I'm still a little kid," he says. He's a little kid in my mind too, but since Matt hit his growth spurt, he towers over me and my father. If the two did get into an actual fight, there would be no competition. Matt would take him out easily. He's not a lanky teenager anymore, I mean he's a teenager, just not lanky. He grew into his height, putting on pounds of muscle over the last few months.

"He makes his choices, I'm not going to blame you if it comes to that, but please don't get into a physical altercation if you can avoid it," I plead.

"I'll try, for you, not for him," he says.

"Thank you, did you finish your homework?" I ask. He rolls his eyes again, but nods.

"Alright, don't stay up too late, I'm going to bed," I say. I shut his door as he puts the headphones back on and hits play on his video game. He's a good kid, and I wish I could give him the stability in a home that he actually deserves.

I shower quickly and get ready for bed. I can't leave Matt and my dad alone by themselves. I let myself imagine how things would be if I could just run off with a gorgeous stranger, having amazing sex in seclusion, not worrying about barely getting evicted, or how I'm going to afford groceries. It's a nice dream, but not one I can actually indulge in. Maybe when Matt is old enough to live on his own, then I can be selfish. But then I just remember how catastrophic my mother's death was for my father. Do I really want to give someone that type of power over me? A better question is how do I avoid Mathis?

MATHIS

After making sure Heather was safely at home, I returned to my house to get everything in order. Luckily, the four of us siblings have small cabins spread out on our parent's property, reinforced the same way a chimera community is, so they keep trespassers out, but more importantly, they'll keep errant mates in. My cabin only takes a couple of minutes to walk to behind my parent's house. There are no roads that lead to it, but that's not really a consideration when I can teleport.

I made sure the fridge was stocked full, the sheets were changed, there were clean towels and everything else I could think of doing to make sure the place was comfortable for Heather and me to stay at least until we get things a little more sorted. I don't know what her work schedule is, but I don't really care, she doesn't have to work. I have no problem supporting her. In fact, I would prefer her to stay at home and have my children. Something tells me Heather is going to fight me on that one. Something tells me she's going to fight me on everything.

I keep close tabs on her tether all night. I can make the tether so strong and tight that it feels like a physical rope that attaches us, that way if Heather moves, I feel it. That's how I know she woke up in the middle of the night and went for a run in wolf form. I don't think she's doing it to escape me, but still, my mate is not allowed to run through the woods in the middle of the night.

I follow the tether to teleport right in front of her, she skids on her heels to avoid running right into me. Her fur is light brown just like her hair color when in human form. Even in wolf form

I can see the shock on her face to see me. Not the way I was planning on explaining to her what chimeras are, but I guess it works. I pull off my shirt and throw it at her feet. Even though most shifters have no problem with nudity, it does mean more between mates.

"Shift," I command, after I had turned around to give her privacy. I didn't need to be looking at her to feel her energy change, and know she was no longer in wolf form.

"What the hell?" she asks.

"Put on the shirt," I say.

"What did you just do? You came out of thin air," she says.

"You got five seconds to put on my shirt before I turn around," I say. I hear her grunt, before I hear the ruffle of fabric.

"You can turn around," she says. She swims in my large shirt; it covers her to mid-thigh.

"Why are you running alone in the woods in the middle of the night?" I ask.

"None of your business, what are you?" she asks.

"No Honey, I was asking the questions, it's not safe for you to be out here at night," I say. She laughs in response.

"I turn into a rather large wolf, which I'd have assumed was the biggest predator out in these woods, but now I'm not so sure since I have no idea what you are. Are you even a shifter?" she asks, looking at me suspiciously.

"Yes," I say.

"Well, I don't want to be out here anymore, I'm going back to bed," she says.

"Great idea," I say, with a smirk, before grabbing her and teleporting back to my cabin. I hold her steady when she doubles over like she's going to puke. She scurries out of my reach though as soon as she recovers enough to stand on her own.

"Where are we, what just happened?" she asks, her eyes dart around the place, and she sprints to the door when she sees it, frantically wiggling the handle in a futile attempt to escape. I approach her slowly, like I would a cornered animal.

"Get away from me," she shrieks, cowering away from me.

"Heather I'm not going to hurt you," I say, with my hands up in surrender.

"What are you?" she asks. I run my hand through my long dark hair.

"I'm a chimera," I say. I can tell by the look on her face she doesn't recognize the word. Alright, so this wasn't my smoothest plan.

Chapter 62
HEATHER

What. The. Hell? Am I sleeping? I feel awake, but this is all so surreal. My brain is rejecting the sensory input that it's getting since it doesn't make any sense. First Mathis appeared out of thin air, then he surrounded the both of us with some kind of vortex, now we're in what appears to be a medium sized cabin of some sort, kind of like the cabins they use for seclusion, which isn't exactly reassuring.

"Where are we?" I ask, looking around at the unfamiliar setting. I don't know Mathis very well, but I strongly suspect the decoration is a reflection of his personal style. Bold but simple. Dark and masculine. Like the man himself, there's an obvious edge of danger to him.

"My house," he says, looking around as though he's seeing it for the first time too.

"This isn't a house, this is a cabin," I say, probably not an important distinction to make.

"Why do you argue with me so much?" he asks. Because it would be too easy to give into you.

"I'm not arguing, I'm pointing out that you're wrong," I say, since it's easier to deflect and push away than it would be to face my own fears and insecurities.

"Although I'd love to continue to discuss all the ways that I'm wrong, it's the middle of the night and I'd like to go to bed, we can talk more in the morning," he says.

"Oh yeah, absolutely, I'm sure I'll just fall right asleep, nothing makes me sleepier than being kidnapped by a strange man," I say.

"I didn't kidnap you," he says, I notice he didn't dispute me calling him a strange man. Is he even a man? He called himself a chimera, but I don't know what that meant.

"Great, so I can leave?" I challenge. He takes a step closer to me, crowding my personal space. I hate how good he smells. It's strange being around a man so much taller than me too. Sure, the average shifter male is taller than me, but not this much taller than me.

"Do you really think I'd hurt you?" he asks, staring at me with his intense light blue eyes. He's an interesting combination of dark and light features, he reminds me of a fallen angel, or a beautiful demon, attractive but deadly. It's hard not to admire his sculpted chest when he's standing in front of me with no shirt on. He arches a brow when I hesitate to answer.

"I think you could hurt people," I say.

"Yes, I could," he says unapologetically, "but that's not what I asked, do you think I could hurt you?" he repeats his question.

"No," I sigh. I'm confused by what's happening, my thoughts are definitely a little jumbled, but I don't believe Mathis would ever actually hurt me, not just because he's my mate, but the same two people who raised Rain couldn't have raised anyone that bad. A little flicker of hope I don't want to fully acknowledge, has me wondering if being mated into Mathis' family can ensure I don't turn out like my father. Having strong relationships with good, decent people has to have some kind of positive impact.

"Are you afraid of me? Because it doesn't seem like you are based on the attitude you've given me," he says.

"If you don't want attitude, you shouldn't kidnap people," I say.

"Answer the question," he says.

"No, alright, I'm not afraid of you," I say. Not for reasons he thinks anyways.

"If you're not afraid of being here, then we're going to bed," he says.

"I will as soon as you take me home and I can sleep in my own bed," I say. I have to stop myself from stomping my foot.

"No, it's too late," he says.

"Why does that matter if you can time travel?" I ask.

"I can't time travel," he laughs "don't be ridiculous," he says.

"Right, you appear out of thin air, and magically transport me to your creepy serial killer cabin, but suggesting you can time travel is ridiculous," I say. He stares at me, his frustration palpable. Without warning and too quick for me to process until it's already done, he grabs me by my hips and throws me over his broad shoulder.

"Stop it," I shriek, hitting his muscular ass with as much force as I can in my current position.

"If you wanted to touch my ass you could have just asked," he chuckles, while walking me to what I would assume is his bedroom, but it's hard to see anything while hanging over his shoulder. I keep struggling against him, until he landed one solid smack to my left butt cheek. A butt cheek that was only protected by the thin fabric of his shirt that I was still wearing. One smack that was infinitely more effective than all my struggles combined. I stop my fight, more out of surprise than anything.

"Good girl," he says.

"Oh, fuck off," I say, his words renewing my struggle. He unceremoniously plops me on his oversized bed, I quickly scurry into a sitting position, making sure his shirt is covering everything.

"I don't have any clothes," I say, which really is the least of my problems.

"You can wear my shirt to bed," he says.

"I don't have any panties though," I say with as much dignity as I can.

"That doesn't bother me, in fact I might make a no panties rule," he says, with a seductive smirk over his attractive face.

"Yeah, right like I'm going to follow your rules," I scoff.

"No Beautiful, you don't have to follow my rules, in fact I prefer you don't, but you'll be the only one to blame when you have to face the consequences," he says, the underlying threat evident. God, why is that so hot?

MATHIS

I can smell the slight hint of her arousal. That combined with the knowledge she's only wearing my shirt with nothing underneath is hard to ignore. But it's the middle of the night, and she obviously hasn't slept much. I know she's too agitated to sleep on her own. If tonight's any indication, our relationship will never be dull. I have a feeling she's going to make me work for her submission.

I rarely have ever used it, but I have just the trick to help her sleep. Since I'm male my chimera gene is most dominant, but my mom is half pixie and a fourth fae, which means I inherited some of their abilities, one of which is calming people down. I can't do it as well or as easy as Rain can, but still, it should help her sleep. I let the calming energy flow from me to Heather, and it almost immediately takes effect.

"Did you drug me?" she asks, suspiciously, yeah definitely will never be boring.

"When could I have drugged you?" I ask.

"I don't know, you can appear out of thin air, I imagine you can be pretty stealthy," she says.

"No, it's the middle of the night, and you're probably crashing from your adrenaline rush," I say, I get under the blankets, and Heather reluctantly lets me pull her to my side, before I tuck us both in.

"I guess that's reasonable," she says. I let my calming energy wash over her, she relaxes into me, just her weight on me is deeply reassuring in a foreign way. Her golden-brown hair fans over my arm, as she lets me spoon her. After a little while, I hear her breathing even out when she's finally sleeping. I'm not worried about letting my guard down and sleeping too, the cabin is reinforced, and not that I think she would attack me, but there's nothing that could be used as a weapon in my house, or I guess cabin is more accurate.

Chapter 63
HEATHER

I hear his deep chuckle before I'm fully awake. It's the best I've slept in years, possibly ever, so it takes me a little longer than usual to be conscious of my surroundings. At least, that's the excuse I'm using for why I found myself humping Mathis' leg.

"Don't even pretend like you're still asleep, I know you're awake," he says. This would've been a good time to have panties on. It's kind of a compromising position to be in and I don't want to think about the wet spot I'm leaving on his thigh. Even so, I'm reluctant to disentangle my body from his much larger one. There's just something so quintessentially right about being here in his arms, but I can't tell if I'm just so desperate for a way out of my current situation, that I'm making Mathis into a savior without reason to.

"I need clothes," I say.

"Good morning to you too," he says. Even first thing in the morning, he looks painfully good, enough to make me feel self-conscious since I probably look like a hot mess.

"What's the matter?" he asks. It's strange having someone so intuitive to my emotional state, it almost feels intrusive. I'm so used to no one noticing or caring about me, it's not like my father was ever sober enough to care that I was upset, and I always had to be the strong one for Matt since he was younger. It wouldn't be fair to unload on my little brother when he also had to deal with our dad too.

"Heather?" he says, and the concern in his voice is almost my undoing.

"Nothing's the matter, I just need to go home," I say, trying to shut off my feelings.

"Stop, don't even bother trying to hide from me, I'm not going to let you," Mathis says. Now that my mind is clearer, I can actually dissect all the things that happened last night, and I use that as a distraction.

"What did you say you were?" I ask, pulling up the sheet to use as a shield.

"Don't think I don't realize that you're deflecting and don't think I'll let you get away with it, but I'll answer anyways. I'm a chimera, well half chimera. My mom is a mix of shifter, fae and pixie," he says. I knew there was something off about their family.

"What does that mean?" I ask.

"It just means I can manipulate energy," he says.

"Can you shift?" I ask. I want to ask what our children would be, but I don't want him to know that my mind went in that direction already.

"Yes," he says. Not giving anymore information, it feels like he's trying to not overwhelm me.

"And you can teleport?" I prompt.

"Yes," he says. I don't feel like he's being intentionally evasive, but he isn't exactly being forthcoming either.

"But you can't time travel?" I ask, making him smirk.

"No," he says.

"Any other surprises I should know about you?" I ask. I know there's more when he tries to avoid eye contact with me.

"Part of being able to manipulate energy, I'm able to send you calming energy," he says.

"So, you did drug me," I accuse, grabbing the pillow from behind me and hitting him with it.

MATHIS

Okay, so I am enjoying the bratty side way more than I thought I could.

"You are going to regret doing that," I say, trying but failing to keep the humor out of my voice, as I stalk over the bed as Heather backs up to the headboard. I grab her ankles and pull her to me, forgetting that she's only wearing my shirt, which is now bunched up under her armpits, giving me a full-frontal view of her beautiful body. I wasn't thinking, or maybe this is exactly what my brain wanted to happen, I freeze looking at her exposed body, her perfect tits that are on the smaller side but so perky, her muscular legs and toned waist.

"Like what you see?" she asks, unashamed of her nudity, not that she should be.

"Very much so," I say. The familiar scent of her arousal perfumes the air, and it's already becoming addictive to me. She smirks, then lowers my shirt, and I'm sad at losing the view, but I know I won't be able to think straight with her body on display like that.

"I'm hungry," she says.

"Me too," I say seductively.

"Not for that, for food," she says, rolling her eyes at me.

"Okay, I'll make us breakfast, then you can take a shower, while I grab some of your clothes," I say.

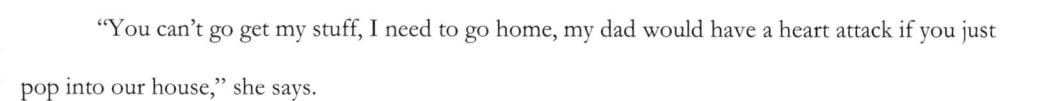

"You can't go get my stuff, I need to go home, my dad would have a heart attack if you just pop into our house," she says.

"Don't worry, I can be stealthy," I say.

"I'm still mad that you drugged me," she says, crossing her arms, over her chest.

"I didn't drug you," I say.

"I don't know if I trust any food you make me either, I don't trust you not to drug me again," she says.

"Fine, you can make me breakfast then, I like the idea of you fulfilling your wife role," I say. I'm just lucky that looks can't actually kill, or I'd be a dead man already.

"I guess I'll take my chances," she says, sighing dramatically.

Chapter 64

MATHIS

Despite her initial reluctance, Heather ended up eating everything I put in front of her. I made us eggs and bacon for breakfast. After we both eat and I clean up our dishes, I grab her a towel and show her the bathroom.

"I need my cellphone, clothes, and my purse. Do not let my father see you. My brother should be at school," she narrows her eyes at me "I really think I should go with you."

"It's fine, take a shower, I'll be back before you're done," I say, before leaving I add the warning "Be good," pinning her with a glare.

"Be quick then," she counters.

"You're just begging for me to spank your ass," I say. She steps closer to me, maintaining eye contact.

"No Baby, you'll know when I'm begging for it," she says, grabbing the towel from my hand, before closing the bathroom door on my face.

"Have you left yet, I'm waiting," she calls from the other side of the bathroom door, then I hear the shower start. Such a brat. It's hard to leave knowing that she'll be naked, and wet, and in great need of some discipline……..and I have to cut off that train of thought.

Usually when I teleport, I do it as quickly as possible, because even though I've been doing it my entire life, I still will get queasy if I'm in a portal for too long, but if I need to be aware of my surroundings before I resurface on the other side, I just go through slower. That way, I can look around without being detected. When I get to the end of the portal I made that leads to Heather's house, I can feel that it's only her dad inside, and it seems like he is sleeping. I resurface in Heather's bedroom. Earlier, she had described her house to me and where her bedroom was located so I knew where to go.

I quickly and very quietly find her phone and purse. I go to her bathroom and grab all the toiletries I can find, putting them in one of the bags I brought, then I go to her dresser for her clothes. I go through each drawer, just grabbing clothes and putting them in a bag I brought. Pants, shirts, pajamas. I open the last drawer and sitting right on top of a pile of bras and underwear, is a hot pink vibrator.

I pick it up, I can tell it's been washed, but I can still smell the hint of Heather's arousal lingering on the impressive sized toy, rummaging through the same drawer, I find condoms, nipple clamps, and a pair of handcuffs. I'm so done. Any ability I had to think was completely eliminated when all the blood in my body decided to be redirected to my penis.

I abandon my task at hand, put the handcuffs in my back pocket, and the toys in the bottom of the bag, and teleport back to my place. I don't hear the water running anymore. That was a pretty quick shower.

"Heather, I have your stuff," I say, knocking on the door.

"Did you bring my brush?" she calls, opening up the bathroom door enough to poke her head out, her hair looking a shade darker being wet, the towel wrapped around her.

"Yeah," I find the bag I threw the toiletries in, and hand her the brush. She grabs a pair of leggings and a shirt from the top of the bag with the clothes.

"No underwear?" she asks, rummaging around. No, the vibrator I found was in the underwear drawer and that stole my attention.

"I actually got distracted by that drawer," I say, pulling the handcuffs from my back pocket, and dangling them from my finger.

"Did you at least bring my vibrator? I might need it if we're going to be here a while," she says, without a hint of shame. Not that I think she should be ashamed in any way, I just expected her to care even a little bit about me finding her toys.

"What?" she asks.

"I just wasn't expecting to find a vibrator," I admit.

"I like to orgasm," she says, so matter of fact. "Do you not enjoy to orgasm?" she asks confused.

"No, I do," I say, rubbing the back of my neck, organizing my thoughts.

"Then what's the problem?" she challenges. I don't know how to articulate my expectations, because I can't quite articulate them to myself.

"No problem, I just wasn't expecting it, I was happily surprised to see it," I say.

"Great, act right and I'll let you watch me use it," she says, before retreating back to the bathroom, closing the door. God, this girl is going to be the death of me.

Chapter 65

RAIN

"I wasn't expecting you so soon after your mating ceremony, you looked beautiful that day, what a lovely event," Mrs. Thomas says, as we both take a seat in her living room.

"Thank you, Mrs. Thomas," I say. I've enjoyed getting to know her better over the past few weeks. She has an interesting way of putting things in perspective.

"I heard there was some excitement at the end of the night," Mrs. Thomas said with a poignant look.

"What do you mean?" I ask.

"I heard Max and an out of towner got into a fight," she says, taking a sip of her tea before placing it back on her coffee table.

"What?" I say surprised, "no one told me, what happened?"

"You'll have to ask your brothers for all the details. We'll just have to see what comes of it," she says in the dismissive manner I've become familiar with "now show me, what you have," she says, taking the rough draft I had brought, excitedly thumbing through. I don't bother pressing her for answers, Mrs. Thomas has an elusive manner about herself, I find she only discloses exactly what she wants to and nothing more.

"I was so excited to show you the first draft of what we've created," I say.

"What you created, Darling, I'm just an old bat with a cat," she says petting her lazy cat by her side affectionately with her free hand.

"It's perfect, I'm so glad Tyler suggested you for this project," she says.

"Thank you," I say.

"Rain, I want to tell you a story, a story I was told as a young girl. Once upon a time," she starts.

"Is this a fairy tale..." I cringe "sorry, I didn't mean to interrupt," I say, I just needed to know if I should take notes.

"Of sorts," she shrugs "once upon a time, well not upon time, but at the beginning of time, all beings lived together, in reasonable harmony, regardless of their otherness. At a time when you didn't have to hide your true nature, there was no division, not like there is now, no shifter versus chimera. In fact, there were no separate communities at all, sure some beings mated with similar heritage, but cross matches were as equally common if not more so," she says. My suspicions were confirmed, she did know about chimeras.

"What happened?" I ask.

"Now remember, this was a long time ago, eons ago, simpler times, but as the populations grew and became more sophisticated, there was a need for formal governance. It was necessary, but unfortunately poised a new problem. You see, what's best for a vampire isn't always what's best for a shifter and each faction felt like they weren't being represented fairly, it created discourse and division. Each group thought it'd strengthen them to purify their bloodline, make their own community with their own hierarchy, but something completely different happened. It's not known why but their otherness became diluted and that's how humans evolved, or I should say devolved. It's like the different genes had a symbiotic relationship with each other. As though they were needed to activate each other," she says, pausing to take another sip of her tea. Wait, did she say vampire?

"It's speculation, but people that are the creation of several species coming together, were spoken of as the revolutionaries," she says.

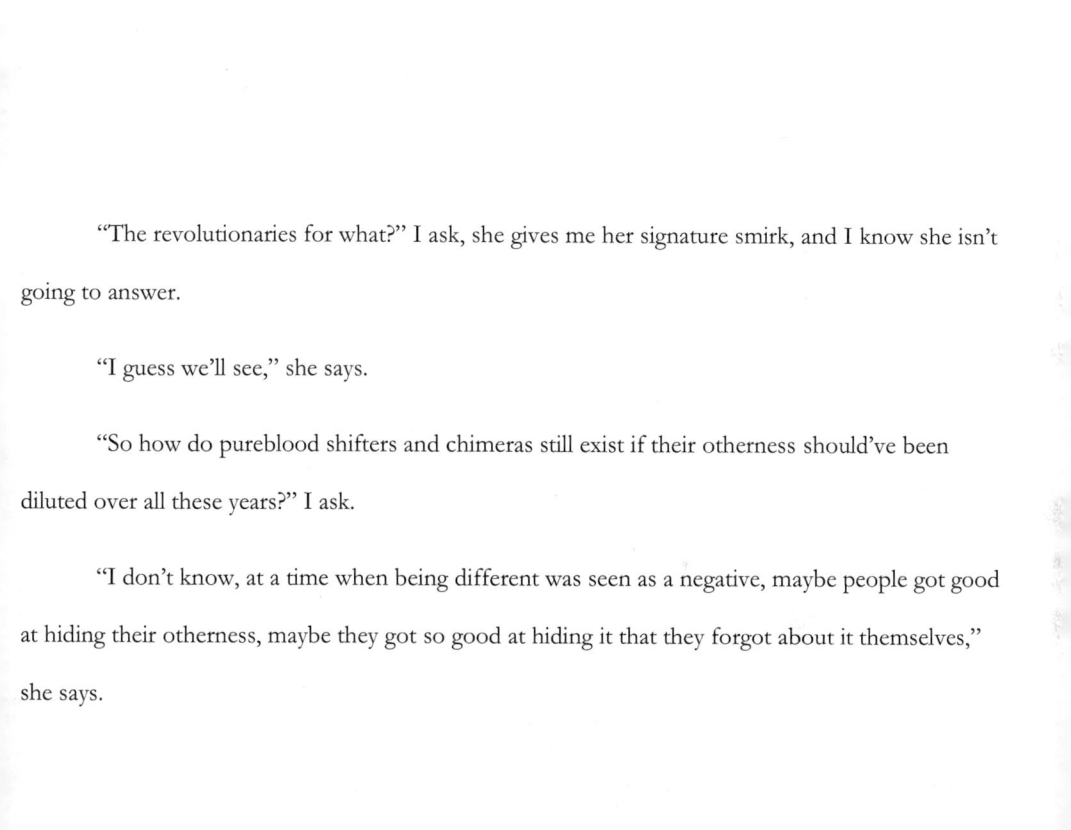

"The revolutionaries for what?" I ask, she gives me her signature smirk, and I know she isn't going to answer.

"I guess we'll see," she says.

"So how do pureblood shifters and chimeras still exist if their otherness should've been diluted over all these years?" I ask.

"I don't know, at a time when being different was seen as a negative, maybe people got good at hiding their otherness, maybe they got so good at hiding it that they forgot about it themselves," she says.

Thank you so much for reading!

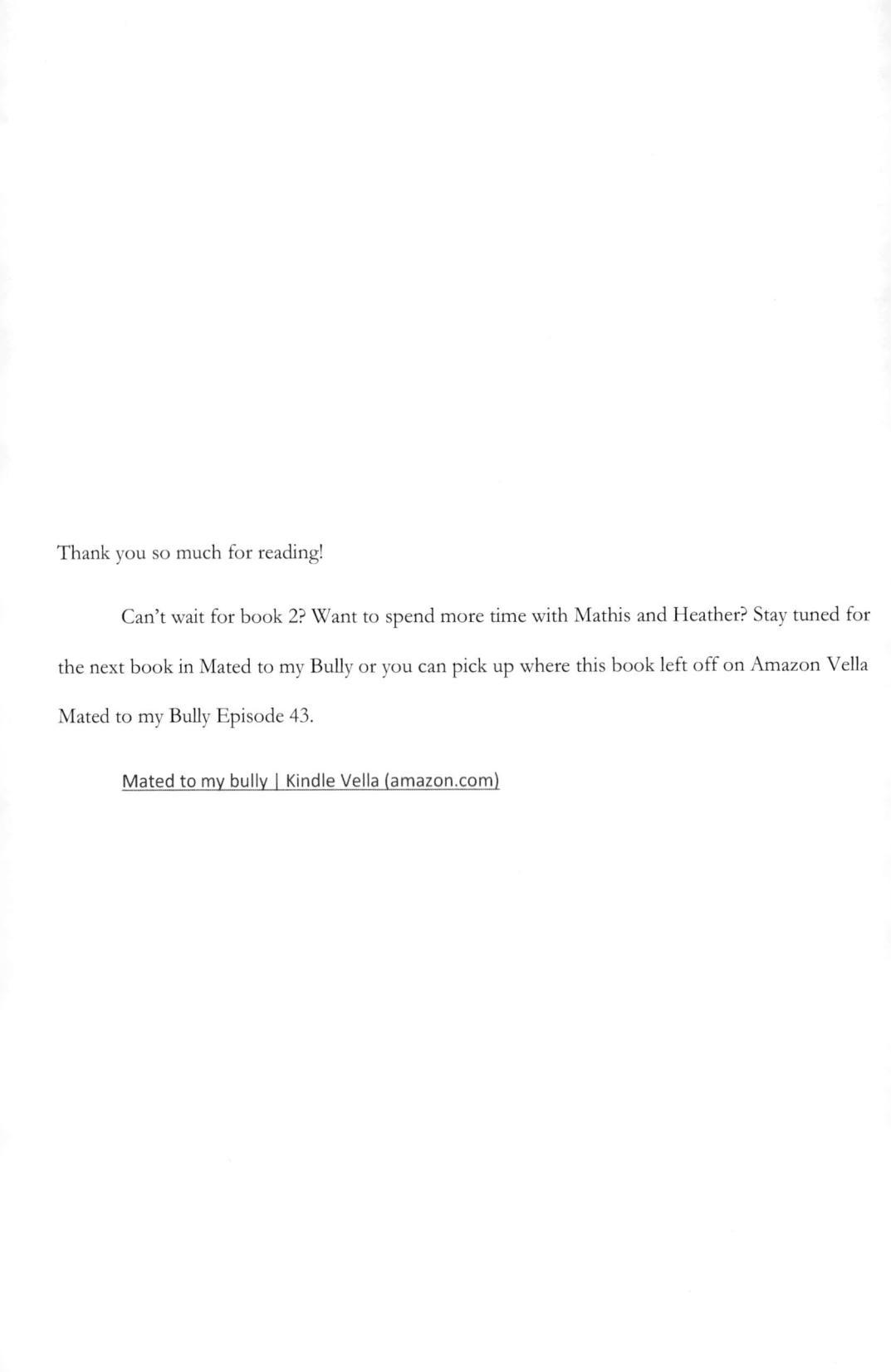

Can't wait for book 2? Want to spend more time with Mathis and Heather? Stay tuned for the next book in Mated to my Bully or you can pick up where this book left off on Amazon Vella Mated to my Bully Episode 43.

[Mated to my bully | Kindle Vella (amazon.com)](amazon.com)

About the author

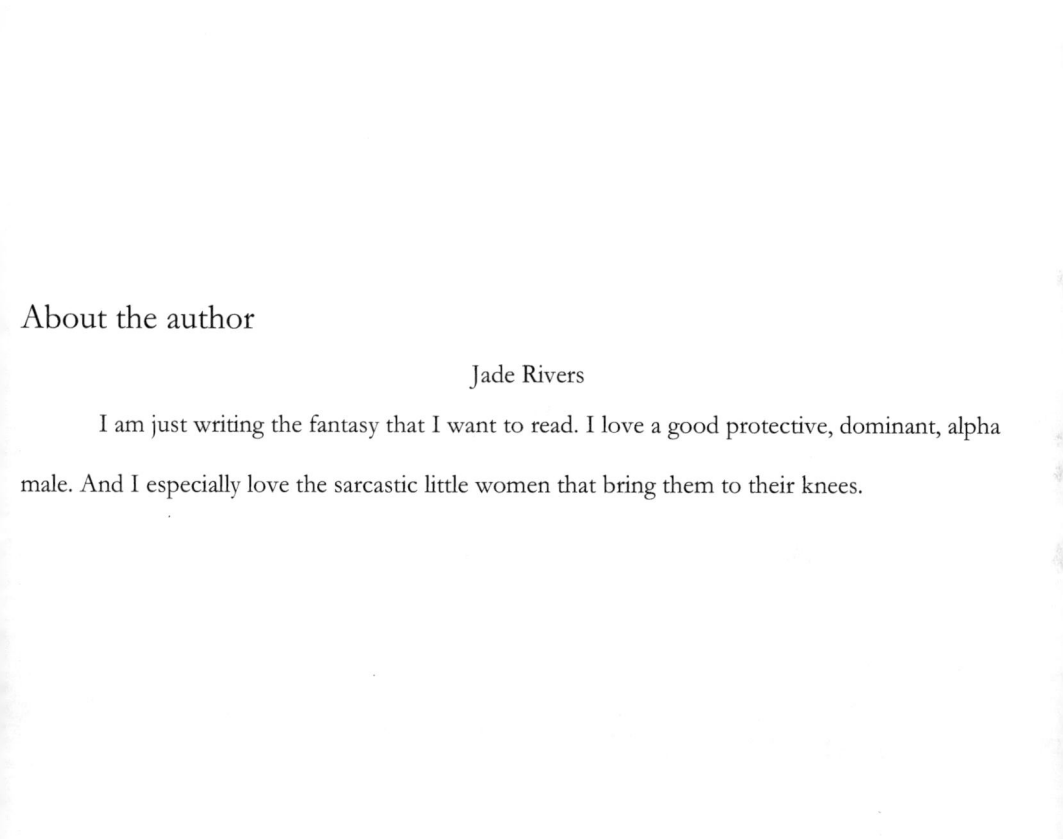

Jade Rivers

I am just writing the fantasy that I want to read. I love a good protective, dominant, alpha male. And I especially love the sarcastic little women that bring them to their knees.

Made in the USA
Coppell, TX
19 May 2025

49628284R00144